# THE RIVAL ROMEO

BOOK #3 THE PUGET SOUND PILOTS

SIERRA HILL

TEN28 PUBLISHING LLC

Trigger Warning:

This story deals with a sensitive subject matter and the effects of PTSD from the aftermath of a sexual assault.

Reader discretion advised.

# PROLOGUE

Jaeger – Post Championship Win

"You are such a dick, Jaeger Matlin! A real world-class asshole."

I have to admit, I'm a bit surprised to hear these words coming from the woman I just hooked up with last night. One, in fact, I know I satisfied quite nicely several times based on the number of times she screamed my name. Usually, the comments I hear are a bit more complimentary and involve my amazing stamina and the size of my dick. Not that I am one.

They usually don't call me a dick until after our hookup concludes and I make it very clear it was a one-time thing, and they shouldn't expect to hear from me again. I'm sure that's when they have a few choice words to say about me.

But that's how I roll. I'm a one and done kind of guy. No second timers. No repeat sessions. No commitments.

Jaeger Bomb and Meister, the nicknames fans have given me, are fitting for my rookie year with the Puget Sound Pilots. Mostly because I'm one of the best basketball players in the league and when I play, I knock my opponents on their asses with my quick moves and fast reflexes. I prove my MVP status every time I step out on the court.

As for the women I hook up with? Well, those nicknames hold true just as often in the bedroom. So the fact that this chick is calling me a dick and an asshole is a little disconcerting. Especially since I've done nothing to deserve it.

"Whoa, whoa, whoa, baby. Come on now. Don't be like that," I say in my charm-her-panties-off voice, showing her my devilish smile. I slowly rise onto my elbows, my morning wood straining between my legs and tenting the hotel sheets, and I hold out my hand to coax her back to bed with me. "Come on back to bed and I'll show you that I can give you something far more valuable than a picture to remember me by."

I grab the top sheet and pull it back so she can see just what she'll miss if she continues to remain mad at me for simply putting a stop to her unapproved dick pic.

I'd been asleep until just moments ago, when I woke to find her aiming her camera phone down at my cock, taking snaps of both it and my face. Apparently as a way to prove she slept with the Championship MVP.

Which, fine...okay, I get, but when I brought her to the hotel last night, I specifically told her there was to be no photo evidence of our night together and had her shut off her phone and stick it in the drawer.

She understood and agreed to the rules. We had a very memorable night together and then she decided to break that rule this morning.

If you don't have trust, what is there?

The word trust is the one and only tattoo I have on my chest. Because trust means everything between people. I learned early on in my professional career who I could and couldn't rely on. I'd not be fooled by anyone.

She stands at the end of the bed, biting her plump bottom lip, staring at my erection. There's a scowl on her face but an interested gleam in her eye.

I think I'm in the clear and she's about to succumb to my request. No such luck.

Instead, I have to use my quick reflexes that I normally reserve for the court to duck my head just in time to avoid being hit with the pillow that she picks up and hurls at me.

Truth be told, I don't know how we went from the fun we made last night together to this uncalled-for hostility. But I do know she wasn't the least bit angry with me last night, from the moment she wandered over and made her presence known at the bar.

No, siree. I made sure of that.

She wasn't calling me an asshole then—or any other curse word, for that matter. The words falling from her lips on repeat were "*Oh God,*" and "*Fuck yes, Jaeger,*" and "*Don't stop. Harder, Meister.*"

How quickly things can change from one moment to the next. One minute she's sucking my dick, and the next she's calling me one. *Go figure.*

It was obvious the minute she came up and started chatting with me at the after-party that she was DTF and wanted a ride on my dick. In fact, that was pretty much word for word what she said that got my attention and had me bringing her back to the hotel.

*"Hey, Jaeger...I have a question for you. What kind of Internet do you use?"*

*I shrugged, checking her out over the rim of my beer bottle. "I don't know."*

*"Well, if you need reliable and fast, I've got your DSL right here, baby."*

*Dick-sucking lips.*

Then she licked the outline of her red-painted lips with the tip of her tongue and grabbed my crotch. I was hard in an instant. And true to her word, we were up to my private room where she was sucking my cock within fifteen minutes.

And damn, it was a good fucking night. She was down with it, I was up for whatever, and we enjoyed several rounds of celebratory sex.

Isn't that the best part of being a professional athlete? I'm a championship-winning, league-MVP rookie. I wasn't going to pass up a hot woman on the take.

Which is why, in the light of day, I'm thoroughly confused by how she went from singing my praises at the top of her lungs when she climaxed last night to the antics she's throwing at me right now.

All because I caught her trying to get a picture of me naked in bed and I told her she didn't have permission to use it or share it. That's when she freaked out.

"Listen, darlin'," I offer with a soothing voice, hoping to persuade her to let go of the flying objects and see reason. "I can't have you walking around with a picture of my dick print in your camera roll. Otherwise, I'd have to get my lawyers involved and that could get messy. So let's say you delete it now and I'll give you something more valuable."

I raise my eyebrows and let my eyes travel suggestively over her sexy body.

She crosses her arms. "You can't sue me over one picture. I'll go to the press...I'll make you look like a womanizing man-whore," she shrills in a high-pitched squawk that rivals nails down a chalkboard. "It will ruin your reputation, Jaeger *Meister*."

*Fucking ball bunnies and their selfies.*

I'd just given this chick a night to remember with a fantastic boning and that isn't good enough for her? She wants to remain stubborn and fight over this simple request?

How does it make me the bad guy here because I won't allow her to keep an unauthorized photo of me naked in bed?

Christ, it's true what they say...there is a steep price to pay for fame.

And based on this woman's antics, I'm about to pay the fine.

I raise one hand in surrender as I stand up slowly, holding the edge of the sheet up to cover my junk. Don't need anything else flying and hitting those jewels. The chick glares at me suspiciously. I lift my brows, tipping my head to the side, and give her the sexy smirk I know makes women lose their motherfucking minds.

"Hey, come on now, baby. Don't be like that." I saunter toward her, licking the corner of my mouth and reaching out to stroke a hand down her arm.

I'm trying to be the decent guy here, even though I could just as easily act like the asshole she claims I am. One call to hotel security and she'd be kicked out of here so fast her head would spin.

But I remember the advice my dad gave me when I hit puberty on ways to handle hot-headed women. He said, *"Son, you attract more bees with honey. And those honey pots are special. So be nice. Be respectful. And for God's sake, be careful."*

I may be a cocky son-of-a-bitch for a myriad of reasons, one of which is my sexual appetite, but I'm not an idiot. I know these girls talk, and if word gets around that I'm a dirtbag and treat women disrespectfully, well then, there goes my reputation.

Brushing her wild, sexed-up hair off her shoulder, I cup the back of her neck, bring her in close, and lower my head so my lips brush over her forehead.

Then I lock my eyes with hers, which are smeared with last night's eye makeup, and lower my head further to murmur in her ear, "Don't leave mad, sweetheart. I'd hate to know I caused you distress. I'd rather you leave a satisfied woman."

Then I kiss her neck, feeling the long slender cords relax, and she tilts her head to give me more access.

I know the moment I've got her because she lets out a soft gasp.

*Works like a charm every single time.*

I drop the sheet and crush my mouth to hers, sweeping my tongue through her swollen lips as I wedge my growing erection between her thighs.

"That's right, honey. You know you want more of the Jaeger Bomb. Don't you, baby?"

She nods her head eagerly, parting her legs to give me access to my very own happy place.

Because there's only two places I love to be.

On the court and between a woman's legs.

And lucky for me, I get to do them with regular frequency.

They don't call me the Meister for nothing.

Jade

As I have almost every morning for the past five years, I walk from my apartment on Queen Anne Hill into downtown Seattle—past the basketball arena, the waterfront, and all my favorite local Seattle coffee shops and restaurants—on my way to work.

This time of morning is relatively quiet, far enough from the freeway where the only sounds are the seagulls squawking overhead looking for their morning breakfasts. I look up to the sky where the sun tries valiantly to peek out from underneath the heavy marine layer of clouds, the grayness a welcome sight for me.

They call it the June gloom for a reason. For most Seattleites, the dreariness of this time of year is annoying but easily forgiven because of the vibrant grandeur of the surrounding natural beauty. The snow-capped Olympic mountains over on the peninsula toward the west make their presence known and the gray-blue waters of the Puget Sound make way into the lush greens of the forests that surround the Pacific Northwest.

It's not a bad place to live as long as you don't melt under the daily precipitation or have a strong need to see the sun most of the year.

I don't mind the weather because most days I'm indoors managing my gym, the business I dreamed of owning since I was a sophomore in college and finally made a reality five years ago.

It's been a dream come to fruition through blood, sweat, and tears——not to mention capital. But it's all been worth it because this is the year I hope to be featured in Seattle's Top 30 under 30, as well as be in contention for the annual Young Entrepreneurs Award presented by Seattle Digs Biz magazine.

The thought of that possibility fills me with gleeful optimism as I respond to the damp drizzle and chill seeping into my bones by tugging at the collar of my rain jacket up to my chin. It would be everything I've dreamed of and would allow me to open another location of Seattle Circuit.

Rounding the corner on Second Avenue, a smile lifts at the corners of my mouth as I peer down to the end of the street and see Mary Q sitting on the old milk crate I gave her a few weeks back, her trusty dog Perkins sitting dutifully by her side.

Plunging my hand in the tote I have draped over my arm, I rifle around at the bottom in search of the reusable shopping bag I placed in there before I left my apartment this morning. I locate it with ease and pull it out as Perkins swings his head around and gives me those puppy-dog eyes of his that hold recognition and happiness. While he doesn't move from his spot, his mouth opens in a pant and his tail wags wildly behind him, thumping against the white crate.

I sift through the tote once more, rummaging at the

bottom for the bone I purchased at the pet supply store this weekend and hold it out for his inspection.

He sniffs at it dubiously before opening his mouth and gently taking it from my open palm.

"Good morning, Perkins," I greet, patting his head before he plops down on his blanket stretched out at Mary's feet and begins gnawing at his new treat. "Hello, Mary. You hungry for some breakfast?"

In nearly the same manner that Perkins assessed me, Mary lifts her head from its bent position, removing her hoodie from her mess of tangled hair, and gives me a short grunt.

Mary Q doesn't speak. Whether that's based on her unwillingness to engage with others or from a sense of self-preservation from past traumas, I'll never know. Whatever has caused her to shut down verbally hasn't prevented me from communicating with her, though. We manage just fine with simple questions and answers.

I place the bag I have in my hand gently on her lap, which is covered with the wool blanket I brought her a few days ago that's now filthy. I add exchanging it with a clean one tomorrow to my mental checklist. Living on the streets and in alleys doesn't give her access to clean laundry on the regular.

"Mary, I brought you some bagels and cream cheese this morning, along with a few bananas and an apple." I wink at her. "I know how much you love bananas."

Mary nods her head, her tangled hair covering her eyes, and hums. That means she's in agreement.

"There's also some water and a few personal products in there, too." I motion to the bag and she cautiously peers inside. Even after all this time, she's still extremely wary around people. I get it. Trust is a huge issue for those who have been hurt.

I know the feeling.

"By the way, were you and Perkins able to get into the new shelter on Lenora Street I mentioned to you last week? The one for women only?"

She ducks her head further, rooting around in the bag to extract one of the bananas, peels it open and wolfing it down like she hasn't eaten in a few days. But I'm confident that's not the case since I bring her food nearly every day on my way to the gym.

While chewing ferociously, she shakes her head and grunts, pieces of banana falling from her mouth.

I crouch down next to her and offer her a napkin from my tote, concerned about this news. I'd read about the newest shelter that opened a few blocks from here in a local blog I follow. This one is specifically for women, trans women, and children, offering them a safe place to stay. While there are plenty of available options, they aren't always the best environments for women like Mary Q.

Seattle's homeless population has exploded over the past ten years. With an ever-expanding population of unhoused people due to skyrocketing housing costs and gentrification, the city hasn't been able to keep up with missions or shelters. Currently, the 2300 shelter spaces in the downtown vicinity is still not enough and unable to provide for women.

I'd done some research to help Mary locate something closer to her corner so she doesn't have to go far each night to find a safe place to sleep. When I learned about the Lenora Street women's shelter, I was elated and gave Mary the details.

The news that she didn't get in has me troubled. And

more than a little pissed off. If I find out they didn't allow her in, I'll have some choice words with the administrator.

"Why not? Why couldn't you get a bed?"

Mary raises her hand and points down at Perkins, who chews and slobbers loudly over his bone, his body pressed tightly against Mary's leg.

My jaw drops open and then closes in a frown.

"Oh no. They don't allow pets?"

She shakes her head and mimics my frown.

I want more than anything to be able to hug Mary. To place my hand on her shoulder in a show of my support. But I learned early on that Mary doesn't like to be touched in any way. She cowers and scares easily. So I keep the space between us to a safe and tolerable distance. But Perkins never minds a good scratch behind the ear or belly rub.

"I'm so sorry, Mary. I know how much you love Perkins. He's your family and it's not fair there are not many pet-friendly shelters around here."

I add contacting the city's Social Welfare department to find out if there are programs to help in these situations to that ever-growing checklist of mine. Mary has a hard enough time already with her mental health and communication issues. Her only constant is having Perkins with her at all times and vice versa. Which means that, if she can't bring him with her to the shelter, they sleep out on the street. My heart clenches with anguish at the thought.

I rise to my feet and dust off my hands, taking the moment to peer at my watch and check the time. It's five-fifteen a.m. My gym opens at five-thirty every day.

"I've gotta get to work, Mary. But let me see if I can work something out for you and Perkins this week. I can't promise anything, but I'll do what I can."

She nods and gives me what looks like a small appreciative smile. It warms something inside my chest.

"Oh, and I'll bring a clean blanket tomorrow morning so we can wash this one. You can include any other clothes you want me to wash, too."

I blow them both kisses, bending down to also pat Perkins on the head. He whines his thanks. "See you both tomorrow. Be safe."

And then I turn to cross the street at the light, my emotional state a little more fragile than it had been fifteen minutes earlier.

I hate the fact that I can't do anything more substantial for Mary and her dog. Or that there are women who seek help and refuge who can't get the support they need to turn their lives around.

The only thing I can do currently is keep my personal commitment to being there for them in whatever way I can. Helping one by one. Volunteering at the local soup kitchen. Incorporating free programs into my business strategy for those vulnerable female and trans populations in the community. And plugging away at building my business so that someday, I will be able to fund my own shelter for those in need.

Because when you are fortunate to have more than others, you have a responsibility to be a kind human and give back.

Without that, what's the point?

## 2

———

Jaeger

I had just returned from a run with my roommate, Henri, who has jumped in the shower while I stand in the kitchen, slamming my protein drink and sorting through the mail that's been stacking up on our kitchen counter for a better part of the week.

Most of the stack is addressed to Henri-Pierre Garnier, with postmarks from France. I can't figure out who it's from, though, since everything is written in French.

The only French I know is the kissing kind. And while I'm a pro at that, the language kind I am not.

I chuckle at my twelve-year-old humor, picking up one of the lone envelopes addressed to me. I nearly discard it until I notice the official-looking emblem in the top left corner.

Fuck yeah. The news I've been waiting for since I started this process earlier this year. My excitement is palpable as I snatch the letter from the counter and head over to the couch to stretch out, throwing my legs over the new sofa table I recently purchased, and rip open the letter.

It's taken over eight weeks to get an answer on the building permits from the City Planning and Development Offices. Ever since I had purchased an old, dilapidated downtown apartment building that had been vacant for years and need of serious repairs, I'd been waiting for the approval to start on the renovations. With the help of my brother, Jesse, a business and construction major, we filed the application under my new company name, JJ Enterprises, and had just been waiting on the commercial land use permit so we could get started.

Some might ask what a guy like me, a professional basketball player, is doing buying and renovating buildings?

Well, it's mostly due to my dad and brother, who have encouraged me to invest my money wisely in real estate and other property-holding businesses, knowing that ball careers rarely last long.

Having made some major bank my first season as a rookie with the Pilots, my agent, Fred Lovelace, renegotiated my contract after we won the championship and I earned the title of league MVP, so now I've doubled my salary with a tidy twenty-million-dollar three-year agreement. Fred worked out all the details less than a month ago, which is what led to me making some serious business decisions to solidify my future.

The first one is opening my first business, one my younger brother will help me manage once he graduates from Stanford next fall. Jesse and I had thrown around no less than fifty different business ideas after I'd signed my contract with the Pilots last June, and we ended up landing on two ventures. The one nearest and dearest to my heart is opening gyms across the country that will cater to the wealthy and elite. With my name tied to the business front, I don't have any doubt we'll bring in the kind of clientele we want: the rich and famous.

The second is restaurants, which we've yet to land on anything substantial. Jesse is actually writing a thesis and business proposal that will be our spring board into the gym-owning and franchising business.

Until then, this letter holds the news that will get me one step closer to achieving my goal. I smile in anticipation of knowing this letter is just a simple formality in the process, as was implied by the lady in the city administration building when I filed it. The location is perfect, but after looking further into the existing building structure and foundation and knowing we would need both commercial and residential zoning for the gym and spa plus living spaces on the higher floors for tenants, we started from scratch with our architectural plans. Which means I expect there to be a few more hoops to jump through.

But I'm up for the task. I am a hoops player, after all. Plus, what else do I have to do this summer? I already took a short vacation after the championship win and am now looking to dive into these projects until the fall training camps begin.

Opening the envelope, I extract and unfold the letter and scan the first few lines, my smile quickly dissolving. I blink. Then my eyebrows squeeze together in confusion.

"What the fuck is this?" I say, only to myself since Henri is still in the shower and can't hear me.

I read the remaining content and jump to my feet, my heel hitting the table leg and nearly sending my plastic tumbler perched on the table sailing to the floor. I grab it before it spills and set it up right before pulling my phone out of my pocket.

I punch in my brother's contact and hit the call button, pacing while I wait for him to answer.

It rings a few times before he picks up. I can hear he's clearly out of breath and there's a muffled noise on the other end. "Yo. I'm busy, can I call you back later?"

I check the time on the microwave clock. It's just after six p.m. here and we're both on West Coast time.

"No, you can't. This is important, bro," I argue, perturbed by both the letter and his brush-off.

An aggrieved sigh rattles from his throat and I can hear a grunt. "Fine, just a second."

There's a rustling sound, and even more murmurs on the other end. It sounds like I may have caught him in bed with someone. I grin proudly. That's my baby brother, following in my footsteps. Chick magnet extraordinaire.

Technically, it runs in our family, and we come by it honestly. A gift from dear old Dad.

Our father, Jensen Matlin, is the king of pussy. He taught us everything we know when it comes to women: how to get them, how to please them, how to respect them, and how to avoid getting trapped when they want to settle down. Both Jesse and I acquired the Matlin charm and have done well in all the lessons we learned.

That may seem like strange accolades for a son to say about a father, but it's not all he's done for us. He raised us on his own after my mom's untimely death when I was just a young kid and Jesse was barely out of diapers.

During our childhood, while my dad was building his growing marketing empire, we did have a stepmom for a short time, after he married his twenty-four-year-old secretary, Shellea, because he thought it required a woman's touch to raise boys. But that relationship lasted barely long enough for the ink to dry on the marriage certificate and from what my dad has told us, Shellea realized quickly that she didn't want to be his secretary, housekeeper, and in-home childcare provider, and high-tailed it out of there a year later.

After that, Dad decided he was much better off as a single father and didn't need any woman to replace our mother. He hired nannies throughout our formative years, which, due to his good looks, charm, and overly active sex drive, we went through with astounding regularity after he fell for them, slept with them, and then broke their hearts when he moved on.

By the time I was ten and Jesse was eight, we were basically old enough to manage on our own. My dad did everything he could to be an involved parent, starting me off in basketball camp when I was six, and everything after that revolved around the sport for me.

Jesse, on the other hand, wasn't into sports at all. He was clearly the academic in the household, becoming a math, computer, and chess whiz by the time he turned four. It didn't, however, affect his ability to be a chick magnet like me and our dad. Girls for Jesse were just as easy for him as a math problem.

I hear a door click closed in the background and Jesse returns to the line.

"This better be fucking good, J, because I was just about to get Celeste Garfield naked, and now I have a case of massive blue balls thanks to you."

I sift through my memory bank to see if that name rings a bell. It doesn't. He goes through a plethora of them every school year. But I chuckle at his plight.

"I wouldn't call your walnut-sized balls massive, bro. But I am sorry for interrupting your fuck fest. I'm sure you'll be able to get into her pants and good graces again later. But right now I need your help." I hold the open letter in my hand and place it on the table, flattening my palm over the creases to keep it flat. "I got a Notice of Application in the mail today about the construction permit. It gives the file number, the building address, and mentions a public hearing date. What the hell does that mean?"

Although I have impressive skills in basketball and sex, this whole application process is a little outside my wheelhouse. I don't have a lot of real-life experience in business aside from the contracts I've signed for the team and various endorsement deals. And let's face it, my agent handled those for me. This type of thing is way over my head.

My brother, on the other hand, is smart as fuck and knows this shit because it's all he does in his business management program.

"You couldn't have called Dad for this?" he sputters disgruntledly, still apparently pissed that I ran off his girl.

"He's in Jamaica for that conference."

"Oh, right. Fine. Read it to me," he insists with a huff. "What does it say?"

I read through the letter, which basically says that, because I won't just be renovating the building for the residential part, there is a requirement for a Land Use Action and public hearing to allow the public to give their statements to the city planning committee about the land use. Which could mess everything up if someone opposes the build-out.

"The hearing date is next week. Fuck, am I supposed to be there? Do you think I need to hire an attorney?"

My brother, with his infinite knowledge of the inner workings of business, and who also interned for the state of California during his junior year of college, is the only one I trust to be completely open and honest with. He won't judge me too harshly for sounding dumb or ignorant. He might bust my balls, but I'll dish it out to him just as hard.

"Nah, just show up and have all your proposal paperwork, the permits and plans, in hand. No one ever shows up at those public hearings except the people who wear tinfoil hats."

I bark out a laugh just as Henri strides into the living room, looking fresh and clean shaven. He eyes me curiously as he passes me on the couch and I lift my chin, watching as he heads into the kitchen to start dinner.

That's the other bonus about having a roommate. He loves to cook. And not just mac and cheese boxed shit, but honest to God three-course meals that smell like they're from a French eatery.

"Oh good," I muse. "I'll make sure to keep my alien-sighting and conspiracy theories on the down-low while there."

"Good idea," Jesse says, then changes the subject on me. "Hey, do you know when Dad is supposed to get back? I have my upcoming semester tuition and need him to write a check."

"Do I look like his personal assistant?" I snort.

"No, you look like an asshat, but that doesn't mean you might not know his itinerary."

This is how brotherly love works. You can do each other a solid one minute and then bust each other's balls the next.

"I honestly didn't pay that much attention when I spoke with him last. He mentioned something about being in Jamaica and then off to some place for a client presentation. I really don't remember."

It's rare that the three of us are ever in the same spot at the same time with how busy our schedules can be. While Jesse and I were both in college, we did spend time with

Dad over the holidays. But once I started playing ball, my travel schedule was constantly chaotic, leaving our family time brief and infrequent. But the one thing my brother knows he can always count on is me.

"Hey, if you're in a bind, you know I can help you out with tuition this semester. It's no big deal. Just tell me what you need."

There's a pause, as if Jesse has to weigh out the viability of this option. It kind of pisses me off that there's any hesitation on his part about asking me for the money. I've got it coming out of my pores and this is the least I can do for him. My brother is my best friend and I'd do anything for him and I know the feeling is mutual.

"No, I don't need your money—"

"—but you'll take Dad's?" I interrupt with an irritated grunt. "Don't be an idiot, Jess. Just let me pay the fucking tuition so you're not overdue. Consider it payment for the work you've already done for me and what you'll be doing after you've graduated and are running my empire."

Jesse relents, as I knew he would. That's what family does. Helps each other out when they need it. If you can't rely on family, who can you rely on?

"Okay, okay...fine. But I think you're getting ahead of yourself on the whole empire thing. You've always been an arrogant and over-confident asshole," he says, pointing out my favorite personality traits about myself. But it doesn't bother me a bit because I am all that and more. I eat that shit up. "I'll send you the Registrar's information today. But make sure you get it in before next Tuesday."

"When have I ever failed you, little brother?"

This makes him wheeze with laughter. "Don't get me started. I don't have time to recount all your idiotic moments in life."

"Dude, don't bite the hand that feeds you," I reply authoritatively, moving toward the large bank of living room windows that face the Puget Sound. "I can always fire your ass before you start your job with JJ Enterprises."

I wouldn't and he knows it, but it's a good threat, nonetheless.

When Jesse does graduate, the plan is for him to move to Seattle and we will buy a house. For now, living with Henri has made the most sense, since we both initially only signed up for a year when we started as rookies last year. The Parks is a newer high-rise complex that's unofficially become the team's residence of choice for those of us who are single or don't have families.

Our teammate Trenton Ashford, another rookie, lives on the floor below, along with two of the team's veteran players, Carch Anderson and Ansel Werner, who also happen to still be single. And I hear that our incoming rookies, Tra'Von Matthews and Xander Williams, may be moving in soon, too.

So far, living here with Henri has panned out and I consider him one of my closest teammates, although Henri is far more introverted than I originally assumed. That surprised me because when he's out on the court, he's a loud-mouthed trash talker. But off the court, he's reserved, keeping to himself except when he goes out to the clubs looking for action, and is the tidiest motherfucker I've ever known.

I always kid him that he was born a French maid. He doesn't think that joke is funny.

"Fuck off," my brother mutters in response to my baseless warning. "But thanks for taking care of this for me. And call me next week and tell me what happens at the hearing, okay?"

"Yeah, for sure. I will. Thanks, bro."

"Now I gotta go take a cold shower because my dumbass brother ruined my chances of getting laid tonight."

"Pfft. It's still early." I chortle. "I'm sure you've got a few others on the bench you can text for a booty call."

Which reminds me. I invited Henri and Trenton to go out with me tonight to a new club in Belltown. It's been a few weeks since I've had some action outside of my own hand myself.

"That's your department, bro. I'm a hell of a lot more selective than your slutty ass."

"You've got a point there," I muse. "Mmm-kay. Talk at you later."

As soon as I hang up, I set the letter aside and head down the hall to my bedroom to get ready for our night out, jumping in the shower to wash away all my concerns about the upcoming hearing in favor of having a good time.

What every twenty-four-year-old dude lives for.

**3**

———

Jade

"Let me get this straight," I hear from my bestie, Harper, who stands in a stall behind me. "You call being knee-deep in shit and covered in the odiferous stench of urine a good time? Where did I fail you as a friend?"

I lift my chin and throw a glance over my shoulder at Harper as I laugh over her response, even though she's glowering at me with a shovel in hand. If looks could kill... she just might murder me with both the shovel to the head and that death glare.

I suppose I wouldn't blame her, considering it does stink of dog piss in these cement cages we've been cleaning the past two hours. She may have been under the impression I had something more relaxing planned for our girls' day, like drinking cocktails at the bar, not mucking dog shit.

Doing my best to make Harper smile and see the difference we're making, I give her a lopsided grin that says, *"But I know you love me anyway."*

"Ahh, come on now, babes. It's not that bad...you are,

after all, surrounded by all these pretty puppies and me." I give her a cheesy grin and motion with an outstretched arm to the surrounding kennels as we're serenaded by a chorus of barks and yipes from the furry inhabitants.

Harper shakes her head and lets out a dramatic groan, bending forward to scoop up a pile of poo left over from the dog that was just taken out for a romp in the yard by Sam, another volunteer.

"You've gotten me into a lot of shit over the years, girl," she laments, tilting her hip sideways with a hand gripped around the shovel handle, her eyes glaring me down. "But never did I think it would be *actual fucking shit*. You're the worst best friend ever and you're not getting a Christmas gift this year."

I snort out a laugh and then pout. "What? That's just plain mean. I thought you'd want to do this together today. Obviously, I was wrong and I'm dropping you as my wingwoman."

She squeals loudly when I pick up a wet tennis ball left behind by a dog and toss it at her calf. But she's fast and jumps out of the way with a swift twist of her hips. Not fast enough to avoid the slobber that sprays over her leg, though. I can barely hear the curse that slides from her mouth over my loud laughter as she leans down to wipe off the wet residue.

We continue to work through our inside jokes and laughter for another thirty minutes, chatting about the previous week's escapades in our life, until the conversation veers to my upcoming City Planning meeting and Marek's annual Fourth of July bash. Which also happens to be Harper and Marek's engagement party.

"So, tell me about this meeting and why you have to attend."

I turn off the water spigot used to hose down the dirty cage and begin to replace all the bedding and toys for the next doggie guest.

"The City Planning Board sent a notification out to all businesses who might be impacted by the new development. I wouldn't normally go to these things, because those meetings can be boring as fuck, but according to my friend who works for the city, the new owner has submitted plans to tear down the building, rebuild, and develop it into a gym and spa situation."

Harper sniffs in disbelief. "What? Can they even do that? I mean, build a gym so close to an existing gym?"

I pick up the bucket at my feet and rinse it out before setting it back in the supply closet.

"Sure, with the city planning commissions approval. It's a free country and capitalism is at work." I sigh, flicking a lock of my curly springy air out of my face. "That's why I need to show up with my stats and arguments to prove how it could be detrimental to my Black woman-owned business. It's going to be a tough sell, though."

"Why's that? Sounds easy enough for you."

I wish I felt a smidgen of her confidence in me, but it isn't like that.

"The council won't care about the competitive factors. I'll have to find a counterpoint to get them to reject the build. I just haven't found it yet."

Harper removes her rubber gloves, ditching them in the wastebasket in the hallway as we pass. We push through the front doors of the shelter as I wave a hand in the air at Tricia, the Volunteer Coordinator at the front desk, as we leave. Our volunteer time is up and I promised Harper a bottle of wine and a cheese plate out on my balcony to watch the sunset for her efforts to help me.

"Well, I have faith you can convince them otherwise," Harper says, slipping on her sunglasses to hide from the glare of the late afternoon sun and throwing an arm around my shoulders. "You'll find a way. We are not going to allow some yahoo corporation sweep in and wipe out all you've done. No one has worked harder than you have."

I give her a wan smile and bump her hip with mine. "Yeah, but regardless, they won't care. I just wish whoever owns the building wouldn't be in direct opposition to me, ya know? Why can't they open a laundromat or something?"

We hop in the Uber I'd ordered to take us back to my place, sliding into the backseat next to one another.

"I hear ya. But they have no idea who they're up against. No one takes on Jade Russell and lives to tell the story."

Her comment reminds me of when we were in college and the two of us together pulled out a win for the record books. And then, because we're always on the same wave length, we turn our heads to face each other.

"Western—" Harper says with a smile, and I reach out and bump her fist, mirroring her grin with one of my own.

"We were invincible."

It was the game that took us to the Final Four that year and solidified our friendship. And also sparked the same fierceness and drive to win that we both possess to this day.

"Hell yeah, we were," Harper agrees, spouting off the stats I pulled out in that game after she suffered a sprained ankle and had to sit on the sidelines for a good portion of the game.

I felt unstoppable and was at the top of my game that day.

Sadly, though, that toughness on my part has only been a veneer. I'm only a portion of my former self after the night that irrevocably damaged my heart and how I trust others.

Harper may be the closest thing I have to a sister, but that is something I've never shared with her. Not that I haven't wanted to or tried in the past, but this secret was too big. Too shameful to ever expose, even to my best friend.

Because if I do ever let her in on what happened, all the walls will collapse. Like a house of cards, my façade will crumble, and everyone will see the empty shell I've become.

Instead, I've let her believe I'm invincible, tough, and always down for a good time, when in reality, my soul was crushed to smithereens and is still lying on the floor withered and rotting.

Maybe if Harper had been with me that night...if I hadn't been so naive...if I hadn't trusted a wolf in sheep's clothing...

I shake off the thoughts because it doesn't matter now and does me absolutely no good rehashing it over and over again in my mind. It wasn't Harper's fault that she wasn't around much for me that semester. She was dealing with her own family problems and living back at home, leaving me to handle life on campus and the aftermath and consequences of my decisions. And I hadn't wanted to add to her list of problems.

I kept it to myself and buried it deep. Harper knows me too well, though, and is intuitive enough to know something happened to me. She confronted me several times throughout that summer but I shut her down. I thought if I could bury it deep enough and never discuss it, then maybe it never happened.

It changed me though. I was no longer the easy-going, fun-loving girl I'd once been, the one quick to joke or the girl who enjoyed attention. I no longer trust men or myself around men. I put up barriers to hide my vulnerabilities. It seemed to have worked because after a while, Harper stopped asking if I was okay all the time. I forced myself to smile and worked my way out of a deep depression by focusing on the one and only thing that mattered to me.

Turning my life from a mess to a success. Which is what I've been doing the last five years until this potential new competitor showed up.

The Uber stops in front of my building and lets us out. We exit the car and head through the locked front doors, climbing the stairs to my third-floor apartment.

I can hear Tubby scrambling up from his bed by the window and the clickety-clack of his nails skittering along my hardwood floor as he races to the door.

"There's my little man," I coo once I open the door, scooping his tiny four-pound body into my arms and kissing the top of his head. "Who's my good boy?"

He swipes a lick on my chin with his tiny tongue before he snarls like a savage at Harper, showing his canines with an aggressive growl. Harper closes the door behind me and puts up her fists like she's about to fight him in the ring.

"I hate you too, Tubby boy," she sing-songs in a sweet voice, dropping down on my couch with a thump.

"Now you two get along tonight. Or else." I wag my finger at them both as I set Tubs back on his feet and he follows at my heels as I enter the kitchen.

"White or red?" I ask, opening the cabinets to extract two extra-large wine goblets. It is definitely going to be a night for *extra*.

"Either is fine. But I need some water first."

I swivel around and give her a wink. "Coming right up, Your Highness."

She shoots me a scowly look and hoots from the living room but stands up and strides into the kitchen as I fill up our glasses with a red.

"What's up with that sarcasm?" Harper bumps a hip against mine. "Does doth thinketh I've become used to my new lavish living arrangements?"

"If the shoe fits, Miss Bougie-I'm-engaged-to a-millionaire High-and-Mighty." I tease her with a waggle of my ass in her direction, laughing when she protests over my comment.

"Whatever...you know that's not true," Harper grumbles, but then leans in over my shoulder with a conspiratorial whisper and a giggle. "But I have to admit, it's really nice to have a boyfriend who's rich and handsome."

"Fiancé!" I correct with a laugh, grabbing her hand in mine to examine the brilliant sparkle of her engagement ring that he gave her on live TV less than a month ago. "He's your fiancé now, Harp. Oh my God, you're engaged!"

We both stare down at the glint on her finger in awe over how this even happened. A little over a year ago, I was helping Harper pin down an exclusive interview with Marek Talbert, the GM of the Seattle Pilots basketball team, and now she's engaged to be married to him. It's crazy how fate can intervene so beautifully in the lives of people.

While I'm truly so happy for my friend, it stings a bit knowing I'll never have what she has. You can't love someone if you don't trust them, and my trust meter was broken years ago and can't be rebuilt.

I take my glass with me to my small outside balcony, where we take our usual spots that overlook the water. Tubby jumps up on my lap, making himself comfortable as I look out across the incredible view that never gets old. But it's nothing compared to the water view of Marek's and now Harper's home on Lake Washington. Which reminds me of their engagement slash Fourth of July party next week.

"Is there anything you need help with for the party? I've

never been a maid of honor before, obviously. Are there rules and etiquette I need to know?"

Harper waves a hand and takes a sip of her wine, propping her legs up on the wrought-iron balcony railing.

"Trust me, Marek has everything planned out. He asked me what I wanted, and I told him a good old-fashioned BBQ and s'more-making station and that's it. He took it from there."

I tip my head and motion up to the sky with my chin.

"And fireworks, of course."

She laughs. "Well, duh. That's a given. Only the best for this bougie-ass bitch."

We laugh over her joke, but it has taken quite a bit of getting use to being around so many rich and famous people, most of whom are local athletes and bigwig sports execs.

Although my business caters exclusively to wealthy clientele, I grew up an Army brat, living in military housing both on and off base. And Harper is a farm girl born and bred, now in the sports broadcasting field. There are times we've both felt out of our league when around these guys.

But for Harper, I will do whatever she needs me to do and go wherever she wants me to go. Because that's what friends do for each other. She's had my back from day one and I've had hers. And I hope that doesn't change when she gets married.

"Well, if I don't need to bring anything, just tell me when you want me there."

Harper lifts her shoulder and taps her finger on the rim of her glass.

"How about noon? Everyone else won't arrive until after five. That gives us some alone time at the pool."

"Sounds perfect," I agree with the clink of my glass against hers. "I'll drink to that."

4

J aeger

I have no idea what to expect when I walk into city hall in search of the conference room where the meeting will be held. But I'm stopped short immediately once I'm through the doors by the beefed-up armed police officers who search and screen people before they leave the foyer.

Checking the time, I sigh at this unexpected inconvenience. There's a line ten-deep as we wait for an idiot who can't figure out what's in his pants that's sending the machine in a tizzy. The officer has sent him through three times so far.

My irritation is on the rise when suddenly a man in a gray suit with his phone in hand pushes through the doors like his ass is on fire, dangles his badge in front of my face, and bumps me in the shoulder to move ahead of me in the line. The physical contact is not only rude, but it's hard enough that it propels me forward enough that my body smacks into the woman in front of me.

On instinct, I extend my hands in search of something to

grab onto to keep myself upright, and that something just so happens to be the woman's lower back. Well, technically, my fingers latch around her waist. Quickly finding my balance, I bounce back onto my heels, the momentum unintentionally tugging her along with me. My elbows lock at my sides and it tucks her securely against my chest.

She immediately struggles like a fish on a line trying to get free, the tension ricocheting through her stiff body. I let my hands fall to my sides the moment she wheels around, a curse slipping from her lips as her hazel-gold eyes throw daggers my way. Or maybe they're golden brown with flecks of copper? I'm so mesmerized by the color, I stand there like a fool.

"What the hell, buddy?"

"Whoa, whoa, whoa," I throw my palms in front of me in a defensive gesture, although it might be wiser to cover my junk by how mad she looks for being accidentally groped. Not that it was my fault, which I try to explain by pointing toward the douchewad who set this entire thing in motion. Problem is, he's already skirted through security and is halfway down the hall, leaving me to look like the asshole here.

"Hey, I'm sorry. Are you okay?" I look her over to see that she isn't physically hurt. She looks fine but far from happy over my intrusion into her personal space. I wisely step back to offer some distance. "I didn't do that intentionally. It was that asshat who hip-checked me. I swear I wasn't trying to cop a feel."

I give her my most disarming smile and a wink for good measure, which usually works on women but doesn't quite seem to have the intended effect this time. Instead, her gaze studies me skeptically. But even that glare doesn't detract from the fierce beauty of this woman.

Holy fucking hell. She is a goddess in a business suit.

"I'm fine, thanks for your concern. Just be more careful next time," she says, righting her jacket by tugging at the hem before turning around to effectively dismiss me.

Before she does, though, the tugging action has me automatically homing in at the way her full breasts pop out from behind her lapels. I examine her from head to toe, scanning her features and admiring how fucking gorgeous she is. Even her profile is shockingly perfect. I've seen a lot of filter-perfect women on Instagram and such, but this woman's the real deal.

She may be wearing a demure navy blazer and matching pants, a white blouse peeking out at the collar, but it does little to hide her smokin' body. Underneath the prim and proper business attire, she's clearly rocking a supremely hot body. And my cock becomes aware of it, as well.

The skin of her neck and face is a light shade of brown with a shimmery rose hue spanning along her cheekbones, and she has the most delicious-looking cherry-red lips I've ever seen. Her hair is done up in some tight braided twist on the top of her head, giving her a regal flare. A dainty silvery necklace wraps around her slender neck, paired with silver diamond studs.

*Something goes haywire in my head because I'm shook. I want to bow and worship at her feet.*

"Next time. I like the sound of that," I offer with a wink. "How about—"

"Next."

My words are interrupted when the security officer gestures the woman forward, putting an end to our hot exchange that has left me winded like I just did suicide drills down the court. Okay, and technically, maybe I'm the only one between us who found it to be hot. The feeling may not have been mutual.

Which confounds me. I'm not used to literally being disregarded. My fame makes me a pretty fucking recognizable celebrity in this town, and I get a lot of second looks from both men and women.

Not from this woman, though. Which leaves me unsettled.

She flicks her chin to give me one last side-eye and places her purse on the conveyor belt that feeds it through the X-ray machine and spits it out the other end. Then she moves forward through the metal detector.

Her strange reaction and disregard has me wanting to chase her down to talk with her. To find out who she is. Maybe even to ask her out for a coffee or drink later. I dare not blink for fear she'll disappear, and I won't get my chance to catch up and talk to her.

My interest to pursue her has my eyes dropping to her firm ass, the perfection of it making me salivate.

My eyes haven't left her for a second. I watch her intently as she exits the detector and retrieves her purse at the other end. When I haven't moved, the security officer motions me through the metal detector with a grunt. As if hypnotized, I walk through, completely oblivious to anything except the beauty in front of me.

The loud blare of the machine's alarm wakes me from my stupor and has me jerking backwards a step. The officer briskly moves toward me, a menacing dip of his brows indicating his displeasure with me.

"Did you empty your pockets like it says?" he asks, gesturing to the sign on the wall with an irritated scowl. Then he motions me off to the side, waving a wand over my front pockets and crotch area, then down the length of my hips, then behind my back over my butt.

I hear someone in line behind me groan in annoyance as the officer's wand chirps again. I was so focused on finding a way to meet the woman that I failed to remove my keys from my pocket. Jesus, what's gotten into me? Like some strange voodoo spell was cast over me and I have swirling cartoon eyes spinning in my head.

Soon a second officer joins in on the fun, flanking me on both sides as I'm ushered through the archway, the metal detector sounding off with a screeching blare.

My view of the mystery woman is now completely blocked by the broad shoulders of the first officer who steps in front of me, arms crossed over his chest, preventing me from proceeding ahead.

He gives me an authoritative head nod. "Empty your pockets, sir. Nice and slow."

A laugh bubbles up from my chest. What exactly do they think I'm going to do? Hurl my keys at their heads and run off like an escaped convict?

I stick my hands in my pocket and rifle around until my hand lands on my keys and the forgotten change the barista returned to me this morning after I paid for my coffee. I don't know why I didn't leave it in her tip jar like I normally do, but I was nervous about this meeting and forgot.

"Sorry," I offer up in apology, extracting the handful of change and my keys and placing them in the basket. Neither officer seems to give a shit about my apology or recognizes who I am. They just think I'm some asshole holding up their line because I couldn't follow directions.

By the time I repeat the entire walk-through again and gather up my belongs, the gorgeous mystery woman is no longer in sight.

"Goddammit," I mutter a little too loudly as I shove everything back into my pockets. This scores me another dirty look from the officer before he returns to his screening duties and all the frustrated people behind me.

I shake my head, annoyed with myself for missing a prime opportunity to introduce myself to the incredibly tall, goddess-like beauty.

She's literally vanished into thin air. Hating to give up on my quest to locate her, I scan the corridor as I walk through the mezzanine but don't see any sign of her. If she were around, she wouldn't be too hard to spot, considering how tall she is. That was the second thing I noticed after being entranced with her golden eyes.

Most women barely measure to the top of my chest. It happens when the average woman is around five-foot-four and I'm freaking six-foot-seven. I'm a giant by almost any standard.

But this chick was tall. Maybe even six feet? I suppose she could've been wearing heels to exaggerate her height, but I didn't get a good look down at her feet because I was too mesmerized by her face and the fact she didn't recognize me.

Not only was she hot, but her lack of fawning over me like other women tend to do intrigued me. Once they recognize me, I never know if they want to get to know me for me or just my basketball-hero status.

But surprisingly, this woman didn't seem to know who I am.

And those eyes of her. *Damn.* They shined with some kind of golden sparkle, like rays from the sun ringing around her irises.

Jesus, I'm pathetic. I'm waxing poetic about her eyes?

That right there is a sure sign I need to go out and have

some fun with Henri and the guys tonight. I've been so consumed with this business venture lately that I haven't spent much time with my boys.

After all that happened with the chick post-championship fuck, I promised myself I would take a break from hooking up with randos. And unlike Henri, who has a few local chicks on his go-to list for occasional hookups, I've been staunchly celibate, a little freaked out to try anything new with any unfamiliar women.

But I'd make an exception for the mystery woman.

Standing in the middle of the open mezzanine, I resign myself to the fact that I'll probably never see her again and decide to give up the search. Unfolding the piece of paper from my back pocket, I verify the room assignment that was listed for this public hearing.

The Rainier Room. Second floor, west corridor.

A bank of elevators behind me hosts a half dozen or more people waiting to ride upstairs, so I locate the nearest stairwell, taking the stairs two-by-two until I reach the second floor. Reaching the landing, I open the door and enter the hallway, reading the placard on the wall that directs me to the left and toward the Rainier Room.

Upon entering, the first thing I notice is that it appears to be a courtroom. Which make me even more nervous than I was to begin with. I guess I expected it to be a conference room, not so formal. Instead, it looks like one of those rooms from the senate committee hearings you see on CNN.

I take a few tentative steps forward, uncertain whether I should sit toward the front or the back. Straight ahead of me at the end of the aisle is a podium with a mic and behind that on either of the aisle are rows of seating.

I slowly lumber down the aisle and take a spot on the right, third row from the front. Now that I'm seated, I scan the room and see two other people in the auditorium, an older gentleman that could probably win a look-a-like contest for Albert Einstein and an older woman who wears a colorful crocheted shawl like they wore back in the '70s.

No aluminum hats to be found. I snicker to myself at the image in my head.

I check the time on the phone again and see I'm still a few minutes early, even with the difficulties I had in security, so I start playing a game on my phone while I wait.

Five minutes later, the creaking noise from the large wood door at the front of the room draws my attention and I cast an upwards glance to see three people entering the room, someone's rubber-soled shoes making a squeaking noise as they walk.

A man with dark hair and glasses, possibly in his early forties, sits at the center chair in the U-shaped desk and the other two people flank him on either side.

He leans into a microphone and begins the meeting.

"Good morning. Today is June 23rd and the Seattle City Planning, Land Use and Zoning Committee will come to order. It's 9:01 a.m. I'm Tom Chan, chair of the committee, and with me are Dale Martins, and Sandra Ho." Tom motions toward each of them and they nod their heads. Tom clears his throat. "Today's meeting is a public forum to discuss zoning on several new land use development opportunities as proposed to the City Council and Planning Commission. We will hear out the legislative and environmental factors related to these proposed developments, then open it up to the public for questions, opposition, and counter arguments."

I swallow thickly, already feeling the sweat dripping down the back of my dress shirt and pooling near the waistband of my briefs.

I'm suddenly feeling completely unprepared for whatever is about to happen. Jesse said this whole thing would just be a formality required by the city, but this sounds like I'll be expected to speak in favor of my project. Shit. I have no idea what to say.

It's not like I'm inept at public speaking or anything like that—as a professional ball player I've been interviewed on TV and sports channels countless times in my career. That's different. I just use my cocksure attitude and basketball experience, add in a little swagger and my charm, and I'm golden.

This right here?

Fuck, I'm not sure my cocky self will be able to argue my way out a box if it comes down to it.

Let's just hope no one opposes me on this project.

**5**

___

Jade

I stare down at the notes I've carefully crafted in preparation for this meeting, confident that I'm ready to speak on my business's behalf.

As a business owner, I've spoken in many public forums. I've been invited to present at various women's business groups and organizations, was the keynote speaker at a Seattle independent fitness event, and even gave at talk at a local high school's career day fair. That was a blast, and all due to an invitation from my college friend, Letitia, now a teacher and the girls' basketball coach at that particular high school.

But today is different. The outcome is bigger and there's more at stake for me professionally. If my arguments aren't strong enough to get the council to change their minds, and they allow the new building owner to continue their development plans, I'm screwed. It will have a direct impact on my bottom line. All my financial security and my future business aspirations could be bulldozed, right along with the old building down the street.

I can't let that happen. I have too much at stake and far too much to lose. Not only my current business but my hope of one day starting a non-profit women's shelter.

The toe of my high heel taps wildly as I wait for the meeting to convene, my fingers nervously fiddling with my notecards as I read over them for the bazillionth time. That weird experience down at security rattled me, and I had gone straight into the bathroom to freshen up my lipstick.

That entire situation with that guy threw me off-balance —literally. Had he not grabbed onto my waist and kept me upright, I would have tumbled onto the floor.

When I turned around to give the guy hell—righting myself with a palm to his chest—he seemed so apologetic that I let it go. Plus, one look into his bright blue eyes framing his handsome face had me willing to forgive and forget.

*Those baby blues could make a girl forget her own name.*

There was no use getting upset over an accident, even if he did put his hands on me without permission. All of it happened quickly, so I didn't get a chance to pinpoint his vague familiarity to me. There was something in his face that seemed recognizable. As I washed up in the bathroom, I tried to place him but came up empty. With so many young athletic guys coming into the gym on a regular basis, it could've been any one of them.

But there was something about him—beyond his attractiveness—that niggled in my belly and the back of my mind. I just couldn't put a finger on it.

Now as I wait in my seat, inhaling and exhaling in a meditative breathing exercise to calm the jittery nerves residing in my stomach, I lift my gaze to the front of the room as I hear the sound of the anterior door opening and then slamming shut. Three people walk in and take their places at the horseshoe-shaped desk. Taking a quick glance around at the rows in front of me, my attention is drawn to the guy sitting across the aisle and one row ahead.

He's the guy. The hot one who ran into me earlier.

Due to the circumstances and timing of it all, I hadn't stuck around to check him out. At this angle, though, I have an unobstructed view of his profile.

His hair is a light brown with swaths of blond and auburn weaving through the tousled strands. From all appearances, it looks like he did nothing when he woke up this morning except slide a hand through it.

I make a soft scoff under my breath. *Men.* They have it so easy in the grooming department. I spent an hour on my appearance, including makeup application and hair, which is now in tight braids due to the hair appointment I sat through yesterday and pinned up in a knot at the top of my head.

I continue searching the guy's profile with an assessing gaze. He has a strong, angular jawline with a light shadow of stubble. The slope of his nose is proportional to the length of his face, but there's a bump at the bridge which suggests it's been broken in the past.

He's a big guy. Tall and clearly muscular based on the stretch of his pant leg over his thigh, and it's...*unsettling.* There are visible bulges that strain against the tight cling of the material. His legs are so long they can't even be confined to his row because his feet are crossed at the ankles and his body is twisted so that his legs stick out into aisleway, leaving his knees to still touch the backside of the chair in front of him.

And the way the charcoal suit jacket pulls over his broad shoulders clearly says he is blessed with a very athletic physique. I'm keenly aware of just exactly what he was packing under that suit when my palm landed on his abs during our accidental tussle at security.

I swallow. Either I'm parched from the nerves taking up residence in my bloodstream or this guy is a thirst trap. My pulse throbs in my throat...and elsewhere.

I shake my head to clear my thoughts.

*Focus, Jade.*

To shift my thoughts from this attractive but untimely distraction, I scan the room in search of anyone who looks like they're here representing JJ Enterprises, the company that owns the building and that I'm here to oppose today.

All I see are a few older citizens and the young hottie I've been ogling.

Weird. Maybe the reps or lawyer for JJ Enterprises couldn't make it or skipped out entirely, thinking it would be a slam dunk. Too bad they didn't know they'd be dealing with me. A confident grin ticks up at the corners of my mouth.

This day might actually turn out to be an easy win for me, which would be a first. Everything else I've ever done in life has cost a piece of me. Blood, sweat, and tears. Nothing has ever been handed to me without me having to work for it.

My dad has always told me it makes you appreciate things more when you have to work for it. But just once, maybe this one time, I'd like something to go easily for me.

I cast a speculative glance at the hottie again, wondering what the hell a guy like him is doing here. Although he's clad in a suit, he appears younger than me. Maybe early twenties. It's a strange juxtaposition to the type of people I'd expect to see in this hearing.

"This meeting is called to order," the meeting chair

announces, using a gavel to gain everyone's attention. "Looks like we have two agenda items today and they are both about new Land Use Actions under City Ordinance Number 2293 related to the demolition and tear down of an existing building, and the environmental and economic factors of this new project. As this is open to the public, speakers are limited to two minutes of public comment. If the speaker's comments exceed two minutes, the microphone will be turned off. First on our list is regarding the Land Use Action at 14237 South Vine and Bell Street in the Belltown district."

I shift in my seat, straightening against the back of the wood bench as I wait to be invited to the podium.

"First on our list is Ms. Jade Russell, owner of Seattle Circuit, followed by Mr. Jaeger Matlin, owner of JJ Enterprises."

I jump to my feet upon hearing my name and brush a hand down the front of my blazer to calm myself and keep myself in the present. As I step into the aisle, ready to go to battle, the second name the speaker mentioned nearly stops me in my tracks.

That name.

I've heard it before.

Jaeger isn't a very common name in most circles. Unless you hear it used regularly on every local media station in the greater Seattle area.

*Jaeger Bomb. Jaeger Meister.* Jaeger Matlin. Star rookie player for the Puget Sound Pilots.

Holy shit. That's why I recognize him...

My eyes snap to Jaeger, whose head whips around to look at me so fast it's almost comical, his eyes flaring wide. In surprise? Or panic? I'm not sure why either would be expressed but it's then I put two and two together.

There's no big wig corporate attorney here to represent the interests of JJ Enterprises.

It's Jaeger Matlin.

The cocky multi-million-dollar basketball player.

The rumored Romeo playboy and man-whore.

And apparently, the owner of JJ Enterprises and my new competitor.

I suck in a harsh breath as I walk by his row, locking eyes with him on my way to the podium.

He blinks and his mouth falls open as I size up my opponent.

I curl my lips up into a side smirk. It's the same one I'd give my rivals out on the basketball court in my college days.

The one that says, "*I'm going to wipe the floor with your ass.*"

And then I mouth, "You're going down, Rookie."

My body lights up like a hundred-watt bulb with the same level of adrenaline I used to get before a big game as this young cocky player turns a ghostly white.

I love to compete.

But I love to win more.

Based on the way his eyes flash in shock and his brows crinkle in confusion, I think this is going to be an easy win. Regardless of his superstar athlete status, the way he's sizing me up right now tells me there's a good chance he's just realized what he's up against. He realizes he's met his match.

It's how I've presented myself to get as far as I have in my career. I started with a paltry five thousand dollars, a high-interest bank loan, and a dream. When most of my college friends were getting married and starting new jobs, I was out busting my ass, teaching kickboxing five days a week, training women in their thirties and forties, building a brand. The odds were stacked against me to move into my own business.

I was a young Black woman trying to compete against national gym chains and corporate men in suits who'd never had to be scrappy and self-invested.

They underestimated my drive to win and my desire to be the best. I'm a woman who doesn't take no for an answer and will find an alternative way in if one door is closed in my face.

Which means if Jaeger Matlin thinks he can bulldoze me out of my business, using his name and notoriety, he has another thing coming.

He will soon find out I won't quit, I won't give in, and I won't give up without a fight.

And the first punch in this fight is with my statement in opposition to his land use proposal.

I stand in front of the podium's mic, positioning it closer to my mouth, and offer a soft smile to the committee members in front of me.

"Thank you for your time today. My name is Jade Russell, and I am the owner of a local gym called Seattle Circuit on Bell Street, kitty-corner to the property now owned by JJ Enterprises and Mr. Matlin." I snap a quick glance over my shoulder at Jaeger, who appears to have leaned forward in his chair, intently listening to what I have to say.

"I began my business five years ago, using my meager savings and a bank loan, to build my fitness business from the ground up. To date, I have helped hundreds of clients become healthier and stronger to live better lives." I stare pointedly at Tom Chan, who comes in three times a week to work with one of my trainers. When he first started, he was nearing fifty, just finalizing a divorce, and had a spare tire worthy of a Mack truck. Since then, with the help of my training staff, he's turned his body into something that even most thirty-year-olds would admire.

I continue. "Outside of the fitness programs I offer for profit, I have also used proceeds to work with inner city schools to promote healthier lifestyles within their student bodies. In addition, I open up my gym for specialized activities, like self-defense classes for women and girls currently residing in shelters, a vulnerable population in our city."

The woman in front seems to perk up at this point, tilting her head and nodding her thorough agreement. The expressions on the men, however, even Tom's, have changed little from their original disinterested observations.

"The reason I share this is because it's important to remember that as a small business owner, specifically a Black woman business owner," I say with emphasis, "I am only able to make these things happen by the continued development of my business. According to the permits, it appears that JJ Enterprises plans to open and run both a commercial and residential development that could potentially hurt my business and put an end to the community programs I currently offer."

This, while very true, won't likely sway the committee in my direction. As I told Harper, they won't care about the competition or my bottom line. That's just a fact of life in business. It's all about property taxes for them. I only throw in this tidbit as a ploy to soften their hearts before I go in for the real kill shot.

The one objection that can't be disputed in this case, and the one I owe my friend Mialani a debt of gratitude for giving to me, is a snafu in their original permitting. The city fucked up and I'm about to let them know it.

"Aside from that, I'm sure you are all very aware that Mr.

Matlin's proposes to create a multi-use building, featuring a gym and spa at street level and potentially apartments on the upper three levels. But it's my understanding that the existing building is only two floors, which is what meets the height restrictions in this neighborhood. The current zoning is specifically for residential, and not commercial space. Which means"—I pause, knowing my two minutes are nearly up, and flip my notecard to read the last part of my statement—"that JJ Enterprises cannot be allowed to build it under those specifications."

There's a collective murmur from the members up front and I hear someone cough behind me. I swivel my head just slightly to the side to once again see the pale face of Jaeger. This time, however, there are beads of sweat at his temples and he hangs his head looking like a defeated man.

I give an internal *Praise Jesus and Hallelujah*, followed by invisible jazz hands.

"Thank you for your time."

I pivot on my heels, turning back down the aisle with an easy and graceful stride, and flick my gaze to Jaeger as I pass his row. He stares at me with a flabbergasted look.

This is my moment of triumph. I tilt my head and give him a patronizing pat on the shoulder, knowing I just won this round.

"Sorry, not sorry."

And then I sit down and wait for his rebuttal.

My inner Queen rejoices over my win.

## 6

———

J aeger

"Mr. Matlin, would you like to address the concerns brought forth by Ms. Russell? If so, now is your chance to make your statement."

I swallow the lump in my throat, completely thrown off course at this unexpected turn of events, and wonder what the fuck just happened.

One minute I think I'm going to build a gym and the next thing I know, I'm being taken down by a beautiful woman.

I hear my name being called again, this time in a more impatient tone, and I look up to find the committee chair staring at me expectantly. Oh, that's right. I'm supposed to go up to the podium.

If I were out on a basketball court standing at the free throw line, it would be an easy shot. At this moment, I feel like a beaten and bruised gladiator in the middle of the Coliseum, up against a giant with only a pebble in my hand.

The only thing I can do is wing it. Otherwise, I'm basically throwing away my chance of making good on my first business investment.

I slowly rise to my feet, legs shaky, and I walk toward the podium. I adjust the mic as high as it can go and still have to bend down so my mouth is level with it.

My voice blasts loudly and sounds raspy with a nervous rattle.

I clear my throat. "Thank you, Tom, and Committee. While I am surprised to learn of this zoning requirement, I'm sure I can go back and readjust the plans to meet these codes. I will meet with my architect this week and if you'll allow the extension, I can resubmit new plans before the next meeting."

The Chairmen covers his microphone with his palm and turns to the two other members to confer and seek their approvals. Then he returns his focus on me and responds to my request with a nod.

"Very well, Mr. Matlin. Due to this unfortunate error in our zoning process, you are hereby granted an extension to make whatever necessary revisions are needed. You may submit it before the next month's agenda timeline. Thank you. You may be seated."

I nod with a grateful smile and turn around, my eyes immediately snagging on my very worthy adversary.

The very beautiful, very gloating adversary. The one whose smile has just changed into something closely resembling righteously indignant.

Maybe she thought she was going to walk out of here victorious. Like the 1990s Chicago Bulls dynasty who squashed every team that decade to win time and time again. But thanks to my luck, I was able to fake her out and swerve to the net to deliver a "not so fast, lady" reply to her earlier taunting.

There's no doubt she gave a compelling speech, and maybe I'll feel bad if my new gym interferes with her business. But that's life. Regardless of that sob story she gave, I'm not going to roll over for her and pass on my business interests.

Doesn't she know who I am? I'm Jaeger "The Bomb" Matlin. I came in and took this city by storm, giving the team and our fans our first championship title. It may not be an apples-to-apples comparison, but I'm no stranger to hard work either. Nothing's been given to me that I haven't earned through perseverance and commitment.

I take my seat and as the chairman gives his parting remarks, I pull out my phone and set it in my lap, angrily typing out a text to Jesse.

> Me: Motherfucker. I got hosed in this City meeting today. Thanks a lot.

I see the three dots begin and then disappear and start again.

> Jesse: What? I'm at a study session right now. I'll call you later tonight.

Clenching my jaw hard enough to break a tooth, I slip my phone back into my suit jacket pocket and decide I need to figure out my next steps on my own. I am, after all, the owner of this property. I'm not a complete idiot. I can figure out a solution without always having to run to my dad or brother.

The gavel hits the desk to adjourn the meeting and I jolt upright in the row. This may seem like a loss right now, but I won't let that stand for too long.

I push to my feet and turn into the aisle, ready to

confront my newly appointed arch-nemesis, when a man appears in front of me.

"Hey, Jaeger Bomb. Wow, it's so cool to meet you," the man says with the familiar eager excitement that fans get when they meet me in person. He sticks out his hand to shake mine.

Jesus, why do fans always have the worst timing?

I hide my impatience with a tight smile and clasp his hand, doing the honorable thing even as I keep my gaze fixated over his shoulder at Jade, who books it out of the room. When she gets to the door, she flips her head around and smirks at me.

And goddamn if I don't want to go chasing after her. But this time, instead of drinks, I want something else. An idea forms inside my head as the man babbles on and gushes over me in that starstruck manner so many seem to get.

Maybe there doesn't have to be a winner and a loser in this situation or even a competitive impasse. Maybe instead of rivals she'd be willing to be partners. We could find a way to work together instead of against each other.

Based on the speech she gave, Jade's obviously worried about how my gym would interfere with her business. Perhaps there's a chance I could entice her to join forces with the opportunity of more space and money at her disposal. Sweeten the pot so she could have her cake and eat it too.

The man continues to quote all my stats from this past season. *Blah, blah, blah.*

"I just wanted to shake your hand and tell you congratulations. You really earned that salary of yours in the post-season games."

I think there's a compliment somewhere in there.

"Thanks," I say, hoping to move this along quickly. "Do

you want a picture with me or something? I've really got to go."

The guy seems to fluster, nearly dropping his phone from his hand when he fishes it out of his pocket.

He sidles up next to me, him a full foot shorter, and positions the phone up, then wraps his arm around my back. I give the camera my trademark smile and the number one sign with my finger.

After taking a few snaps, I dislodge myself from his hold and nod toward the set of double doors leading into the hallway where Jade disappeared moments earlier.

"Nice to meet you. I've gotta run."

The guy slaps me on the back. "Yeah, yeah. Thanks, Jaeger. My son will totally freak out when he sees these pictures. Go, Pilots!"

I pivot on my heel and give him a wave over one shoulder, hightailing it out of the doors in hopes of miraculously finding her waiting for me in the hallway.

No such luck.

I walk swiftly toward the stairwell and take them three at a time down to the main corridor, rushing past some people in a serious discussion, and heading out the main entrance and into the street.

The clouds from earlier have dissipated, leaving a clear blue sky, and bright sunlight blinds me as I hit the sidewalk. I shield my eyes with my hand, wishing I'd thought to bring my shades, and scan the sidewalks left and right, then search across the street.

And then I see her.

She stands on the corner, waiting at the crosswalk and talking to someone on the phone. And she's wearing a huge smile.

A smile I know all too well because I've worn it myself. The one that says, "*I won.*"

Ignoring all pedestrian safety laws, I dash across the street, throwing my palm out to stop a car heading in my direction. The driver honks, but I've already reached the other side as he whizzes by and am less than ten feet behind where Jade stands.

The light turns green, and the crosswalk blinks with the walk sign. I shove my way through the other pedestrians, reaching a hand out without even thinking to grab her arm to stop her.

"Hey, Jade. Wait up for a second. I need to talk to you!" I shout, but that's the only words I get out because the next thing I know, Jade whirls around and clocks me in the nose with her right fist, followed by a kick to the shin.

*Holy shit. I did not see that coming.*

**7**

———————

J ade

"What in the hell were you thinking, grabbing a woman like that from behind?"

Jesus, what the hell is wrong with this guy? He had that punch coming, if you ask me.

I reluctantly offer a hand to Jaeger, who toppled backwards in the middle of the street the second after I punched him in the nose and kicked him in the leg. I should just leave him, but I don't want to be the woman responsible for Jaeger Meister's untimely death. Basketball fans would hate me.

It is kind of funny, though, to know I landed a professional basketball player on his ass. I can see the headlines now: "Pro baller gets knocked out by a badass babe." I smile internally at my badassery.

But the sight of the blood pouring from his nose interrupts my reverie as I watch it drip onto the front of his clean white shirt.

I give a heave-up to help Jaeger to his feet. He blinks

several times and wipes at his nose, the blood now clotting enough to stop streaming down his face.

"Come on, rookie. Let's get out of the road before we both end up laid out flat."

I direct him with a gesture to the other side of the street, finding a spot at the end of a bus bench for him to take a seat.

He still looks a little blurry-eyed and in shock.

I rifle through my purse and pull out a packet of tissues, placing one in his hand.

"Here, use this to clean up and tip your head back to stop the blood flow."

He blindly accepts the tissue, his head falling back between his shoulders, his eyes closing. He stretches out his long legs in front of him.

A low, throaty laugh snags my gaze back to his eyes and sends a shiver down my spine.

He opens one eyelid, his voice a mixture of awe and humor. "I've never been decked by a girl before."

I snort with amusement and note his gigantic NBA championship ring, the diamonds surrounding the circular Pilots emblem sparkling in a blinding light of brilliance.

"That is surprising, considering you're kind of a fool," I counter with a bit of sass. "Serves you right for touching a woman without permission. I gave you a pass the first time because it was an accident."

His dark eyebrows furrow and his mouth turns down into a frown. I hate to admit it, but he is cute. Jaeger looks like a little boy who's been scolded, his full lips turning down in a pout like he's trying to get out of it.

"I know. You're right," he agrees, shaking his head, his change in demeanor giving me a case of whiplash. What is it with this guy? "I'm sorry about that. I got so focused on stopping you from leaving so I could have a conversation with you that I didn't think."

He bends his head forward, blotting the remaining blood. I take his chin in my hand and inspect his nose, giving him a nod of approval.

The corners of Jaeger's mouth curl up into an adorable smile. "I have a tendency to act first, think second. I'm a bit impetuous."

"Ya think?" I quirk an eyebrow and drop my hand, my fingers still tingling from where his stubble prickled my skin.

Sighing, I look down at my phone and notice the time. I need to be back to the gym soon to give Siena her morning break. I've already been gone longer than I anticipated. But it was well worth it based on the outcome of the hearing.

Although it feels like only a temporary win because the sad truth is that Jaeger will probably get the star treatment in the end and be given exactly what he wants.

If he were any other Joe Schmo, who failed to know the city code, and not a star basketball player, he would've been given an immediate rejection from the council.

*Or, if he were a Black woman.*

That's the problem in this world. As a Black woman business owner, I have to know the rules, play by the rules, and not ever break rules. And work twice as hard to go half as far. Others, however, can get away with just about anything and be given grace and exceptions for their actions.

It's hard not to let it get me down, not to give up when I see these inequities happening. But what good would that do me?

Up until now, I've done exactly what I set out to do,

without any favors, handouts, or exceptions like what Jaeger just got today.

But because he is who he is, the council gave him a pass.

If the tables were turned and the situation were reversed, I doubt they would've given me the same consideration.

It's enough to make my blood boil and my irritation rise. It may be a systemic societal issue and not at all Jaeger's fault that he receives the benefits his privilege provides, but in the end, he is the recipient.

"Listen, Jaeger. I've got to go." I pause to cast a quick glance up the street where, just two blocks away, is my gym. "Sorry about your nose but I'm sure you'll survive."

I spin on my heel and wave a hand behind me as I take off down the street, believing I've heard the last of Jaeger Matlin, when suddenly out of nowhere, he appears at my side again, his long strides keeping up with mine. Damn heels for slowing me down. If I were in my gym shoes, I'd leave him eating my dust.

"Dude, stop following me," I grouse, giving him a flick of my hand. "There's a line between polite inquiry and stalking...and you're getting mighty close to that line."

I don't stop as I speak. I don't turn to look at him. I just keep walking straight ahead, increasing my pace and hoping he'll leave.

"Jade, please. Don't be like that. I just want to talk to you. I have an idea you might be interested in hearing."

Now I do stop, so abruptly that he's two steps ahead of me before he realizes it and turns back around, his facial expression registering surprise. I place my fists on my hips and shake my head in annoyance.

Probably more at myself than him because I still find him attractive even though he's a clueless asshat.

"Be like what, exactly? Concerned that you won't leave me alone?"

This seems to stump him. "Well...you're being rude. I've asked politely to talk to you."

I give a rueful laugh, my voice edging on hysterical. "*Rude*? You think *I'm* rude? Why? Because I don't want to chitchat"—I use air quotes—"with the guy who's out to ruin my business? Huh."

Jaeger's eyes grow wide and he noticeably stiffens, consciously or unconsciously, and takes a step backwards, granting me space.

He bows his head, his shoulders deflating before he returns his gaze to mine. "I swear, I'm not out to ruin yours or anyone else's business, Jade. I'm just a guy who has his own dreams to own a gym. And I have a proposal you might be interested in."

I pinch my lips together tightly and throw my hands in the air, giving him a look that I know displays my incredible disbelief.

"Why? You're a freaking millionaire. Why in the world do you need a gym on the same street as mine?" My voice breaks in desperation. I hate that he's gotten to me like this. I'm losing my confidence and control with every additional moment of this conversation.

"Can't you just find something to put your celebrity brand name to instead of trying to drive my business into the ground? It's just not fair."

Oh shit. I went there. That word is not supposed to be part of my vocabulary.

Since the day I was old enough to understand what life was about, my father taught me never to expect anything to be fair. There is no such word in my race's dictionary. Nothing will ever be fair. There will always be inequalities, especially for a Back woman in business. It's the reason I work as hard as I do. Why I fight for the things I believe in and stand up against the Establishment.

But a guy like Jaeger will never understand that because he was born a white man with an athletic gift that people now worship him for. They put him on a pedestal and give him everything he wants, whenever he wants it.

"I'm not trying to ruin you or steal anything from you, babe. That's not how business works."

Oh no...he did not just say that. *Seriously*? Did he just call me babe?

"Listen up, Jaeger *Meister*." I take a menacing step forward, encroaching on his space, quirking my eyebrow up. "First off, I am *not* your babe. That term is demeaning and insulting to full-grown women." He has the decency to look apologetic, his mouth turning into a regretful grimace, as if he's realized he fucked up. *Again.*

And now he looks nervous.

Good.

I poke him in the middle of his chest with my fingernail. *Hard.*

Jaeger winces but then turns his face and mutters into his shoulder. "Sorry, it slipped out. Most chicks like it when I call them babe."

I shouldn't even play this game of back-and-forth. What I should do is walk away right now and leave him with his foot stuck squarely in his mouth. But there's something about him that makes me both abnormally infuriated and maybe even a little hot. And not just hot under the collar, I mean like hot, hot. My panties may even be wet.

Shit. I need to reclaim my sanity and get the hell away from this dude once and for all.

"I am not one of your chicks, *Romeo*," I retort, throwing

in the name the tabloids call him when discussing his revolving door of hookups and notorious conquests. "And secondly, are you actually mansplaining business to me? Wow. That's rich coming from the guy who obviously wasn't prepared back there."

I hook my thumb over my shoulder before I bend over in laughter. When I stand back up, I swipe away at the fake tears that have left invisible rivulets down my face.

"That's so funny, Jaeger, considering one of us is a successful business owner. And you... aren't."

I poke at his chest to emphasize my last words, hoping he wises up and actually hear the truth in my words. His mouth opens and closes, his chin dropping to his chest to watch my finger burrow into his pec.

"Jaeger Matlin, all you are is a rich dude who plays basketball. I have been in business for five years." I emphasize this by spreading my fingers wide in front of his face, then ticking them off one by one. "That's more than you, rookie."

His gaze shifts to my hand and back to my face, his lips tightening into a grimace as if I just hit a nerve with my observation.

"I'm more than a basketball player. That's what I'm trying to prove with this business start-up. But I could use your help."

"At my expense." I shake my head with an exasperated laugh. "No thank you."

I raise an eyebrow daring him to say more. Our eyes lock, our jaws tighten, and we're stuck in a staring contest where someone probably needs to say Uncle, but it sure as hell won't be me.

*Stalemate.*

I will not let this rookie beat me at a game I've played for years before he ever stepped foot on the court.

Finally, without a word, he drops his eyes and growls, testily admitting defeat.

I shake my shoulders to adjust the strap of my purse. "I think we're done here. I wish you well, Jaeger, I really do. But if you're looking for business help, take some online classes or hire a consultant. I'm not here to do your work for you."

Jaeger's face turns a bright red. He sucks in a breath, his chest heaves in exertion.

"That's not what I want from you." He says matter-of-factly, his voice changing into a deep and almost sensual throaty sound.

My smile waivers. Here I thought I could win this pissing contest.

But what would I win?

There's nothing I want or need from Jaeger Matlin.

Jaeger's expression is transformative. One minute it's apologetic. The next moment there's heat in his gaze that turns my pent-up annoyance from a flicker into a raging inferno where I feel dizzy and lightheaded. My body ignites with a snap, like lightning hitting an exposed electrical box, turning me into a detonating device.

I'm suddenly at a loss for words, staring back at his mouth Those full, sensual lips, slightly parted. The tip of his tongue as it peeks out, wet and pink.

I do the only thing I can do to protect myself from falling for this Romeo's obvious charms. I cross my arms over my chest and take a step back, the atmosphere changing between us from a need to fight to the desire to fuck.

I try to swallow down the hundred-pound lump that has

found itself lodged in my throat. I don't even sound like myself when I respond.

I sound...turned on?

"I don't care what you want from me, Jaeger. I'm not giving you anything," I assert with a nod of my chin. "So I'll consider this conversation over. We can say goodbye and get on with our lives."

I hold out my hand and his eyes drift down as he lifts his and it meets mine.

The shock of our touch burns up my arm and I quickly yank my hand away before taking one final step back and turning. I can feel his heated gaze on my backside as I head up the street without a backward glance and take a sharp right at the next corner.

The minute I'm out of his sight, I press my back against a brick building and let out a long exhale. I don't know what that was, but I need to collect myself before going back to work because my heart is racing like I just ran a marathon.

But even with the chaos and busy work with all the daily responsibilities I have to manage the rest of the day, I can't shake Jaeger from my thoughts.

If I ever see him again, which I hope isn't any time soon, I need to remember to not allow his attractiveness to blind me into forgetting he's my business rival and nothing more.

I will not fall for a ball player or his Romeo ways.

## 8

J aeger

"Is that what you're wearing to the party?"

I look up from the television as Henri saunters into the living room, dressed with his usual French flare. I glance down at my attire and consider his question with a laugh.

"What are you, the fashion police for this soiree? It's an outdoor barbeque, dickwad. Yeah, this is what I'm wearing."

Henri's dressed in a pair of chinos and a striped polo with a light sweater draped around his shoulders, his dark strands brushed in thick waves off his face. He could easily pass as one of those J Crew or Calvin Klein catalog models.

He grouses and says something in French that I don't understand, but it's likely an insult. His opinion doesn't bother me in the least. We may be heading off to Marek Talbert's three-million-dollar home on Lake Washington, but I'm not there to impress anyone. As far as I know, the only people in attendance will be the players and team staff and their guests. It's a BBQ and I'm looking to relax and have a good time with my friends. No need to make a fashion statement.

Henri picks up his keys from the dish on the counter and twirls them around his finger.

"I'll drive."

I jump off the couch and join him at the apartment door, then swing it open and gesture with a hand to allow him to go first, following closely behind him into the hallway.

"Cool," I remark with enthusiasm, clapping him on the back as we head to the elevator. "That means I can party and enjoy myself as much as I want."

He sniffs and punches at the button.

When the elevator car arrives and the doors open, we're greeted with the sight of one of the senior members of the team, Carch Anderson. In his hands is a nicely wrapped gift.

"What's that for?" I ask lamely, staring at the shimmering silver wrapping paper and bow. There's no fucking way he wrapped that gift. It's too precise for a guy to do.

Carch rolls his eyes with a look that says, *"You're an idiot."*

"It's an engagement gift, you moron. We are going to the same party, are we not?"

I exchange a look with Henri, who smirks and says, "Mine is already in the car."

My mouth gapes open. "What? Jesus. No one said anything about gifts. How was I supposed to know this?"

Both Carch and Henri burst out in laughter at my expense.

Carch lays a big hand on my shoulder. "Were you raised in a barn or something, Rook? When you get an invite to celebrate a birthday, wedding engagement, or retirement, it's customary to bring a gift."

"Fuck," I lament, threading a rough hand through my hair. "I'm going to look like an asshole. Why didn't you assholes tell me? Or better yet, why didn't it get mentioned on the invitation?"

Henri makes a throaty noise. "Technically, the invitation did say no gifts—"

I huff out in gloating triumph. "See! Exactly. They don't want gifts. Marek's fucking rich enough already. He doesn't need anything."

Carch clucks his tongue. "Doesn't mean you don't bring something. It's customary, bro."

"That's the dumbest thing I've ever heard. Do they have these customs in France, too, HP?"

"*Oui.* You don't think the Americans came up with this idea on your own, do you?" He snorts as if it's a ridiculous thought.

"You're both assholes." I elbow them each in the ribs just as the elevator stops at the next floor and standing there is Ansel Werner, another player from the team. I'm surprised to see him since I thought he was back in Germany for the summer. He holds a small gift in his hands, shifting it to hold in front of his stomach as he gets on.

"You too? Goddamn it."

Ansel steps on the elevator car as I let out the long-suffering sigh to emphasize my complaint. Both Carch and Henri wail out in laughter as Ansel looks around with a curious expression.

"What's so funny?" he asks before his gaze lands on me and scans me from head to toe. "If it's Jaeg's outfit, I see the humor."

And then they all start belly-laughing loudly as I groan like a child.

This is the start of what could be a grueling evening.

"We're stopping at the mall, bro," I confirm with an elbow to Henri's side. I'm not going to walk in to Marek's house looking like a fool as the only one with my hands empty.

This only leads to more laughter.

My teammates are such assholes.

I T  TOOK  the inside of twenty minutes for me to get a salesperson to help me find a nice expensive gift and get it gift-wrapped before we got back out on the road and drove across Lake Washington toward Mercer Island.

I may not be dressed up like some of the other guests, but at least I won't show up looking like a complete loser who didn't bring a gift. I can thank my teammates for that, I guess. I suppose this is another downside to not being raised with a mother. I never learned these particular social skills like others did.

I make a mental note to impart this new-found wisdom to my brother later.

When we arrive, we drop our gifts on a table inside the main living space and grab beers from the nearby open bar. We all split up and go our separate ways, and Henri and I head out to the pool area in search of Marek and Harper. Outside we see some other guys from the team and their significant others milling about in clusters around the yard.

Kids' laughter and yelling carry through the yard and the splashing of water draws my attention to the shallow end of the pool, where I find Zeke Foster waist-deep in the water. He's throwing his son in the air, the kid's arms flailing, and his squeals of delight ripple across the air before he lands in the pool with a splash.

I smile at the scene. His little boy, Gus, is a cute kid, and Zeke recently shared the news that he and his wife Kendall are expecting another, with Kendall four months along. I scan around the backyard so I can give her my congratulations when I notice her sitting on a deck chair, chatting with Logan Edwards, the wife of my teammate Carver. She, too, looks pregnant, with a round belly protruding from underneath a snug swimsuit wrap.

Another splash and a loud "Bombs away!" draw my attention back to the pool. This time, though, I find it's our new team rookie, Xander Williams, who is entertaining his audience by doing a cannonball into the deep end.

Zeke whips his head in X's direction and glares him down. "Dude, there's kids in the pool. Take it down a notch."

Xander wipes the water from his eyes, slicks back his dark hair, and mumbles a contrite apology.

"Sorry, Zeke. Didn't think it would get you."

"It's fine...just be more careful around the kids, okay, man?"

"You got it, Cap."

Zeke harrumphs and smoothly glides through the pool with his son in his hands, the boy wearing those floaty wings on his arms as they make their way toward the shallow end and a safer distance from our new rookie.

I chuckle to myself because just last summer I was the one doing cannonballs and juvenile antics. It just goes to show that under the right leadership and direction, maturity can happen. Speaking of a mature adult men, Henri shakes his head next to me.

"Dumb fuck."

Clinking my beer bottle to his, I nod in agreement. "Yeah, so immature."

Henri raises an eyebrow at me but then laughs. Even though he's only a year older, he acts more like he's in his mid-thirties. He's wise beyond his years and doesn't seem to demonstrate the same traits I did when I started with the team. He's more of a silent observer and enjoys staying out of the limelight. He definitely doesn't want to be the center of attention like me or Xander.

"I'm heading over to say hi to Marek and Harper. You want to come?"

The bottle in my hand is almost empty and I decide to grab another beer from the bar inside before I do. "Yeah, but I'm gonna grab another beer inside first."

Henri waves his bottle in the air as he heads off, a silent invitation for me to get him another one too.

Turning back around, I say hello to a few people as I make my way back through the open accordion-style glass patio doors toward the bar.

Due to the change in brightness from outdoors to inside, I slide my shades up my nose and prop them on top of my head so my eyes can adjust to the light. As I round the corner into the kitchen, though, I still don't see the person in front of me until it's too late, barreling straight into them.

"Oof," the woman says, her hands landing on my chest. "Watch where you're—"

I know that voice because it's been stuck in my head for days. After the conversation we had the day we met, how could I possibly forget the sound of it? It's laced with a sweet huskiness that sends bolts of arousal to my cock. It also prompts me to be on the defensive, swiftly moving a hand in front of my crotch, in case she tries that same kickboxing move on me again.

"Jade? Shit, I'm sorry. I couldn't see."

"YOU. Again." The words are said like an exasperated curse.

I smile at my good fortune. "What are the chances of this? I'm one lucky guy."

Although I am very careful to keep my distance—and nonchalantly keep my hand covering my junk—I prop a hand along the hallway wall, trying to look cool and casual, even though my heart is racing a mile a minute at my good fortune.

Jade rolls her eyes and drops her chin forward, steepling her fingers together at her mouth in almost a prayer position as she voices her incredulousness.

"What did I ever do to deserve this, Lord?"

I don't fail to catch the note of sarcasm lacing her tone and chuckle at the humor of it. It gives me hope that I'm growing on her. She might think I'm more like a wart, but hey, it's a start.

"I'd like to say we have to stop meeting like this, but it's kind of a funny coincidence, don't you think?"

Her lips pucker in annoyance, brows narrowing as she tilts her head to the side.

"Funny? Mmm...I'd say it's just plain annoying, Romeo."

I smile at the use of the nickname. Normally it annoys me when the media calls me that, but in this case, I like how it sounds slipping from her tongue. It also doesn't hold the same level of irritation it did the other day. She's warming up to me. Maybe I have a chance after all.

Jade motions with her chin and tries to move around me but there's not much room and I'm blocking most of the space with my broad body.

She throws me a glance. "Do you mind? Or would you like another kick to the shin?"

I snicker, bending to rub at the spot just below my knee as her eyes follows the path. "Still got a nice bruise."

"I should've aimed higher," she says, a hint of humor lacing her words as she motions toward my crotch with a sexy smirk and the bat of her eyelashes. "Unless you want to give me a second chance now."

Damn, I like this Jade. She's sexy and funny.

"Nah, I'm all good, thanks." I notice her hands are empty. "But how about you let me grab you a drink and we can head out together."

Jade laughs. "Yeah, no thanks, Romeo. I already have a cold one waiting out there for me."

She crooks an elbow and pushes her forearm into my stomach, trying to get me to move so she can squeeze past me. The direct contact has my abs contracting from the heat of her skin. She wiggles through the open space against the wall.

And whoa. Now that my eyes have adjusted, I get a good look at what she's wearing. Her bright pink bikini top has my mouth in serious need of a cold drink and my cock stirs in my shorts. Her breasts are full and lush, spilling out over the barely there swimwear.

Whether it's from the friction of our contact or the cold air-conditioning blowing on us from the vent above, I can't be sure, but her nipples pebble tightly and poke through the skimpy material.

I inhale sharply, trying to get a handle on my body's reaction to her close proximity, but what I get is something even more desirable. Her scent—a mixture of coconut sunscreen and other tropical flavors—infiltrates my senses and has my pulse speeding up as I let out a shaky breath.

She motions with her hands out wide. "Jesus, rookie. It's like you've never seen a girl in a swimsuit before. Get a grip."

The words leave my mouth without a second thought.

"Not one as sexy as you."

Jade's eyes flash with something I can't quite pinpoint. Did I push this too far?

*Shit. Me and my mouth.*

"Jaeger, you can stop it with the whole player attitude. I am not one of your ball bunnies who is going to swoon and fall all over you when you say something flirty and charming."

I cock an eyebrow. "You think I'm charming?"

Jade smacks her forehead. "No, that's the point. You're a fool."

I seem to be hearing that a lot today.

Jade whips passed me as I move out of her way. But as she moves down the hallway, she gives me a clear and unfettered view of her ass. I slap a palm against the wall beside me to keep myself upright and ball up my fist at my mouth, letting out a hoarse and croaked curse.

Then she stops suddenly when she reaches the end of the hallway, peering over her shoulder to give me one last look. But this time it's punctuated with a wickedly sexy smile.

"And for the record, Romeo. I don't need a player to tell me I'm hot. I already know it."

If I didn't have the wall holding me up, I'd be on my knees right now. Because that right there, folks, is what in basketball is called an uncontested shot.

I think she just broke my winning streak.

**9**

———

J ade

"Are you okay, babes? You look a little flushed and overheated," Harper says when I take my seat next to her on the patio chairs. She reaches over and draws a finger across my temple, wiping away the sweat dotting my brow. "You're even sweating. Do you need a hat? Some water?"

I shove her hand out of my face, annoyed with my rattled nerves. Even my hand is trembling when I reach for my margarita glass and take a long pull to cool me down.

My entire body is jittery and wired. All because of Jaeger Matlin.

Emotions war within me over the unexpected confrontation we had in the hallway. I'm both heavily aggravated over Jaeger's presence and inexplicably turned on.

*I am not attracted to ball players.*

And certainly not the kind of players who think they are God's gift to womankind and believe that they can get panties to drop with a single smile.

But I'll admit it, that crooked smile of his could be categorized at a panty-dropping level, and I understand why the hoops honeys clamor to call them their Romeo. It makes me shudder with disgust. Or maybe something else.

God, it's so confusing. I'm stuck in this perplexing state of chaos around him. I don't know whether to deal with him as my evil business adversary or view him for the hot guy that he is.

I suck in a sharp breath and let it out slowly. "Yeah, maybe I have had a bit too much sun." I shield my eyes from the bright sunlight casting over us. Harper lucked out with a perfect day for her BBQ slash engagement party.

"Come on, then" Harper says, encircling my wrist to tug me up on my feet and drag me behind her. "Let's head over to the shady side of the pool and I'll go get you some water."

I yank my hand free. "I'm fine, Harp. This is your party, you don't have to dote on me. Go enjoy yourself. I can manage on my own just fine."

She gives me a haughty stare but then it turns into delight when we hear the voices of two little girls calling out to their auntie. We both turn to see Harper's nieces, Holly and Hazel, walking with fast-clipped speed and skirting around the pool toward us, followed by their mother, Hannah.

"Slow down, girls," Hannah encourages in a motherly tone, adjusting the wide brim of her hat. The hat hides her face but I'm sure she wears a smile.

"Auntie Harper! We're here!" The older one, Holly, shouts out as the little one, Hazel, bounce-walks on her tiptoes like she's done since the day she learned to walk.

"When can we go swimming?"

They run up to Harper, flanking her on each side, and wrap their arms around her legs in greeting.

I smile at the love and adoration that exists between them all. Knowing Harper for as long as I have, I'm very aware of the difficulties her sister, Hannah, has overcome to take care of her daughters. Harper has been there for them every step along the way, always putting their needs ahead of her own.

"Hey, girlies! Come give your auntie Jade some love too," I say, smiling with open arms as the two unfold from Harper's embrace and run to my chair, where I envelope them both in hugs, as well. They smell of sunshine and cotton candy.

"You're just in time for a swim before we chow down on hamburgers and hot dogs and then roast marshmallows at the s'mores-making station later tonight."

They both jump up and down excitedly and my own stomach growls at the mention of food.

Hannah catches up as I stand from the chair and she gives me a big sister hug while the two little girls dash off, chucking off their clothes to reveal their bright-colored swimsuits underneath, and jump in the pool like it was the only thing they've had on their mind for days.

It probably is.

Just like Jaeger has been the only thing on my mind for days too. Well, not all the time, but most.

But instead of cooling me off like the pool does for the girls, all he does is get me riled up and hot under the collar.

And if I'm being completely honest with myself, other places, too.

"Hey, Han. It's so good to see you," I greet, stepping out of her embrace and looking her over. "How was the drive?"

Hannah unfurls herself from all the tote bags she has slung over her shoulders and sets them down before adjusting the long-sleeved cover-up that swallows her up. She looks a thousand times better than she did a year ago, before her first surgery and subsequent cancer treatment for a brain tumor.

Her skin appears to have a healthy glow and her smile is wide and no longer weary. But if I had to guess, the big hat she has on is purposeful and is meant to hide the long scar behind her ear where they opened up her skull. At least her hair has begun to grow back out and is now just past her earlobes.

Hannah gives an exasperated groan. "Good grief. It was three hours of non-stop *'are we there yet, 'how much further?',* and *'can we stop for ice cream?'.* I'm so glad we aren't going back tonight."

Harper claps her hands together enthusiastically. "Yeah! It's a slumber party."

"I'm sure Marek doesn't share your enthusiasm," Hannah says with an arched brow and a trace of laughter in her voice. "Especially once you get them all sugared up tonight with s'mores."

"Emphatically not true," Harper insists. "He's been talking about it all week and even got them their own Petey Pilot plush toys from the team store."

We both make swoony sounds over his thoughtful gesture. That's when you know you've found a good guy, when he accepts not only your flaws and quirks, but all the baggage your family brings along for the ride, too.

"Aww, that's so sweet. You found a good one, Harp." My voice is wistful and dreamy.

My friend blushes and shrugs. "I know. I'm so happy. You'll find your man someday soon, too."

I snort. "Not looking, thank you very much."

Hannah smiles, catching my gaze. "We need to catch up, J. Are you going to stay the night with us, too?"

"That would be so much fun, but Tubby is home alone.

My neighbor, Stella, is going to feed him and take him out to pee later, but he can't be alone overnight. Plus, I have to be at the gym tomorrow morning at stupid o'clock in the morning."

"Boo," Harper groans sadly. "All work and no play make Jade a…"

"Badass boss bitch."

Harper snorts. "True, that you are. But as the boss, couldn't you have scheduled someone else to open?"

I shake my head. This is one of those times where owning my own business puts a damper on my social life, what little I have.

"No. It's the holiday weekend and I gave Siena and Lars the time off. That leaves me to steer the ship solo. But I did reduce the hours to give myself a break."

"Well, that's good. And at least we have tonight together. Just like old times." She hooks one arm through my elbow and the other through Hannah's and guides us over to the pool bar that's been staffed with a bartender.

She orders us three frozen margaritas and we all happily toast one another as we look out over the grounds and Lake Washington.

And what an amazing view it is because toward the end of the yard is a corn hole game, where Jaeger and his buddies play a raucous game. All shirtless.

Holy hell, that man's physique is nothing short of cut.

As the three of us sip our drinks and keep an eye on the girls in the pool, our conversation naturally gravitates to Marek and their wedding plans. While Harper has been busy establishing herself as a local Seattle sports broadcaster, she admittedly hasn't had time to plan a wedding.

"I don't know, you guys. This is so not my thing. I've never been the type of girl who dreams of a big wedding.

And because of who Marek is, I think the expectation is that it'll be a lavish affair."

I take a sip from the icy glass and hum, cluing into what she's not saying by the reticent tone of her voice.

"But is that what you want, Harp?" I ask gently, withholding judgment. "It's your wedding, after all, and as the bride, you should have the day of your dreams. What does Marek want?"

"That's the problem. He just wants me to be happy with whatever I want. But I don't know what I want." She throws her hands up in the air. "It's so frustrating."

"Have you considered a small intimate wedding, then hosting a bigger reception later?"

Harper lifts a shoulder, her skin a shimmery golden hue. I can see her looking incredible in a strapless, body-hugging wedding gown.

"That's an idea to consider," Hannah says, her eyes growing wide as if the wheels are turning. "Maybe even a destination wedding."

For as long as we've been friends, neither one of us have ever put much emphasis on weddings or babies. We've been more career-minded and hyper-focused on making our mark in the world rather than looking to find a lifelong partner.

Plus, finding an ideal man for me has always felt like a difficult prospect.

Not impossible, considering Harper found the perfect soulmate in Marek. And just like Harper, I won't settle for anyone less than a man who will value my independence and support me as his equal. Not just a woman who will be his sidekick.

I need a man who isn't afraid of a strong woman who speaks her mind. A man who will respect my opinions, even when he may not agree with them. But someone who will take control in the bedroom. That's not asking too much, right?

The handful of men I've tried dating since college have not satisfied both my needs. They've been intimidated by my size, stature, and ability to think for myself or are men I just can't trust.

Harper and Hannah continue talking over wedding plans as I zone out, already a little bored with the talk of dresses and venues. I take another sip and lift my gaze over the rim of my glass to see Jaeger staring straight at me from across the lawn.

Not staring at me like a stalker would but with an admiring, sexy gaze. He doesn't even look embarrassed or look away when I catch him. Instead, his hungry gaze travels up and down the length of my body, roaming sensually over my skin. I can feel the prickle of heat radiating down my bare arms as if it were his fingertips brushing over the warmth of my flesh.

My stomach flips and something wild and turbulent brews inside my chest. Lust permeates the air like a thick fog between us.

My nipples pucker against the Lycra material of my bikini top, and I know the moment he notices because his tongue licks over his full lips and he quirks an appreciative eyebrow, capping it off with a boyish grin.

I don't know why I'm playing this stupid game with him. Is it because he's dangerously handsome with a virile power that is attractive as fuck? It's obvious why women find him deliciously appealing. He's young and cocky and carries an almost overwhelming air of confidence.

Is that the reason I'm being pulled to him like a moth to a flame?

Lifting one corner of my mouth, I lower my sunglasses down my nose so he can see my eyes and return the sentiment with an arch of my brow. Then I slowly trail my fingertip over the indent of my throat, seductively lowering it between my cleavage.

He's chatting with one of the players that I don't know, but Jaeger's eyes remain on me, following my every move. A muscle ticks in his jaw and his burning eyes hold me still. I should look away, but I can't. I'm caught in the tractor beam of his gaze.

God, why is this so ridiculously hot? How can this staring contest turn me into a needy, horny mess?

The way he looks at me gets under my skin like no one else I've ever known. And I barely know him. Regardless, Jaeger's mouth is the only thing I seem to want on my skin. I want to feel his tongue dip in the same spot where my finger grazes between my breasts.

"Jade? What do you think?"

I jolt as if I've been caught doing something naughty, and I spill the contents of my drink over the edge of the glass and onto my stomach.

I reach for the edge of my towel and dab away the liquid on my belly, feeling Jaeger's eyes still on me. Then I snap my head toward Harper. "Huh? What do I think about what?"

She gives me a look that says, "*What is wrong with you today?*"

"About going dress shopping next weekend?"

Oh right. Wedding plans. Dresses. Venues. *Blah de blah blah.*

Sounds boring as hell but at least it will give me something else to focus on besides Jaeger. He's already taking up way too much real estate in my head.

It will keep me from spending useless energy and time

on a baller like him, my rival, who is probably just trying to meet with me to veer me off course with his chiseled looks and come-hither gaze.

He's just playing me so he can find a way to beat me at this game.

How can I possibly fall for this trap so easily again?

Didn't I learn my lesson the first and last time I openly flirted with a cocky basketball player? When I got exactly what I deserved because I wasn't careful with my heart or my body?

**10**

———

J ade – College Senior Year

"One more shot!" shouts my friend and teammate, Lennie, as she raises a bottle of tequila in the air before topping off everyone's shot glasses.

I don't normally drink to excess but tonight we are celebrating the end of the semester.

And I am officially drunk.

I giggle and throw back the shot and then cough. For some reason this makes me laugh harder at the story my friend Courtney is telling us about how she lost her virginity in a rowboat on a lake when she was fifteen.

It's not uproariously funny, but I think it's hilarious, especially the punchline.

"So, there he is, balancing on his knees between my legs and trying to slip the condom over his erection just as something bites me in my ass. I scream because fuck it hurt, and I jerked too quickly, making the boat rock. The unexpected motion had Rory falling to the side, slipping when he lost his balance, and then slamming his mouth against the side of the boat. He ended up with a chipped tooth and a swollen lip!"

Someone pipes in. "But did he get to finish?"

"Hells yeah! I wasn't about to let that interfere with him popping my cherry."

Everyone hoots in hysterics, cheering her on as I fold my body over in laughter and end up pitching forward. Right before I topple into Courtney, two strong hands latch around my hips and pull me back to an upright position. The move has me pinned to the hot sturdy body of Matt "Ripp" Rippling.

Ripp is the six-foot-ten men's basketball player I've silently crushed on since my sophomore year when he transferred to our school. Every girl swooned over Ripp and he took advantage of that fact.

Which is the reason why I turned Ripp down last year at a party when he asked me if I wanted to hook up. Sure, he's hot and all, but I wasn't going to be one of his many conquests. Ripp had plenty of girls at his disposal and he didn't need to add me to his list.

Since then, every time we run into each other, he gives me the stink eye like he loathes me. Like he can't stand to be around me. Or is just pissed that I turned him down because no one else ever has.

But tonight, he's been hanging around, giving me lots of attention, even getting me drinks when my beer cup is empty. Admittedly, I was initially suspicious of the attentiveness, but after a few drinks in my system, it felt nice to be taken care of so thoughtfully. Ripp has been making me feel special tonight, something I've needed this semester in light of Harper's absence.

Due to no fault of her own, my best friend and roommate couldn't return to school after the winter break, having just lost her dad. Instead, she chose to stay home and help her mom in the aftermath of her father's death manage and run their farm.

"You doing okay, Jade?" Ripp's deep, smoky voice murmurs close to my ear and sends a thrill down my spine. I try to stand up and fall back against his chest.

I twist my neck to look up at him, not sure if the weightless dizziness is from his dark blue eyes on me or the alcohol. I grin and wave him off, a gurgle bubbling up from my throat.

"Absolutely," I say, but I don't think it sounds right. The word gets mangled on my tongue and then I giggle again, my body so loose it feels like I'm a ragdoll bobbing up and down. I snuggle in close to his chest, his arms locked tightly around my middle. "I think I just need to lie down for a bit."

Ripp chuckles and helps me stand, then tucks me under his arm and directs me down the hallway of the frat house and to the stairs. I stop at the bottom, my head flopping back, mouth opening in question.

"Where are we going?"

"You said you wanted to lie down." He points up the stairs and shrugs. "I'll find a quiet place for you."

Hmm...that does sound nice. I nod in agreement, my response warbled and thick. Like molasses syrup dripping out of a container.

"Okay," I slur and drop my head down to look at my feet that feel glued to the floor. "But I don't think my feet work."

Ripp must find this funny because he laughs but resolves the issue by lifting me into his strong arms to carry me up the flight of stairs.

"You're like Superman," I say out loud, wrapping my arms around his neck and pressing my face into his neck. "I've never been carried before."

This truth pops out of my mouth without thought. I've always been a tall, sporty girl, and not many guys of average stature can manage my height.

Ripp seems to ignore this in favor of searching out a room for me.

What a nice guy...

"You smell good," I mumble into the crook of his throat, breathing in his cologne scented skin.

"So do you, baby. And I bet you'll taste even better."

My head swims with weird and complex thoughts that muddle together in a big alphabet soup. I blink, trying to clear my head and my vision, which has gone kind of hazy. A huge yawn overtakes me, and I close my eyes for just a second, my mind still trying to understand why he said that.

I WAKE SOMETIME LATER, face down, my cheek smushed into a pillow that smells like stale beer and sweat.

I blink, my eyes coming open slowly but falling closed again as if weights were attached to the lids. I do this several times until they can stay open, and I take in my surroundings. I'm not sure how long I've been asleep, and I don't know where I am. When I try to rise, I push my palms into the mattress, but my elbows cave and I crash back onto the musty-smelling sheets.

My body feels like it's filled with sludge running through my bloodstream.

It's quiet and dark wherever I am. I know it's a bedroom but whose bedroom is the question.

How the hell did I get here? And why won't my body move?

Oh right. I was drunk last night. Frat party. Frat house. Laughter. Music.

Ripp refilling my drinks.

Ripp carrying me upstairs.

Ripp dropping me on the bed.

Ripp holding me down.

Ripp on top of me.

Flipping me over onto my stomach.

Cursing low in my ear.

*"You're such a fucking cock tease..."*

*"You make me so fucking hard."*

*"You think you're better than me, don't you?"*

*"How does your cock tease cunt like me now, baby?"*

I jolt upright, both the movement and the flashes of memory turning my stomach, and I know I'm about to vomit. I roll to my side and then off the bed, landing on my knees to crawl in search of a wastebasket.

I scurry around in the dark until I locate one underneath a desk, barely making it in time as I empty out the contents from last night. Finally, the heaving stops and the nausea dissipates as I sit back against the side of the bed, clutching my knees to my chest, and realize for the first time that I'm completely naked.

Tears roll down my face and another wave of nausea hits me.

*"That's it, baby. Take me all the way."*

The words come unbidden in my head, and I shove the trash can between my knees and retch and heave again until I'm completely dry and there's nothing left.

I'm completely void.

Just like the inside of my soul. Scraped and emptied by what happened.

I may only have a vague recollection of what happened,

like a blurry dream I've woken up from, but I do know one thing. It didn't happen with my consent. He took a part of me that I will never get back.

*My trust.*

My heart may still beat, and physically my body may still be alive, but inside, I feel dead.

And I will never be able to trust a man again.

**11**

———

J aeger
I am so fucking hot I can't stand it. And it's not from the heat of the sun.

That honor goes to Jade.

Watching her from across Marek's backyard today was the biggest turn-on of my life.

I'm not naïve enough to think she miraculously changed her mind about me. It's clear she still views me with contempt, and this cat-and-mouse game was just her way to prove her superiority and control over me and to get me horny. It did the trick.

She stared me down with the perfect mix of pure animosity and raw sex appeal. I wanted to find a way to get her alone and let her shove me against the wall and fuck me senseless.

If only...

Sadly, that didn't happen. She remained tightly ensconced with Harper and her family the remainder of the evening, carefully avoiding me at every pass before she departed right after the fireworks show over Lake Washington. Henri and I stayed until a little after midnight, smoking cigars and drinking bourbon with Marek and the guys.

Part of me wanted to get Jade alone to talk with her. To find a compromise to end this standoff between us. But until I know the final decision and outcome from the city planning committee, I should probably keep my distance, even if it's the last thing I want to do.

So instead of going out to one of the clubs in Belltown with Henri and the guys after we get back into Seattle, I'm taking care of my raging hard-on Jade left me with by jerking off to the memory of her perfect ass and those luscious tits that spilled out over the top of her bright pink bikini. The tits that played peek-a-boo with me all afternoon and revved me up to the point of distraction.

I envision her swimming up to me in the pool after everyone's left the party, just the two of us in the shimmering water, the moonlight and bright explosions of fireworks lighting up the sky. Her hand roams over my pecs and down my stomach, her long tapered fingernails gliding over every ripple and chiseled dip of my abs as her lips part on a sigh.

"You feel so good, Jaeger," she says, toying with the edge of my swim trunks. My cock lengthens, straining upwards, as if trying to reach out to meet her touch.

"I'll feel better with your hand wrapped around my cock."

"Oh yeah?" she asks with a sultry grin. "Show me."

I push down my trunks, grab her hand, and place it over my erection. She encircles it with her fist and rubs up and down with leisurely strokes.

"I want to touch your tits, Jade."

Her bikini top magically disappears, and my hands

instantly mold around each firm breast, plumping gently as I flick her taut nipples with my thumbnails.

Her moan of pure pleasure has me growing even harder in her hand. Something about Jade makes me believe she is deserving of everything. I'll give her anything she wants as long as she doesn't stop the motion of her hand.

Her skin is slick and wet, and I want to find out if she's wet everywhere.

I slide my hand down her sexy stomach, slipping my fingers inside her bikini bottoms. She's molten lava between her legs and when I move my finger through her entrance, her fist tightens around my length with a keening cry.

"Oh fuck, Jade. You're going to make me come if you keep making those noises."

"That's what I want...I want to make you come..."

I slap my hand against the cold tile of my shower, my hand jerking my cock in fast strokes as my release barrels out of me and down the shower drain.

"Fuck."

Have I ever fantasized about a woman like that before?

I finish rinsing off and jump out of the shower, reaching for my towel that hangs on the wall peg to dry myself off.

As I stand in the middle of my bathroom, I wonder what it is about Jade that I find so fucking distracting that I'm jerking off to a fantasy like some high school kid?

I mean, obviously, she's sexy as hell. Whether she's in a business suit or showing off her spectacular body in a bikini, her beauty is unrivaled. None of the women I've been with in the past can hold a candle to Jade's radiance.

The thing is, I've been with beautiful women in my life. Models, actresses, musicians, influencers. All ages, shapes, sizes, skin colors. They're everywhere I look and most often, they want a piece of me. And I'm okay with that.

Jade Russell, though, is unlike any of them, and I feel there should be a shrine dedicated in her honor. Yet her external beauty is only a small part of why I find her so fascinating.

All those other women? They chase me down. They come to me and make it known they'll do anything to be with me.

Not Jade.

She's a challenge.

Isn't that what I love about the game of basketball and now my business?

Challenges make life interesting. That's what my dad has always taught me. If you're always given an easy go at it, you'll never appreciate what you have.

Speaking of my dad, I need to check in with him soon. He should be back from his conference in Jamaica this week. I head into my bedroom and grab a pair of shorts, pulling them on before I walk barefoot into my kitchen to get my phone.

It's going on one a.m. so it's a sure bet my brother is either at a party or has someone in his bed, but I text him anyway.

Me: Hey bro. Sup? You awake?

Jesse: Just barely. What's up?

Me: Nothing. Just bored. Wanted to check in.

Jesse: No fuck buddy tonight?

I snort, typing my response.

Me: I could ask the same thing. And no. Not tonight. Just got back from Marek's party. You?

The next message I get has an attachment. I click on it and it's a dark photo of a head of blonde hair asleep next to my brother.

Me: Atta boy, killer. Remember what I taught you. Buy her breakfast in the morning.

Jesse: Middle finger emoji

I laugh but feel a sense of nostalgia for my college life. Back then, the only responsibilities I had were basketball practice, studying (which I did little of), and getting laid (which I did a lot of). It was all so simple.

Adulting is so much harder.

Although I'm feeling relaxed after my self-induced orgasm, I don't think I can fall asleep yet. So I flip on the television and find a sports station broadcasting footage of some rugby match in Australia. It's not basketball but it'll do.

With my mind now buzzing and body still full of something close to adrenaline from my interactions with Jade today, I decide to do a Google search. I want to see what's out there about her. For curiosity's sake, of course. To size up my business competition. Nothing else, not at all.

I type in Jade Russell and a list of hundreds pop up.

Narrowing my search, I add *Seattle. Business owner. Seattle Circuit.*

Bingo.

Images of her beautiful face appear on the screen. She looks gorgeous in every one of them, but they don't come close to doing her justice. In person she is a fucking goddess.

I click on the Seattle Circuit website and peruse the details of the gym, finding another photo displayed under the About Us page.

It provides Jade's bio, and I'm enthralled as I read through it. Goddamn, this woman is accomplished. My shame punches me in the gut as I remember my comments last week that made it seem like I knew more about business than she did.

Jesus, I'm a dickhead.

As she told me the other day, she started Seattle Circuit five years ago and graduated college a year before that. I do the math in my head and realize that makes her older than me—I'm twenty-four and she'd be, I guess, maybe around twenty-eight or twenty-nine.

I snicker to myself. An older woman.

I continue scrolling and find another interesting fact. She, too, played college basketball, on the women's team at a university in Eastern Washington.

Typing in the school's name, I click on the athletics department, scroll through the rosters by year, and find Jade's senior year team photo.

*Aha*. That's how she knows Harper Conrad, and by proxy, Marek Talbert. It all makes sense now why she was at the party and looked like she was thick as thieves with Marek's fiancée.

It's also now cleared up my question on why she opened a gym. According to her profile, she graduated with a degree in sports kinesiology and minored in business, then parlayed that into her own fitness business. Which proves she loves basketball and athletics as much as I do.

Regardless of our rival business ventures, I'm still very

much in awe of her success and what she's accomplished in such a short time, and we have something in common with our love of athletics.

Not many first-time business owners, much less female entrepreneurs, will make it on their first go at a new business. Based on what I know of my dad's past business ventures, he's failed on multiple occasions and lost loads of money in the process. He wasn't always the rich and savvy businessman he is today. Which is exactly why I want to learn from his mistakes and avoid them at all costs.

I may have more disposable income to put toward my ventures than the typical new business owner, but it doesn't mean I want to lose it by making dumb rookie mistakes.

As long as the city's red tape they have me weeding through isn't too difficult to manage, and I can find a way to smooth things over with my beautiful adversary, then I don't see why I shouldn't be able to get my business off the ground before my second professional season begins.

**12**

———

J ade

"Dad! What are you doing here and why didn't you call me?"

I step out of the big bear hug my dad, former Army Staff Sergeant Mel Russell, gives me and smile up at his familiar face.

To me, it's warm, comforting, compassionate.

To anyone else who knew him during his stint in the military, it was likely called scary and intimidating.

He returns my smile with an even bigger one and shrugs those brick shoulders of his. For a retired man in his late fifties, he's still in amazing shape, rarely missing his daily workouts and his part-time job teaching Taekwondo. The man did not retire to slow down. In fact, he also invested in a construction business but insists he is only a paper pusher.

On top of that, both he and my mom, Annie, take care of themselves physically with daily walks with their dog, Hildy, hiking and camping in the mountains, and even the occasional square dancing. Which I find hilarious and give them crap about all the time.

Now that they live over on Vashon Island, an hour and a half commute that includes a ferry boat ride across the Sound from Seattle, I unfortunately don't get to see them as often as I'd like, with visits limited pretty much to holidays, special occasions, and weekends when they venture across the Sound.

But usually, the visits are announced in advance and thoroughly planned out, unlike this surprise. Which has me narrowing my eyes at him skeptically as I wonder why he didn't let me know he'd be in Seattle today.

"I meant it to be a surprise. I wanted to check in and see how my beautiful daughter is doing."

Our height difference isn't much, but he still tips his head down and pinches his furry brows together in that assessing way only fathers can do. It's his go-to interrogation tactic learned through years in the Army. It may or may not have been used quite a lot on me, as well, when I was in high school and tried to pull a fast one over on him and my mom.

I grant him a bright and cheerful smile, gesturing with my outstretched arm to the busy gym.

"As you can see, things are doing well and are very busy."

He harrumphs, crossing his beefy arms in front of his chest as if he doesn't believe me.

"I mean, how are *you* doing, not your gym."

I roll my eyes like I am still his teenage daughter instead of a full-grown ass woman, and nod my head toward my office along the inner gym wall.

"Come on, let's get out of this noise so we can talk."

He follows closely behind, scanning the busy gym as we go. We pass Siena coming out of the laundry room with her head buried in her phone.

"Hey, Siena. Can you watch the front for me while I'm in my office?"

Siena Stewart, the young twenty-something college student I hired a little over a year ago as our receptionist, lifts her head and blinks at me. And then her eyes latch onto my dad.

"You remember my dad, Mel Russell, right? Dad, this is Siena."

Siena brightens in that flirtatious manner of hers. It drives me crazy the way she so openly flirts with men of all ages, but mostly older men. She always seems overly eager to gain their attention with a pout of her lips, a flick of her hair, or a sway of her hips.

But truthfully, it's good for business. Men and their egos love Siena's kittenish vibe.

She wiggles her fingers in a cutesy wave. "Hi, Mel. Nice to see you again. Don't forget to stop by the front before you leave so I can make you my special green smoothie. It's good for your gut." She cups the side of her mouth and winks. "And your libido."

This makes my dad laugh and I groan. He plays along by making a show of patting his belly, as if he has a dad bod, which he doesn't. The man still has ripped abdominals like a friggin' thirty-year-old.

But ewww...is he flirting back with her? Now I do feel like a teenager and want to hurl because it's just gross to see my father act like an idiot around Siena. Plus, he's a married man. To my mother.

"I wouldn't want to miss out on your specialty, don't you worry." He winks back and now I really do want to throw up.

I give him a tug on his forearm. "Dad, stop flirting with my employee. Come on."

He lifts his dark eyebrows, his brown eyes blowing wide and the wrinkles on his forehead popping out.

"For your information, as happily married as I may be, I am still a man, and there is no law that says I can't chat with a pretty girl."

I swing my office door open, and he steps in behind me and then closes the door, leaving us in relative silence.

I choke out a cough as I sit down at my desk chair and throw my head forward theatrically and into my palms.

"Yeah, well, that pretty girl is practically jailbait. Plus, there are some things a daughter cannot unsee, and that's one of them, old man." I shudder and he snickers at my jab.

Turning serious, I prop my chin in my hands. "Sometimes I do worry that Siena is on the hunt for a Daddy of her own, if you know what I mean."

His expression turns mortified, and he drops his mouth open and then closes it. He glances back out through my office window, which is a one-way only so it offers privacy, and notices how Siena has now latched on to another older man. She's clearly giving him the same Little Bo Beep eyes and peek-a-boos of her tits in the V-neck Seattle Circuit T-shirt as she leans over the counter.

"She sure is quite the vixen, isn't she?"

"That she is. I'm not slut-shaming or passing judgement or anything, but I get the sense it's why she wanted a job here." I shrug, straightening back up in the seat. "To be fair, she is a good employee, very reliable and is good with all the clients. Although she does add a bit more flare with the older, wealthier men."

My dad chuckles. "Well, then, she's barking up the wrong tree with me."

I give a dismissive wave. "Anyway, so what's up with your

drop-in? Why didn't you at least call me, so I could've scheduled some time away?"

My dad leans back in the chair and crosses a foot over his thigh, the move causing a flex of the dense muscles in his legs.

It's no wonder I never dated any boys back in high school when he was still in the military. He's a big, strong man with tatted arms who looks like he would kick any boy's ass if they did anything without my consent.

Which is exactly why I never mentioned what happened with Ripp to anyone. Not to Harper, who would have certainly told my mom. Not to my parents. And not to school security.

I knew, without a doubt, my dad would have done something he'd regret to protect my honor. And what good would it have done? Even now, I don't remember much of anything that night, nor could I positively said that I had been assaulted. Which is the reason I kept quiet and tried my best to move on and forget that anything ever happened.

My dad hooks a thumb over his shoulder, gesturing toward the street, and his forehead wrinkles with concern.

"I came here to meet with Jim about a new project."

"Oh, cool. What is it?"

A few years ago, my dad's former military buddy, Jim Presley, asked my dad to invest in his construction company. My dad knew nothing about the construction industry but also didn't want to pass up on the opportunity, so he put in some of his retirement money and became primarily a silent partner. Jim runs the day-to-day operations but with every new commercial project they take on, they meet to review the job requirements, plans, and timelines.

It's no surprise to me then that he's in town to meet with Jim. But it's strange there's an apprehension over it.

He scrubs a hand down his face, lowering his deep-timbered voice. "You're not going to like it."

I tilt my head to the side, eyeing him suspiciously. "Why not? What does it have to do with me?"

He clears his throat but doesn't veer from looking me straight in the eyes.

"It's a bid for the project down the street. The one Jaeger Matlin is building."

There is no doubt that everyone out on the gym floor—and maybe even halfway down the block—hears my obscenely loud curse.

It may have been directed at my dad, but it was meant for my business rival down the goddamn street.

*Jaeger Fucking Matlin.*

# 13

Jaeger

"Goddammit," I mutter aloud as I crinkle the letter and ball it up in my fist, ready to toss it on the floor like a two-year-old having a tantrum.

I knew it was a stupidly premature idea to meet with the construction companies about the project before I heard back from the city with an approval. But I folded under pressure from my dad and brother's suggestion to get a head start on things.

Now here I am, two days later, the rejection letter on my building plans I had drawn up to turn the building into a live/work space that would potentially meet the zoning requirements.

Spoiler alert: it didn't.

Henri looks up from his laptop, where he's been camped out all afternoon doing God knows what. Games? Porn? Dating website? I have no clue.

"Problem?"

I snap my head in his direction, scowling at him with a

toothy snarl. "Yes. Problems, as in plural. The city shot down my proposal, which I thought was fucking brilliant, by the way, and said no can do. It's zoned for residential only. Fuck me and fuck them."

He shoots me an empathetic look. "Sorry, bro. What do you think you're going to do now?"

"I don't know. I'm back to square one without a way to open my gym. I've had my mind set on this for years."

I know I'm whining over something most people would just move on from. Even my dad suggested I let it go and find a different business venture to start there. But I've had my heart set on this forever.

Rejection is something I've never encountered in my life. Everything I've ever wanted, I've gotten. I've worked hard, of course, but even with the challenges and hurdles to jump, look where my determination got me? I'm a league MVP who has a great basketball career ahead of me.

Yet for some reason, that doesn't extend to anything outside of the sport. I wanted to venture into business ownership and become an entrepreneur so that when the day comes and I'm no longer to play the sport I love, I have something else to be proud of.

The truth is, I want to be known for something more than being a cocky jock and a playboy. I know what the public perception is of me. They believe I only think with my dick and my ego. But I know that's not all I am. And it won't be the person I want to be five or ten years from now.

This entire side hustle was a chance for me to grow up and prove I was worth more than just an MVP trophy and a good fuck.

Henri casually removes his laptop from his lap and shifts sideways on the couch, his arm and elbow crooked over the back of the leather sofa, giving me a thoughtful glance.

"What about the other gym?"

"What other gym? There is no other gym in this scenario. Remember? I can't build one, idiot."

He rolls his eyes, flicking a hand in the air.

"Mon Dieu," he grievously mutters in French. "The woman who owns the one down the street. Surely you've considered an offer to buy her out?"

I had just taken a giant drink of my orange sports drink and now spew it out on a choking cough.

"Buy it? From Jade Russell?" I wipe the liquid off my chin with the back of my hand. "I like my balls where God placed them, thank you very much. She'd cut them off before giving up ownership of her business."

If Henri had any idea how much Jade despises me and how little she thinks of me, he'd see the lunacy in his suggestion.

With the exception of her fascinating and sexy turn-about at Marek's party, Jade hates me on general principle and would never in a million years consider selling to me.

I swallow down the rest of my drink and then laugh. Big, side-splitting laughter that has me doubling over from the hysterics that burst from my stomach.

"Why is this funny to you? Isn't that what all you rich capitalist Americans do when you want something you don't own? You just wave enough dollar bills in front of the right person, and voilà, it is yours." He presses his fingers to his lips in a chef's kiss.

My laughter dies down and my eyes bore into his, which are staring at me warily.

"HP, let me clue you in on a little something I've learned

about Jade Russell," I offer with a knowing grin. "This isn't like in the movies you've seen where I'm just going to make her an offer she can't refuse. This woman plays hardball. Jesus, she practically chewed me up and spat me out at the public meeting a few weeks ago. And then at Marek's event, her claws came out again, sharper than ever, but this time she used a different type of tactic altogether."

I shake my head as I recall the game she played.

Then an idea hits me like a cartoon lightning bolt from the sky.

Maybe I'm playing the wrong game with her.

Maybe if I went in with the right offer and the right enticements, it could sweeten the deal enough to get her to sign on the bottom line.

Henri turns back around, seemingly done strategizing with me on this topic.

"Well, then. I guess you give up on your gym idea and build a condo or something. I don't know. Tough break."

I stare at the back of his head, considering what he just said and what my other options might include.

Moving behind him at the back of the couch, I clasp the top of his shoulders and give him a good squeeze. "Dude, you just gave me a great idea. Thanks, man."

"Any time. I'll expect my service fee to be paid in beers."

I laugh and head down to my bedroom where I need to come up with my new plan.

Because it's a well-known fact that the best strategy for winning any game is to study your opponent's plays and moves. To find out their strengths and weaknesses, and then execute your own plays to annihilate the competition.

Which is exactly what I plan to do.

"I HAVE TO SAY, Jaeger. Your invitation to meet for lunch surprised the hell out of me." Marek tips his water glass across the table and taps the top of my beer glass. "But I'm glad you called. We didn't get a chance to talk much at the party and I wanted to find out how your summer is going."

I take a swig of my Belgium White beer and grin, gesturing with the mug in my hand toward the sparkling blue waters of the Sound. I'd called the restaurant in advance to ensure we were seated on the outdoor terrace, where we could enjoy the view and some modicum of privacy.

"Yeah, it's been good. And it's the reason I wanted to chat with you. To get your advice."

Marek's eyebrows go skyward. "Oh? What's up?"

I look down at the beer glass in my hand, tracing my finger over the drip of condensation on the outside, suddenly nervous to share my inexperience with him.

"Well, I've run into a few troubles with my plans for the building I purchased. I'd originally planned on gutting and renovating it." I pause, waiting to see if there's any recognition of the situation in his expression and holding back so as not to divulge too much at once. To determine whether he's heard any thirdhand stories from his fiancée, Harper, who probably heard all about it from Jade.

Unless Marek has a great poker face, his expression remains impassive.

"That's a huge project to manage. I'm glad to hear you're putting down roots in the community though. That goes a long way with our fan base."

And there it is. My opening.

I tread lightly, trying to avoid bulldozing my way into this conversation and end up with Marek suspicious of my motives. Truth be told, they are completely selfish and with one goal only: to get what I want from Jade.

"Speaking of community, I heard that Harper has a friend who owns a business down the street from my building. A gym?"

Marek smiles like a proud father. "Yes, she does. Jade Russell is Harper's best friend and owns Seattle Circuit. In fact, it's the gym I belong to and, long story short, it was Jade's intervention that led me to meeting Harper."

I tilt my head, feigning surprise at this bit of news, but I already knew this. I've been digging up dirt through my covert research. I had to obtain all the important intel if I'm going to pull this thing off.

"No way. That's cool. I've never been there but I've heard it's a great place and a good location." I chuckle, tipping my head to the fact I own a building on the same block in Belltown.

"It really is. Jade has turned it into one of the top gyms in the Seattle area. In fact, Harper tells me Jade has been vying for a spot on the Seattle Young Entrepreneurs Award list this year. She'll find out in September if she received a nomination. I'll tell ya, I've never seen anyone work as hard on building a brand and a business than Jade."

I nod. "Jade sounds like a go-getter. Does Harper get to see her much?"

"A lot more when Harper first moved to Seattle. But she got the network job and then we started dating, so now when she is home, I get her spare time." Marek winks, letting me in on a secret bit of his private life.

Marek wasn't always this open. Prior to him getting together with Harper, he was kind of a recluse who didn't talk to anyone about his personal life. If it wasn't about the Pilots team, it was off the table.

It's easy to see Harper has been a good influence on him.

Now that I've warmed him up a bit, I get down to the nitty gritty of what I really want to know. The route I plan to take to get my inside scoop on Jade.

I take a bite of my salmon and moan at the deliciousness of the fresh local catch of the day.

"Besides the gym, what else does Jade do to occupy her time?" I ask in a casual tone, as if only mildly interested.

Marek's fork stops midway to his lips and then he drops it back to his plate, cocking his head to the side and eyeing me suspiciously.

"Why all the questions about Jade? Are you looking to ask her out or something?"

I'm quick to reject that idea. Although I wouldn't mind doing something with her. But date?

I don't date.

"God no. I'm not looking for a relationship. I'm just curious about her and I want to meet other business-minded people in the community."

This seems to do the trick, cooling his protective instincts for his fiancée's friend.

"Jade is a force to be reckoned with and has a good head for business. And damn, she has a heart bigger than the Pacific Ocean." His voice turns warm and tender with a touch of wonder. "She also has a soft spot for the homeless and rescue dogs. Jade's been a volunteer at the Central Soup Kitchen for several years now."

*Bingo.*

It feels like I just struck gold.

"Damn, that's cool. Not many people are that selfless in this world these days."

"I agree. In fact, Glen in PR and I have been talking

about doing some pre-season team event to raise money to promote services like that in the Seattle community."

I raise my hand in the air. "Count me in. I want to help."

But first, I'm going to help myself.

**14**

—————

J ade
   There are times when I know I've stretched myself too thin.

How do I know this?

Mostly from the migraine that wraps around my head and feels like a wrecking ball with its continuous bashing against my skull like it's trying to break down a brick wall.

When I was in high school and college, my mother would encourage me to slow down and listen to my body when it needed rest. But rest is not an option for me right now. Not when there's the constant pressure to keep my business afloat and off the verge of collapse.

Running this gym has taken everything I have emotionally, financially, and personally. There are months where I wonder if I'll even be able to keep the lights on. But somehow, I've managed.

That was before I had the possibility of competition ready to swoop in and take away my clientele. Ever since Jaeger came on the scene, the nasty negative thoughts I'd always worked to keep at bay have been creeping back into my thoughts like water wedging through rock crevices.

*You're not good enough.*

*Not smart enough.*

*You'll never make it in this field as a woman, especially as a Black woman.*

*You're weak and an easy target for men who want to use you.*

I shake my head free from that last thought, turning off the stove and removing the large pot of sauce from the burner, placing it on the counter.

It's times like these when, when I'm not busy and have too much time to think that my mind wanders back to that night. To how stupid and vulnerable I was. What a fool I'd been to trust a player like Ripp. I was a young woman, a victim. It wasn't my fault. I know this. The only one to blame is Ripp.

*Trust.*

I can count on my hand the number of men I trust these days.

That would be two. My dad and Harper's fiancée, Marek.

I learned my lesson the hard way and I'll never let myself fall into that trap again. The walls I've built are strong enough now that I'm able to wear my confident face in public so no one can ever tell just how weak and scared I really am.

Not even Harper.

I've been angry with myself for keeping this from her for all these years. But what good would it do now if I told Harper what happened that night? It's a useless endeavor because I don't remember that much. Only that I am to blame for having let my guard down.

Sharing it now with Harper would serve no purpose but to hurt her and our friendship. While she'd feel betrayed, I also know she'd go all protective warrior girl on me and would track down Matt Rippling and bust his ass.

There's no point. It's over and done with and I've moved on.

Voices and laughter behind me shake me free from my thoughts as I dip the ladle into the industrial-sized pot of spaghetti sauce and stir.

As they enter the kitchen, girlish laughter erupts from the head nun's lungs. I swivel my head in curiosity over what's gotten into Mother Martha, a notoriously soft-spoken and piously solemn woman, to have her giggling like a school girl with a crush.

"We are so pleased to have you here to help, Jaeger. What a treat. Our dinner patrons tonight will be thrilled to meet you."

I drop the kitchen utensil and it plunges into the pot, splashing red sauce all over my hand and exposed arm as I jump away from the stove.

"*Fu*---dge!" I yelp, remembering almost too late that I'm in the presence of a spiritual woman before cursing like a drunken sailor.

My loud outburst has Mother Martha and Jaeger rushing to my side as I blindly search for the towel I'd placed on the counter earlier. My hand lands on the towel but it slips from underneath my sauce-covered palm, falling to the floor at my feet.

"Oh, my dear! Are you okay?" Mother inquires, her wrinkled face etched with worry lines, and Jaeger bends down for the towel, snatching it up before reaching to clasp my arm gently in his hand. I stare in silence as he cleans off the spill, an odd sensation warring inside me.

Jaeger is touching me, and I don't feel the same discomfort I have in our previous entanglements. While I should want to rip my hand free from his grasp and push him away, a bigger part of me melts like a marshmallow, warm and gooey, from this simple gesture. His touch has my body vibrating like a frayed live wire.

Jaeger tugs me toward the sink basin. He flicks on the faucet and asks silently for my consent with the lift of his eyes to mine. I nod, watching with fascination as this man I've come to loathe, who has been nothing but an annoyance to me since the day we met, washes off my arm gently and with so much care.

A competitive silence hangs between us; or maybe it's my stubborn unwillingness to be the first to speak. As if neither of us wants to commit a foul by being the first one to speak.

I stare into the sink, avoiding his gaze, but furtively check him out in my peripheral vision.

He has on a pair of black and grey sweat pants that fit nicely over his long legs. Stretched over his chest is a grey and blue Pilots' team T-shirt that is tugged so tight by his straining biceps and toned torso it's no wonder Mother Martha was swooning. How could you not?

And that dick print is something even a nun couldn't help but notice.

Jaeger finishes up his work, examining my arm for any sauce he may have missed, and with a satisfied grunt, turns off the faucet but doesn't let go of me.

I should pull my arm free of his grasp. But I don't. It feels...nice.

It's been a while since I've had a man touch me with such tender care. For years, I've made up these elaborate stories for Harper, lying about all the men I supposedly meet through dating apps and hook up with. The truth is, I rarely do.

There was a guy who lived in my building for a few years who I considered a booty-call boy. He was not my boyfriend, and we were never in a relationship. We didn't date. It was just a way to have sex on the regular with someone I knew and felt safe with.

He moved to California last year and that was that.

Why the hell am I thinking about sex right now? I'm in a ministry-led soup kitchen with a nun standing over my shoulder and an annoying basketball player who wants to ruin my business.

I'm about to jerk my hand free when the low timber of Jaeger's voice socks me in the gut.

"I'm not a doctor but I think you'll live." His lips curl up in the slightest of smiles and I once again recognize the appeal he has on fans, women in particular. "But you can always call me in the morning if you need me."

He adds a wink.

And there it is. *Jaeger Meister the Romeo.*

Everything in me rationally tells me to walk away and avoid getting sucked into his charm. But I can't help the laugh that pushes up from my throat and rips free, like a water geyser bursting up from the earth.

I'm not sure who is more shocked by my reaction, Jaeger or me. I place my free hand over my mouth to cover up the sound of my mistake, but it's too late.

Jaeger knows he's caught me.

Dammit. I know better than to allow myself to get comfortable around a charming player.

Jaeger's mouth splits wide open into an astonished—and dare I say, sexy—smile.

He tilts his head knowingly.

"Is it my imagination, or did I just make Jade Russell laugh?"

This time, irritated over my lack of restraint, I snort and pull away, spinning quickly on my heel so I can past Mother Martha, who is checking on the meatballs, and walk off toward the refrigerated cooler.

I need to cool off.

Opening the large door, I breathe in the crisp refrigerated air and stick my head just inside in search of the bulk shredded cheese.

"Sorry, Romeo. It was clearly your imagination." I give him one last pointed look before ducking inside the refrigerated cooler. "Because you are not that funny."

As the door latches behind me, the cold burst of air immediately cooling my overheated face and body, I hear him getting in one last word.

I guess that's what rivals do.

They must always find a way to show up their competition.

"*Liar!*"

## 15

Jaeger

"Stop staring at me like some kind of creeper," Jade accuses, snapping her gaze to mine. "I know you're a player but didn't think you were a perv too."

I snort, settling my hip against the counter to face her and giving her a non-committal hand gesture.

"Maybe I was staring, but it doesn't make me a perv. I'm just trying to figure you out."

"Good luck with that, Romeo. I'm a complicated woman."

"I'm beginning to realize that." I pause, tugging the ugly-ass hair net off my head and running a hand through my hair. "But you're a sexy complicated woman, which leads me to a lot of questions."

This right here is exactly why I volunteered tonight, so I could find a way to learn more about Jade and work my way onto her good side. To get her to loosen up around me and see I'm not a bad guy after all.

It won't be easy, based on everything I know so far about Jade. But if she'll at least listen to the business arrangement

I want to propose, then maybe I'll have a chance at making this work out for both of us. It would give us both something we want.

Over the last hour, Jade and I have been on clean-up duty, splitting the chores of bussing the tables and bringing the trays back into the kitchen, where we dispose of the remaining food waste and load the dishes in the industrial dishwasher.

Jade's been relatively quiet since the sauce-spilling incident, responding to my questions with monosyllabic responses.

Now that most of the volunteers have gone home for the evening and Mother Martha is back in her office, it leaves an empty silence between me and Jade.

I place a tub full of dishes on the counter, checking out her profile as she works at scraping off the plates.

If it were any other woman, I could probably get away with making the moves on her with my charming compliments about how sexy I think she is. Or how her smokin' hot body would look underneath mine.

But Jade is not like any other woman I've ever met.

"Fine, Romeo. What do you want to know?"

Her words startle me, piercing the silence like a knife cutting glass, even as her voice has softened with a hint of resignation.

I answer with the first question that comes to mind.

"Are you dating anyone?"

Her eyes snare me with their golden glow.

"No. And I'm not going to date you. Next question…"

I clear my throat of the laughter that bubbles up.

"Okay, then what do you get out this volunteer gig?" I motion with my hand out toward the main room of the mission.

Her hands stop in the soapy water, and she twists her head to stare at me, aghast.

"What do I get out of it?" she asks incredulously, staring at me like I'm an alien life form. "I get to help people who need it. Their survival depends on it."

Something twists in my gut. It's a heavy dose of shame and privilege. White male privilege for that matter.

I hang my head low in disgrace and nod, unable to form an intelligent response.

From underneath my lashes, I see her drying her hands off before grabbing her water bottle and taking a heathy swig. Then she turns around and boosts herself up onto the counter with a push of her palms so she can sit with her legs dangling, her feet nearly touching the floor. She leans forward, forearms on her thighs in a thoughtful pose.

I mimic her position, taking a spot on the opposite counter to face her.

My voice is low and I offer a quiet reflective smile.

"You're a better person than I am, Jade."

Jade's eyes meet mine. "You're here, aren't you?"

I lift a shoulder, not wanting to divulge the real reason I'm here tonight.

Instead, I ask another question.

"How'd you get involved in this place? Are you like, religious or something?"

Jade chuckles, shaking her head.

"Nah, nothing like that. It was actually Zeke Forester's wife, Kendall. You know, the team's sports psychologist?"

I give her a quizzical look as I internally connect all the dots in my head, then nod.

"Yeah, I know her," I add, kicking my legs back and forth, one ankle over the other. "Are you one of her clients?"

Prior to me joining the team last season, Kendall was

brought on by Marek to help Zeke deal with some anxiety-related issues he'd been having that affected his ability to play. Since then, Marek has kept her on retainer to help any of the staff or players who need someone to talk to about their mental health.

But as far as I know, Jade isn't employed by the team or have any professional affiliations with the franchise.

"No. But I know her socially through Harper. We went out for a brunch last season while the guys were at an away game and she mentioned how she uses the act of volunteerism to help her clients. It helps build empathy and compassion when you see the world through a different lens."

"Hmm." I rub my chin. "Kind of a 'walk a mile in their shoes' approach."

She lifts her head from where she stared at her lap to look at me, connecting deep into my eyes as if desperate to appeal to me on an emotional level.

"Yeah, exactly that. I guess I have a soft spot for those in need, especially marginalized women of color, and their animals." She shrugs it off like it's nothing when really it's the most compassionate thing I've ever heard anyone say.

Marek was right when he said Jade has a big heart. I don't feel qualified to respond but do anyways.

"You're pretty fantastic, Jade. In case I haven't mentioned that already."

Jade swings her legs back and forth, and the action draws my attention to her long, lithe thighs and the grace in her body. As my eyes continue up, they land on the flare of her hips and the sensual curves beneath her T-shirt.

She twists her lips into a smile, quirking an eyebrow.

"You're not getting into my pants, Romeo."

I choke out a laugh, raising my hands in the air

innocently.

"Just stating the truth."

"By the way, I'm sorry about your loss."

I'm slightly confused by her sudden change in topic and tilt my head trying to follow her train of thought.

"My loss?"

I haven't played a basketball game since the championship, and obviously we won that one, so I don't know what she's talking about.

"The city's decision on your building. I guess that's it for you, then?"

"I'm sure their decision made you very happy." I give her a wink.

Jade laughs and lifts a toned shoulder.

"I won't lie. It does make me feel better about the future of my gym."

I sniff, shrugging a shoulder in acceptance, leaning in to bump my shoulder against hers.

"For what it's worth, you're a tough opponent and made me work at it, even though I lost out in the end."

"Well, maybe we can put the past behind us and"—she clears her throat—"be friends."

I snap my head behind me and then to both sides, my eyes narrowing dubiously. "Wait a minute. Am I being punked? Did you just suggest that we should be friends? Have I been abducted by aliens from another planet?"

She laughs at my joke and jumps off the counter, landing on her feet. Her words are pointed but they're said with enough inflection that I know she's kidding.

"Forget it, Romeo. You're right. It was a lapse in judgment. Why would I want to be friends with a cocky player like the Jaeger Meister?"

Jade busies herself with one last load of dishes as I sidle

up next to her at the sink, close enough that I can smell her tropical fruit scent, but not close enough to touch, even though my hand yearns to do just that.

And then I pose the question that's been on the tip of my tongue all night, as I waited for the right moment to ask.

"What if, besides friends, I had something else in mind for us?" I say, the words punching through my throat, my pulse racing. Jesus, it's not like I'm proposing marriage or anything. It's just a business proposal.

She jerks sideways in surprise. "Not. Gonna. Sleep. With. You, Romeo. Get that out of your head right now."

I shake my head on a laugh. "That's not what I'm asking. I mean, I would totally accept if you offered...but what if there's a way we could be both friends and maybe even business partners?"

She stops what she's doing, her face impassive, her arms crossed at her chest.

"I don't need a business partner."

All the intel I've gleaned has led to this very crucial moment, when I will wield the ammunition I've stockpiled, using it as a means to an end. To finally step up to the three-point line and make my shot.

"You said it earlier, Jade. People need help." My eyes meet hers, silently begging her to be open to what I have to say. "I'm in the position to help. I want to use my property to build a women's shelter to provide for those in need and even the animals in their care."

It's not easy to read Jade because her expression is guarded and wary around me. All I get is a flash of distrust and the straightening of her proud shoulders.

"In exchange for what, exactly?"

I swallow hard, a goose egg stuck in my throat.

"Your gym."

**16**

———

Jade

"My gym?" I repeat, my tone sharp and justifiably shrieky. "Oh, hell no. You have to be joking."

Jaeger has the audacity to smile. Like he's doing me a solid. Like he's offering me a huge fucking favor or a lifeline, rescuing poor little ol' me from the perils of business ownership.

"No joke. Hear me out, please," he begs, doing that thing he seems to do a lot where he puts up his hands in defense. Like he thinks I'll just roll over and give him what he wants because he's cute and says nice things to me. I turn away but he continues.

"I'd pay you more than fair market value, and in return, I'll keep and renovate my property into living spaces that you can use to establish a shelter. Isn't that what they call a win/win?"

My mind reels with every word that comes out of his mouth. What is it about Jaeger that has my first instinct wanting to knee him in the balls? He's just so arrogantly ignorant.

He truly believes he can get whatever he wants simply by dangling a carrot at me like I'm some dumb bunny, the type of woman who would swoon at his oh-so-generous offer that comes with a side of his charm and good looks. Isn't that the exact definition of arrogance?

Well, Jaeger Matlin doesn't seem to know the woman he's dealing with.

"Not a chance in hell," I snap, slamming the appliance door on the dishwasher and setting it to wash before walking toward the cabinet where I've stored my keys and purse.

"Wait, where are you going?" he asks incredulously. "Don't you even want to hear me out?"

"No thanks. But hey, it's been real." I wave my keys in the air behind me and head toward the door. "Later."

He follows me into the dining area, where I hear him slam his foot or something on a table leg and then he cusses.

"Fuck...Jade, wait," he calls out in frustration. "Can you just hear me out? I think you're missing a great opportunity here."

I spin on my heel and take giant steps toward him, my long legs eating up the space until I'm inches from his face. A face I was just starting to like not thirty minutes ago and now look what it's gone and done.

"Do you not see value in me because of my skin tone? Or is it because I'm a woman?"

Jaeger's expression changes into one of shock, his jaw dropping and eyes popping wide. His head does a little jerk.

"What? Jesus, no. Why would you even suggest that?"

"Because it's obvious you think I'm a sucker." I throw my cross-body bag strap over my shoulders and adjust it in front of me. "One you think you can easily sway with your good looks and money."

He continues to shake his head. "No. That's not it at all. I swear."

I shrug, huffing out my response. "But isn't that how you played me? Because I guarantee you, if I was a white male whose gym you wanted to buy, there's not a chance in hell you'd have proposed this same deal. Period. End of story."

It's easy to see Jaeger's irritation in the way he grinds his molars, his jaw clenching tightly as he rubs at his temple. He knows I'm right, and I simply wait for him to see how it looks from my perspective.

Whether intentional or not, Jaeger Matlin discredited my legitimacy as a business owner by making this offer.

I think he assumed I'd jump all over the offer. I bet he thought I would gladly accept because he's a man and I'm a woman. And gee whiz, maybe I should just put on an apron and get back into the kitchen, eh?

Adding insult to injury, after all the questions he peppered me with as we worked side by side tonight, I thought he was genuinely interested in me as a person and wanted to get to know me.

I'm such a goddamn fool.

He knew exactly what he was doing every step of the way and used my personal interests to try and get something he wanted.

"Jade," he finally says. I can see the wheels turning in the flash of his eyes. That dark blue gaze looks almost sincere. But looks are deceiving. "I can see why you'd think that. And I apologize for the way it looks, but you've got it wrong. You've got me wrong. In fact, I think you and I are a lot alike."

I laugh at this comment, furrowing my brow to give him

a "you're fucking crazy" glare. He tilts his head, undeterred by my obvious low opinion of him.

"Yes, we are." He raises a hand, motioning between us. "We're both ambitious and goal-oriented. But you are heads above me, in a totally different league. You fucking inspire me, and not many other people do. Except maybe LeBron."

I try not to let his comment affect me. I know he doesn't mean it and is just trying to butter me up.

When I don't respond, he continues. "I've seen your dedication, business savvy, and work ethic in action, Jade. And it just makes me want to see what more great things you can do with your own shelter."

He takes a moment, bending his head slightly and folding his hands underneath his chi, inhaling deeply. Then he looks up under his long dark lashes and I think I'm goner.

"I won't be taking the gym out from under you and leaving you with nothing. It's so much bigger than that. *You* are bigger than that."

It's like I'm being spun around in a clothes dryer, my thoughts and emotions whirling around in a frantic tumble. One second, I could kick the guy in the gonads for acting like an arrogant asshole, and the next he's singing my praises and putting me on a pedestal.

I don't want to fall for this...or for him. I've worked too hard to get where I'm at for him to just ride in and sweep it out from under me.

"I appreciate the offer, but I respectfully decline."

His face falls and his chin drops down to his chest in defeat.

I will not feel bad about saying no to him. A woman should never feel bad for voicing her opinion, even when it's not what someone wants to hear.

"You just want the easy part, Jaeger, where I spent years putting in all the hard work."

Jaeger's head pops back up and he nods in agreement.

"You're right, this would be easier. But remember, I tried a different route first, but the city shot that down. So, here I am with my plan B. I've never wavered from my goal of wanting to own a gym. And honestly, I thought you'd jump at an opportunity to make a greater difference in this community."

He shrugs and runs a hand through his hair. Hair I want to pull out in frustration because he's hit the nail on the head. I do want to make a bigger difference in the lives of others. Not just the wealthy and athletic. But those who really need help.

Damn bastard is trying to pander to my need to help people.

"Jade," he says, quieter this time. "All I ask is that you think about it. The choice is yours and it's in your hands, I won't pressure. We don't have to remain rivals. We can be friends and do great things together."

I stare at the wall near the exit, where a poster with a motivational quote hangs in front of me as I wonder what that would even look like. Me and Jaeger, friends and partners. It seems so complicated.

My eyes snap back to Jaeger who appears both nervous and optimistically hopeful. "I wouldn't get your hopes up, rookie But I'll consider the offer."

THE REMAINDER OF THE WEEK, I waffle between two extremes: hating Jaeger for putting this idea in my head and actually considering it.

Especially when things take a swift and sudden nosedive at the gym.

It's late Thursday afternoon when the shitstorm begins.

I'm head down in my office, trying to pay some bills before they become overdue in the next week, when I hear shouting from the front reception area. Glancing up from my monitor, I notice a woman standing at the counter—dressed in a chic yet not quite *Housewives of Beverly Hills* level—outfit, and heels. Her long dark hair sways back and forth across her shoulders with the fury of her movements, her hand waving wildly in Siena's face, as the woman yells at my employee.

I lean further to the side to get a better view and see the horrified expression on Siena's normally chipper face. Something is terribly wrong.

Thinking perhaps the woman is an unhappy client—we have them on occasion, mostly women, who want their membership money returned because they didn't lose the weight they wanted or get in the shape they had hoped to achieve—I'm ready to assist if Siena gives me a call.

Most often, Siena is able to calm the client down and smooth out their ruffled feathers. But other times, I'll step in and work through a solution, sometimes offering a free training session or a month free membership.

But when I reach the door to my office and pry it open a crack, I hear the insults the woman is hysterically throwing Siena's way and head out to act as a human shield.

"He's a married man, you little slut! We have children. You're a home-wrecker!"

Instead of walking around to the other side of the counter, I slowly approach to stand at the woman's side.

"Excuse me, ma'am. I'm Jade Russell. The owner of

Seattle Circuit. Perhaps we can go to my office where there's more privacy so I can help you out?"

I raise both palms to gesture toward my office and her red-rimmed, mascara-smeared eyes glare me down. Clearly, the woman is visibly upset. My gaze bounces between her and Siena, who looks quite relieved that I've jumped in as backup reinforcement for this uninvited attack.

"Privacy? Please..." the woman gripes venomously. "Is that how you conduct your business, Miss Russell? Like a whorehouse where married men can carry on affairs in *private*?" She hooks her fingers into air quotes.

Jesus, what is happening here? My eyes dart to Siena, who has the wisdom to look contrite.

I offer a slight smile. "I don't know about that, Mrs...?"

"Mrs. Jack Harmon."

Oh, dear. This could get ugly very fast.

Jack Harmon is the district attorney, a very influential figure in the Seattle legal arena, and also a known philanderer, if you follow the gossips. He's in his late forties, with silverish-fox good looks, and a very big wallet, and has been a member of the gym since we opened our doors.

Now, I'm not jumping to any conclusions about his involvement with Siena, but he is absolutely the type of man she seems to cling to and with whom I've witnessed her flirting in the past. And he's exactly the kind of man who would encourage it.

"Please, Mrs. Harmon, come with me, so we can discuss this further."

I direct her down the hallway until we reach the seclusion of my office walls, shutting the door behind us to ensure all the private details stay where they belong.

"I want you to fire that girl immediately," Mrs. Harmon asserts, clutching her bag in her lap. "And if you don't, I will bring legal action and file a lawsuit against you and your business."

The floor shifts and moves underneath my feet but my voice remains calm and composed. "On what grounds? This is a private matter, Mrs. Harmon. Whether the facts are there to prove it or not, I don't see how it would involve a lawsuit against my business."

She sniffs and snaps her head around, jutting her long, elegant chin out toward Siena. Then she returns to look at me, her eyes as cold as the glacial ice cap on top of Mount Rainier.

"Facts or not, it'll be your burden to prove you're not running an escort service out of your gym. I'm sure your hussy out there has a plethora of texts and emails to not just my husband, but many of your married clients. And that would look very poorly on you and your business, Ms. Russell."

I swallow hard. She's absolutely right about that. I'm not so sure, if Siena did have affair, that she would have kept it off her work devices, which would be damning for us both. Either way, it would cost me everything to disprove it.

But what I won't do in this moment is give Mrs. Harmon the satisfaction of firing my employee just because she faces humiliation that her husband caused her.

*Trust. You can't trust players or politicians.*

The woman smooths away an errant piece of hair from her face, smiling like the cat that ate the canary.

"So I'd suggest your best option would be to fire that slut-bag whore as soon as possible."

"Thank you, Mrs. Harmon. I will take that under advisement."

Whether a real threat or not, I can't imagine getting

stuck in a legal battle for the next three years over something my flirty receptionist did or didn't do.

Come to think of it, maybe Jaeger's offer to buy my gym sounds pretty good right about now. Employee relations and legal battles would transfer to the new owner.

I smile at the thought.

**17**

―――――

Jaeger

"Are you interested in meeting up with those chicks we just met down at Murphy's later?"

I unlock the door, tossing my keys into the bowl by the front entry, and flick a glance over my shoulder at Henri, punctuating it with a non-committal shrug.

"Yeah, maybe. I could go for a few beers and some laughs."

Henri chuckles, quirking a dark eyebrow at me while whipping off his sweat-drenched T-shirt from the run we just had around Green Lake.

"Is that what we're calling it these days?"

I roll my eyes, not about to respond to his innuendo, as I open the fridge and pull out two water bottles, setting one on the counter for him to collect.

While on our run, we were stopped by a threesome of college girls who wanted selfies and autographs, their cleavage and bare stomachs catching Henri's attention. He asked one of the girls for their Insta handle and has already slid into her DMs to meet up later tonight.

Uncapping the bottle, he tips it back and swallows it down, finishing it within mere seconds. He crunches the plastic bottle in his hand and throws it in the recycling bin at the end of the counter.

"Just beers and laughs? What happened to The Meister we all knew and loved? The guy who could bone down two to three girls a day? One before the game, one after and a third on a booty call. I figured you'd be fucking every bikini-clad hoops honey you could find this summer."

I bend at my waist and grab behind my knees, stretching my overly-tight hamstrings and my aching lower back before returning to a standing position.

"I don't know, bro," I reply. "After that chick posted pictures of me in bed even after I asked her not to, I've been a lot more skeptical. Don't get me wrong, I'm horny as fuck right now, but I'm also trying to reassess things and focus my energies on what I really want."

"Jesus, Marek's pep talks have really gotten through to you, eh?" He tilts his head with a smirk.

Yeah, our team's GM sat me down plenty of times during my rookie season to remind me what easy prey I can be. Having some discretion and keeping my dick in my pants when it came to excess women was something I was encouraged to consider.

"Maybe a little, I guess. But there's other things I want, too, besides getting laid."

I wait for him to make a joke or a sarcastic remark, but Henri recognizes my sincerity and responds in kind.

"Like the gym?"

I chuckle. "Like that gym."

It's been over a week now since I spoke with Jade. Since that time, I've replayed the conversation over and over in my head, wondering what, if anything, will ever get her to change her low opinion of me.

I know I've screwed up plenty of times with her, but I don't think I've ever said anything stupid or disrespectful even when we've argued. I just didn't articulate myself very well around her.

Sure, I have the reputation of being a player. I'm a twenty-four-year-old professional basketball player. But I'm not disrespectful or unkind to women.

But somehow around Jade, I seem to stick my foot in my mouth and say the wrong thing every single fucking time.

I'd never admit it to her or anyone else, but Jade makes me nervous. She gets me tongue-tied.

She's not only beautiful and confident but she owns it. She's a woman who has her shit together, and her business competence is the sexiest thing I've ever encountered.

Unlike me, she's probably never had to rely on help from her family. I couldn't even select the right bid for the building renovation without consulting with my dad first.

I'm still kind of amazed that I successfully narrowed my selection down to three local builders after conducting a handful of interviews all by myself. No advice needed and I felt confident making the final selection on my own.

The one I liked best for a variety of reasons was a company called Brothers in Arms Construction, owned and operated by a former military veteran named Jim Presley, whose business model employs mostly former military personnel and vets. I liked that aspect of their company's mission.

Since my plans were shot down by the city, I've decided to build the residential dwelling after all. Without Jade's agreement to sell me her gym, I can still move forward and build single-family rentals or condominiums, even if it wasn't what I originally wanted to do. I still believe Jade's pride is getting in the way of turning this into something the community could really use. But what can I do? I've given her the best offer I could think of.

I know there's no way in hell I could start and run a non-profit. That's totally outside my level of expertise.

But Jade could do it. Plus, I thought it was her heart's desire.

"You think Jade will come around and sell? Or is she holding out for a better price?"

I shake my head. "Nah, man. It's not a money thing with Jade. She's dug her heels in as a source of pride. I don't blame her."

The idea of Jade digging her heels into something, especially my ass as I pound inside her, sends dirty images straight to my dick. I'm not ashamed to admit that I've thought about that all damn week. The way she'd sound as I rocked into her wet pussy, her long legs thrown around my hips, her nails dragging down the muscles of my expanding and contracting back.

That thought is interrupted when both Henri's and my phones beep with incoming texts. I grab mine from the counter and he reaches for his inside his pants pocket.

> Carch: You two up for an impromptu 4 on 4?

I look up and meet Henri's eyes, who nods. I return my gaze to the phone and begin typing.

> Me: Sure, old man. We're in. Where and when?

> Carch: The arena in 30. Marek, Zeke and a few others will meet us there.

Me: Cool. Stop at our place and we can drive together.

Carch: I call shotgun.

Henri rolls his eyes and grumbles something about "fucker" and turns toward his bedroom, where he disappears to take a shower and get changed.

I do the same, showering quickly as I valiantly try to avoid the thoughts of a naked and wet Jade pressed against my body that are urging my cock to life. I do not have time to rub one out.

But maybe Henri's suggestion of going out and getting laid tonight has merit. I have so much pent-up sexual energy, and with the added pressures of the building renovations, I'm a tightly coiled ball of stress. I need a release.

I need to have some fun, get my mind off this whole side-hustle business, and enjoy the company of a beautiful woman.

And a game of pick-up ball isn't a half-bad idea, either.

As I finish dressing in my T-shirt and track pants, I know I'm just fooling myself into thinking either of these activities will do anything to get Jade off my mind. Or my attention off my aching dick.

The irony is not lost on me, though.

I could have any woman I choose except Jade Russell. She's the only woman I want, and she's made it abundantly clear. She doesn't want me.

## 18

———

J ade
   "Why is it that I always let you talk me into bad ideas?"

I swing open a door marked Pilots Staff Only to allow Harper through first, her laughter an acknowledgment to our formidably long list of questionable history that only best friends can get in together.

"Because bad ideas are the best kind." She plants a kiss on my cheek and breezes by me, tugging me by the arm through the corridor of the stadium and toward the guest team's locker room, which for our purposes today is women only.

I continue whining in hopes I'll gain enough sympathy to get out of playing in this pick-up game Marek arranged today with a few of the players. I guess it was some bet between him and Harper, who cajoled him into proving what an awesome player he once was when he'd played in the NBA back in the day.

"I haven't played in years, Harp. It'll be a miracle if I can still run and dribble the ball at the same time without face-planting."

She stops in front of me and whirls around, her gaze moving over my body with a shrewd, challenging look.

"Oh puh-lease, girl," she says with an eye roll and a dismissive wave of her hand. "You are a fitness instructor and gym owner. You're in better shape now than you were back in college. You are going to run circles around those so-called professional basketball players."

I don't share her opinion, pouting as I watch her set down her duffle bag on the bench and open it to pull out a basketball jersey.

It's the Pilots' team colors of gray, blue and white, and across the back, my name is inscribed in sparkly blinged-out lettering. A loud peel of laughter slips from my chest.

"Jesus Christ. How long have you been planning this?" I hold the jersey up to my shoulders, tipping my chin down to see what the front looks like. Pilots #10. My old number from college.

Harper shimmies with excitement, her voice a sing-song pitch. "Merry Christmas."

"Pfft." I give her a raspberry. "I'm telling ya right now, sista. You're set to marry a millionaire, which means your bestie is expecting something a lot more blingy than just a bedazzled jersey."

I roll up the shirt and give her a good snap against her ass, and she tries to dart out of the way with a high-pitched yelp. Admittedly, my mood has already lightened with this sweet gesture—bling has a way of doing that.

But even more than that, while our lives, careers, and situations have ebbed and flowed these past ten years, the one constant has been my friendship with Harper.

We get to work changing into our gym clothes, me sliding my new basketball jersey over my head, and lace up my sneakers. As I'm bent over, I slide a sidelong glance toward Harper, who is pulling her long dark hair up into a bun, a grin stretched wide across her face.

"You're actually excited about this game, aren't you?"

Swiveling toward me, she smiles gleefully. "I can't wait to show these guys up. They're not going to expect us to be so good."

She stretches out her hand for a knuckle bump. We touch our fists together and mime the explosion sign with laughter ringing between us.

I stand up, some of her eager excitement filtering through my systems, and lift up on the toes of my shoes to work out some kinks in my calves while practicing the arc of my free throw shot.

"If you say so," I mutter grudgingly. "Our college skills aren't really a match for these guys you know. So let's not make any bets we can't make good on."

She clucks her tongue through her teeth and shakes her head.

"Or maybe they're no match for these." She palms her tits and pushes them together, presses her lips into a kissy mouth, and sashays her hips in a seductive walk toward the door. "Or this."

Harper then proves why she is my best friend, shoving her ass in the air behind her and twerking suggestively.

I'm laughing so hard that tears spill from my eyes as we walk out the locker room door together, which is why I don't see the mammoth obstacle in front of me before it's too late.

And I slam smack dab into *him*.

Jaeger smiles widely like he's thrilled to see me. My own laughter dies, and I heave an exaggerated sigh.

"Well, hello, *ba*—Jade." He flinches slightly, catching himself before saying it. "We really need to stop running into each other like this."

"Maybe if you just moved out of state, mansplainer, that would happen." I give him a cheesy, toothy smile.

He chortles. "Lucky for you, I'm committed to Seattle for another three years."

I groan childishly, giving him an elbow in the ribs to brush past him, but he follows closely at my heels. Close enough that I get a whiff of his clean scent and spicy deodorant.

"What were you two laughing about just now?" he asks, bending his lips to my ear, his warm breath fanning over my neck. I shiver.

Harper has already jogged ahead of us to meet up with Marek on the court, leaving me alone with Jaeger at my side, his arm bumping against mine like a boat moored against a dock. He's trying to get me to engage. To talk smack with him. To rekindle what started at the soup kitchen the last time we met and also to get inside my head before the game.

My lips quirk up into a sassy smirk. "We were discussing the size of your dick print, if you must know. How small it appears in those pictures that were posted all over social media."

My comment is meant as a joke, a dig. Because, you know, we're trash-talking. Guys talk about fucking your mama and girls make it all about size and stamina.

But instead of laughing and responding with a comeback, it stops him in his tracks and he briefly glances away.

His dick print was a social media sensation and all over the socials after the championship. As the story goes, apparently Jaeger had slept with some hoops honey who took a very indecent snap of him while he was actually sleeping, a sheet covering his lower extremities. The beauty of the photo and what got all the attention from the masses is that while he may have been dead to the world, his semi-erect cock was indeed wide awake. And that package of his was outlined in all its erect glory for all the lookie-loos to see. And salivate over.

And let me tell you, it was a very complimentary pic. His nickname of Jaeger *The Bomb* has new meaning to his fans —it is the size of a submarine torpedo. That torpedo made its rounds across the world wide web. I bet the cocky bastard was strutting around like a peacock with all that attention on him. What guy wouldn't?

Although, based on the sudden downturn of his mouth, it seems I've hit a sore spot. I steal a look into his eyes and notice a flash of something. Hurt, maybe? Embarrassment?

I can't imagine he's upset by my comment. He must know I'm kidding, right? The Jaeger I've seen around this summer would be crowing like a rooster right now, suggesting his dick is so big even King Kong'd be a FansOnly follower if he had an account.

A moment passes, a strange silence descending between us, until he responds.

"Yeah, my cock's pretty impressive, isn't it? Just like my skills at using it."

I make a gagging noise as we enter the arena floor and Harper turns around to give me a stern warning look.

"Hey, you two, play nice today. Leave the trash-talking 'til we're on the court."

"COME ON, rookie! Is that all you got?"

As it would happen, Jaeger and I are paired up against

each other on opposing teams. The four on four is divided up into Marek's team, which includes him, Harper, Jaeger, and one of Marek's good friends, Ballas Keeney.

Oddly enough, Ballas isn't even a basketball player but a professional hockey player from the Vancouver Vikings. He's in Seattle visiting Marek and Harper for the week before heading off for a two-week trip to the sunny beaches of Belize.

On my team, we have Zeke and Carch, both co-captains of the Pilots, along with me, and Henri Pierre. Admittedly, I nearly swooned when Henri introduced himself with that thick, rich, sexy French accent of his. Jesus, he must have all the girls dropping their panties at every turn.

On the sidelines rooting us on are Zeke's wife, Kendall, and their two-year-old son, Gus, who parrots after me in the way only a toddler can do.

*"C'mon, wookie!"*

The little voice and the sweetness of his mispronunciation has both Jaeger and me cracking up in laughter, our gazes locking on one another. His eyes dance with mischief as he palms the ball between his hands, elbows outward while he shifts back and forth on his feet.

He stands inches from me, shifting back and forth on the balls of his feet, as my palm lays flat against his chest in a defensive move. The heat of his body travels up my arm and straight down my spine. He clasps the ball high, raising it above our heads in a taunting game of keep away, his square jaw set, and his blue eyes pinned on me. His impressive form rivals all other players in the league.

But when his gaze drops to my lips and the light humor gives way to darkened sensuality, I know I've found my rival's weakness.

And fuck if I don't use it against him.

This is the same cat-and-mouse game we've played before off the court, but this time the sexual push-and-pull of this dance makes my head spin.

It's the weirdest dynamic I've ever had with a guy.

Ever since...well, since graduating college, I've kept my distance from men in general. Don't get close. Don't let them see how much you want them. Don't play into their egos or show vulnerability.

Jaeger is different in most ways. He doesn't always come on strong and usually knows when to back off. But he also doesn't give up when I push back and express my opinions. I kind of dig that about him.

In that respect, I feel he's an equal.

I'm so lost in my thoughts and the way his blue eyes roam my face that I don't realize our impromptu ref and replacement player, Trenton, has blown a whistle. Jaeger and I both snap our heads in his direction.

"What the fuck, ref?" Jaeger snaps, pressing the ball against his hip in a defiant gesture.

Trenton chuckles. "Personal fouls on you both. Your eye-fucking is becoming a serious delay of game."

"What?" I grouse in defense of my actions. "Are you blind, ref? There is no eye-fucking happening here. That's ridiculous."

Our teammates erupt in hoots of agreement with Trenton, leaving Jaeger and me on the same side of an argument for once. That's never happened before.

I take the opportunity to snag the ball out of Jaeger's hand so I can post up at the free throw line so I can take my shots, but the ball doesn't come loose, and he doesn't let go. Instead, he tugs me closer, leaning down so I can feel the whiskers of his short stubble abrade lightly against my ear.

Then he whispers, "I'd be up for more than eye-fucking with you."

I swallow hard and grab the ball with a muttered curse.

I miss both shots.

Goddamn Jaeger Matlin.

**19**

---

Jaeger

That game was a motherfucking blast.

When was the last time I had that much fun out on the court? Today wasn't about winning a championship. It wasn't about being the best player or proving to the fans and the team that I'm worthy of my contract.

Today was simply about playing the game for the love of the sport and friendship.

It didn't hurt that I had a spectacularly sexy opponent that ran circles around me.

Jesus Christ. Jade left me speechless with how gracefully she moved out on the court. The style of her ball handling. The preciseness of her shots.

Jade is one phenomenal ball player and the perfect competitor.

She played dirty. She talked smack. She owned the court both offensively and defensively.

And it got me hot and fired up.

Seeing her skillful moves on the court made me want more than anything to see what she'd be like in bed.

"Yo, Jaeger. You hear me?" Henri calls out over the locker room shower stall. I've been zoning out as the hot spray cascades over my well used, tight muscles.

"No, sorry. What'd you say?"

He snickers. "You coming out with me tonight or going over to Zeke's for dinner with the rest of the crew?"

It's an innocuous question but has me feeling like a teenage boy, wanting to know what Jade's plans are first before I make my own decision.

"I'm not sure yet," I say noncommittally, rinsing the suds from my hair until the water runs clear before turning the shower off and drying off with the towel hanging from the hook. "Maybe I'll do both."

That seems like a good call. I could hang over at Zeke's for dinner and if Jade doesn't show, I can head off to the club with Henri.

Henri, however, makes a disgruntled noise at this decision.

"Mmm-hmm. Pussy-whipped already."

"Fuck off." I unwrap the towel from my waist and snap the back of his calf with it. Carch and Trenton finish their showers and join us in the locker area, each adding their own two cents from their observations.

Carch offers up his opinion first. "What exactly is going on between you and Harper's friend? What's her name again? Jane?"

"Jade," I answer, a bit more defensively than necessary, and Carch laughs.

"*Riiiight.* Jade. You seem particularly enamored with her. Is that a thing, Meister?"

I bite my tongue. It drives me nuts when he uses that nickname because it always carries a hint of disapproval from him. Carch has never liked me since I joined the team.

"Is what a thing?"

"You two," he states matter-of-factly. "Are you tapping that?"

I snort testily. "No. And she's not a that. Her name is Jade. Use it."

Carch waves his hands in the air. "Oooh, sticking up for your girl. Must be L.O.V.E."

I flip him off. "What would you know about it, old man? I don't see you with any woman. Probably cause your balls are all wrinkled and shrunk."

Trenton snorts in laughter and decides to pipe in. *Bastard.*

"If it is love, it's only one-sided, man. Jade's too fine and intelligent for the likes of this fuck boy."

I give Trenton the finger too. "Why you be hating on me, bro?"

"Come on, J. We know how you are. You're a player all day, every day. And from the looks of Jade, she's refinement and sophistication." He flicks his wrist in the air. "She's not looking for what you're dishing out."

"Like chlamydia."

I shoot Carch a distasteful glare. "You'd know a thing or two about that, dude."

I slam the locker shut and throw my bag over my shoulder, heading toward the door. "You're all just jealous bitches because you know the ladies love me. And they know exactly what they're getting when I love them back."

I spin halfway around and grab the crotch of my shorts in a lewd gesture before walking out and down to the garage in search of Zeke or Marek, hoping to grab a ride with one of them.

But when I open the door to the garage, I see their parking spots empty and both their cars gone. However, when I turn back around, I'm in luck. Jade is stuffing her gear in the back of a cherry red Jeep Rubicon.

"Hey," I call out from the exit door, taking long strides toward her. "Are you by chance going over to Zeke and Kendall's place for dinner?"

She whips her head around, the movement causing the long black braids flowing loosely down her back to sway. I never noticed how long the braids were until now. Nearly down to the curve of her butt.

And now my eyes naturally gravitate toward her tight ass, which I was lucky enough to feel shoved up against my crotch several times on the court today when I was playing defense against her.

She clears her throat, eyeing me warily and I blink away the dirty thoughts.

"Why?"

Ahh, we're back to that again. I thought after the way the ice thawed between us during the game, we'd be on more neutral ground.

I give her my brightest show-stopping smile. "Because I need a ride."

Jade cuts me a look. "Why not go over with your boys?"

I shrug. "Henri drove us here and the guys aren't going to Zeke's."

"Why don't you go home with them and get your own car?" She hesitates before adding, "I need to stop by my office first anyway, and it'll be an inconvenience for you."

I take another step closer. Close enough to inhale her sweet feminine scent. Close enough to hear the sharp intake of breath she sucks in. Close enough to lean in and kiss all the inane questions from her lips.

Jade is angled between the open door and the car. I raise my arm and hook an elbow over the door frame, my body encroaching on her space, but allowing room if she wants to leave. There was no personal space while we played today. We spent two hours groping each other in the most fantastic ways.

I bend down, my lips to her ear.

"Being with you would never inconvenience me," I murmur. "I'd love to spend more time with you."

If it were possibly any other woman, I'd make my move right this instant. I'd take her earlobe between my teeth and suck. Hard. I'd trail a path along her smooth neck and straight jawbone with my tongue. I'd suck and kiss my way to her lips and then crush her mouth to mine.

But I don't do any of that. I reign in my desire and wait, allowing her the opportunity to decide if she wants any of that.

The game we played today helped in some respects. We touched. We sparred. We blocked and elbowed our way to the ball.

And it was all foreplay.

Jade knows it and so do I. Which is the reason I don't take a step back. I don't move a muscle. I remain still and wait for her consent or her dismissal. While I hope for the first, I'll respect the latter.

My breath fans hotly across her neck and I watch the goosebumps form over the supple skin. I want to trace the dots with my tongue.

If Jade doesn't want this, she'll let me know in no uncertain terms.

Probably with a knee to my balls.

But she doesn't do that.

Instead, she asks a question. It's barely audible, just a shaky wisp of breath, her voice whisper-soft like a feather floating to the ground.

"*Why?*"

Is it my imagination, or did she just move closer? Because now I feel the stiff peaks of her nipples pressed firmly against my chest. Her eyes are half-mast and her mouth parted slightly. An invitation, perhaps.

I repeat the question in a delirious murmur. "Why what?"

An aching throb builds rapidly in my pants, my cock roaring to life as we continue this fervent back-and-forth game between us.

"*Why* do you want to be with me?" She tilts her head to the side in her silent invitation as my lips glide gently along her neck. The moan that rolls off her tongue is pure sex, and I can barely think straight.

"Is it because you want my gym?"

Huh? Gym? *What gym?*

All I want is to capture and devour her mouth with mine and then plant myself between her legs.

My lips coast up her slender neck and before I capture her mouth with mine, I assure her that it has nothing to do with business.

"It's because I want *you*, Jade. You're what I want."

**20**

---

J ade

*Lord have mercy.*

I never knew playing a basketball game could be such an aphrodisiac.

My entire body is electric, amped up from the adrenaline of the game and firing on all cylinders from Jaeger's proximity. The unreal sensations rush up my spine, carrying with them bursts and explosions of shimmering light that have my belly clenching in response. My pussy, as well.

Breath lodges in my throat when his lips stop abruptly along my jawline.

My lips part and the desire to slide my fingers through his hair and slam my mouth to his is so overwhelming my knees nearly buckle with the weight of my need.

Jaeger pulls back and gently skims his fingers over my jawline. He places his thumb in the center of my lower lip and levels me with eyes lazy with lust.

"Do you want me to kiss you, Jade?"

Yes, yes, and hell, yes. I want him to seal his mouth over mine so I can feel the hot slide of his tongue. I want him to wedge his thick cock between my thighs and make me come fast and hard as I writhe against him.

But I don't say any of that. I don't want to give him the upper hand or prove how much power he has over me in this moment.

Instead of conceding to the need that bubbles up from the depths of my stomach, I turn the tables and use a tactic I've used in basketball to gain the advantage, to get the ball back in my court.

"Do you want to kiss *me*, Jaeger?"

He growls, returning his lips to my neck and nipping at the sensitive patch of skin behind my ear.

"Fuck yeah, I do. I've wanted to kiss you since the moment I saw you in the security line with that sexy confidence you wore like a goddess from another world."

"That's very poetic of you, Romeo. But are you suggesting I'm an alien life form?"

My lips curl up into a slightest of smiles. I clasp my hands behind his neck, relishing in the hot feel of his skin, watching his expression turn apologetic.

His face twists with regret. But when he opens his mouth to likely refute the allegation, he doesn't get far because I shut him up.

"Then kiss me already, Jaeger. I want you to—"

Then his mouth crushes over mine.

The straining muscles in his shoulders and neck slowly relax as my mouth parts in an open invitation for him to take more. In this game of sexy demands, we both win, whether I let him control or I take control.

His lips, full and warm, hungrily devour mine, as he lets out a feral moan against my mouth. His tongue sweeps past my parted lips to invade and conquer, ravishing me in hot open kisses. I weave my fingers through his silky, still damp hair, roaming along his scalp as the kiss turns urgent and exploratory. It sends my mind swirling in a wild spiraling motion, as all rational thought flies out the window in favor of more.

The velvet warmth of Jaeger's kiss shocks me. In all my years, I've never been kissed with this much intensity and pent-up desire.

My nails dig into the back of his neck, extracting a low groan from the depths of his chest. The sound vibrates through me, shooting deliciously indecent sensations down to my panties that are already soaked with need.

Without a way to get closer or a sturdy structure to push me against except an open car door, Jaeger's hands scoop me up underneath my ass, boosting me in the air so I can wind my long legs tightly around his waist.

And there it is. The Jaeger Bomb's torpedo-sized dick print come to life and wedged right where I need him most.

"Let's go somewhere we can take this further," he says against my greedy mouth, my breaths coming out in harsh pants.

"Mmm...yeah...that'd be good."

My defenses have clearly weakened and I'm a grinding, needy mess, undulating against his thick cock like a dry-humping teenager.

And then I remember I'd planned on putting in some time at the gym this afternoon. I have work piled on my desk I have to attend to.

I'm about to mention this when the sound of a door slamming and throats clearing somewhere in our midst infiltrates through my hazy thoughts, and I immediately go still in Jaeger's arms.

Glancing over his shoulder, I get an unobstructed view of the trio of players who have stopped motionless in their tracks, staring at us in our compromising position. One of them whistles.

"Uh, Jaeger," I whisper, voice raspy. "Can you put me down now?"

His head swivels around and I can see his brows furrow at his friends.

"Go away, assholes."

Jaeger waves them off with a hand over his head and I pinch his bicep hard, extracting a yelp from him. "Down, please."

He complies reluctantly, and my feet touch back on the ground. I can feel the heat rising in my cheeks, burning with embarrassment over being caught making out with Jaeger. I turn my back to our audience and wipe my lips with the back of my hand to hide the evidence of Jaeger's kisses. It's a ridiculous endeavor, considering they all saw exactly what we were up to just now.

Henri shakes his head, as if disapproving of the situation, and I hear him murmur something about "I figured," and then he says to Carch, "You owe me twenty bucks." Carch makes a noncommittal noise, turning to follow him to the passenger side of Henri's car with disinterest. Trenton simply stares, a huge-ass grin stretched across his face. He will definitely use this as ammunition later to taunt and torment his friend about what he witnessed.

*Boys.* They never truly grow up, do they?

A loud thud on the roof of my Jeep hood makes me jump. Jaeger winks and walks backwards, his gaze never leaving mine until he's on the other side of my car. Opening the door, he tosses his bag in the backseat and hops in the front, calling out over his shoulder to the guys as they get in their vehicle.

"Gonna pass on Murphy's tonight with you guys. Have fun."

Then he slams the door and leans over the driver's seat, ducking down to look up at where I'm still standing in my open door, motionless.

"The car's not gonna drive itself. You ready?"

I shake my head out of the stupor and settle into my seat, starting the engine and putting it in reverse.

"That was unexpected," Jaeger says lightly, a hint of disbelief lacing his tone. Then he leans over so he's inches from my ear. "But I liked it a lot."

My heart hammers wildly—and dare I say, foolishly—my body filled with a foreign inner excitement as I attempt to shift into reverse and exit the parking space. My hands clutch the steering wheel as I try to come to grips over what just happened.

I kissed and mouth-fucked Jaeger Matlin.

It can only be attributed to the adrenaline of the game, right? All the endorphins swimming in my bloodstream and the chemicals in my body sparked a mutinous concoction of horniness and sexual attraction.

That's the only conclusion that explains the oddity of it all.

Otherwise, I'd never in a million years make out with a player with a reputation like Jaeger's.

"Hey, you've gone quiet." Jaeger's palm lands on top of my thigh, his fingertips tickling the bare skin above my knee, exposed by the way my shorts ride up. "Want to tell me what's going on in that head of yours?"

I keep my eyes on the road ahead but pluck his hand off my thigh and drop it in his own lap. There's no way I can concentrate on the drive if he keeps touching me. I'm already a wreck after that phenomenal kiss.

"Sorry," he whispers apologetically, lifting his palms in the air. "Didn't realize the boundaries were back in place again."

I stop at the red light on Bell Street, slowly turning my head to look at him. His tatted arm, nearly a full sleeve of various shapes and images, is visible under his black sports tank. If I had the time, I'd examine every colorful image, the intricacy of each, tracing a finger over their beauty.

Instead, I level him with a soft reflective gaze. "It's just been a while for me. I can't go from zero to sixty like I'm sure some of your hoops honeys do. Just because we kissed doesn't mean you can expect me to be down to fuck."

This does nothing to deter him. He scoots to the edge of his seat, leans over the console, and raises a hand to gently brush a few of my braids behind my ear.

I close my eyes at the intimacy of the touch. It's been so long since I've allowed anything like this that isn't the act of sex.

It has me wavering, wanting more than anything to give into his advances. To let go with him. To enjoy the thrill of flirting with a man who is as hard-headed as I am and can go toe-to-toe with me. But then can turn me into marshmallowy-gooeyness with just a kiss.

Jaeger picks up my hand off the wheel and brings it to his lips to kiss it gently, his eyes pinning me with the fire of his gaze.

"I don't expect anything you don't want to give freely, Jade. If I never get another kiss from you again, that will still be the hottest kiss ever."

I'm so lost in his declaration that I'm zoned out until a loud blare of a horn behind me brings me back to reality.

I press down on the accelerator a little harder than I

mean to and the car lurches forward. Jaeger jerks backwards against the front seat with a laugh.

"What's so funny?" I grumble, embarrassed at the way he has fucked with my driving concentration.

He leans back in the seat, resting his head against the headrest and looking relaxed and casual, whereas I'm a ball of nerves.

Out of my peripheral vision I notice his eyes close with a grin.

"You are, Ms. Lead Foot." He turns his head toward me and raises an eyebrow, a mischievous smile spreading across his mouth. "You just went from zero to sixty, just like that." Jaeger snaps his fingers as I turn at the next corner.

His words are clear, but his voice is raspy. "Maybe it means you're as turned on as I am right now."

If my panties weren't wet already, they're soaked now.

**21**

———

Jaeger

Jade locates a parking spot a half block down the street from her gym, turns off the engine, and literally jumps out of the car like her ass is on fire.

"I'll be right back." She slams the door behind her, practically sprinting toward the entrance of her gym. I chuckle as I watch her gain distance between us. That's fine. I get it. She obviously needs time to collect herself.

And so do I, for that matter.

I'm not sure why she needs to swing by the gym on her way to Zeke's, but it probably won't hurt me to get my raging hard-on in check before we head to dinner. As I slowly saunter down the sidewalk, I work through what just happened, like it's a puzzle in my head and the pieces are clicking into place.

Jade let me kiss her. In fact, she demanded that I kiss her.

I know she enjoyed it too and I think it pisses her off just how much.

If the sultry moans and the tight grip she had on my hair

are any indication, that kiss hit the mark with a bullseye. It was as if I hit a secret latch that unlocked the door and lowered a portion of that steel veneer she wears like armor.

She's already disappeared inside the building when I open the entrance door to the gym, the silvery Seattle Circuit decal sign catching a ray of sun and glinting brightly as I enter.

A blast of cold air hits my face and breezes through my damp finger-tousled hair, sending a shiver down my spine. I lower my sunglasses and scan the front room for signs of Jade.

This is the first time I've ever stepped inside. I looked through the pictures online when I did my research a few weeks ago, but until now, I haven't ventured in, mostly out of concern that Jade would kick me out.

Rows of high-end equipment mark several paths down the main floor and the interior wall is fitted with large reflective mirrors, a typical attribute in a fitness center. It's not uncommon for clients to frequently check on their form and physique while conducting their workouts.

I appreciate the aesthetic of the gym's layout and can see Jade's touch in every facet of the place.

Turning toward the reception desk, I notice a juice bar and shelves of various supplement lines fully stocked for purchase. A good marketing strategy.

"Welcome to Seattle Circuit. It's a pleasure to have you join us..." A young, chipper female voice drags my attention away from the displays, and I turn to find a diminutive woman who looks even younger than me, giving me a welcoming cherry-red-lipped smile.

"Oh my God. Jaeger Matlin. Welcome!" she says, clasping her hands together in awe. "What an honor to have you here."

She prances around the counter on her toes like ballet dancers do on stage and stops in front of me, staring up with admiring eyes and extending her tiny hand out to shake mine. I do the polite thing and clasp my hand with hers, but when I try to let go, she covers my knuckles with her free hand.

I give Siena, according to her name tag, a smile in return. "Hi there."

"Are you here to join the club? I'm sure you've heard all about it from Marek. He's a regular member," she prattles, finally dropping my hand and waving hers around as she speaks. "He's such a great guy. You must love working with him. And we have many other local professional athletes as members, too. You'll fit right in."

I shake my head. "Thanks, but I'm here to find Jade. Did you happen to see where she went?"

Her mouth pouts in a disappointed frown, eyelashes fluttering in the universal sad-baby-doll face.

It's funny how I used to play into coy female tactics. I once found it cute and sexy, drawn to the sex-kitten aspect.

Now it doesn't interest me at all. Jade doesn't do any of that. She doesn't need to.

Siena sweeps her tongue over her bottom lip and leans back on her elbows against the counter behind her, a move meant to push her breasts forward in an enticing pose.

I glance away, avoiding the trap, and notice a short hallway leading to some locker rooms and restrooms. There's a tinted window on the wall facing me and a door with the word Private on the name plaque. That must be Jade's office.

Nodding in that direction, I give Siena a decided glance.

"I bet she's in her office. I'll check there. Thanks, Siena."

"But…" she tries to stop me, but I'm already striding down the hallway without a second look.

The door is shut so I knock once.

"Go away," she says briskly. "I'm…"

I let out a low chuckle and don't let her finish her statement, instead twisting the handle and swinging the door open.

"You can't run away and hide after that kiss and expect me not to follow."

I step inside her office with my declaration of intent but stop short as Jade whips around toward the opposite wall, half naked, crossing her arms in an attempt to cover her breasts.

"Jaeger! Get out."

Her words don't even have time to register in my head because I get an eyeful of side boob. Perfectly pert and bare because she's not wearing a bra or the shirt she had on when she came in here. All I see are the gorgeous curves of her exposed torso, her body tall and trim, her waist tapering into rounded, full hips.

And fuck me, my raging dick is as hard as steel now.

"Oh, shit. Sorry." I immediately turn around and offer her my back and some privacy, but don't leave. "I didn't know you were undressed…"

"Jesus, Jaeger. I told you I was coming in to change."

She did? When?

"Go ahead. I'm not looking."

"Argh…you're so annoying," she grumbles but doesn't kick me out. "At the very least, can you please shut the door behind you? I don't need the entire club seeing me naked."

All the bare skin got me sidetracked and I forgot I'm standing in an open doorway. Keeping my back to her, I reach out and shut the door.

Suddenly my mouth goes dry. All that smooth skin on display and the desire to touch her has me clenching my fists at my sides to prevent myself from doing anything stupid.

"Why are you changing?" I ask, my voice gravelly, gesturing wildly behind my head toward her body.

"I hadn't expected to be invited to dinner and I wanted to wear something more appropriate to their house. I have changes of clothes here and it's closer than my apartment."

"I think you looked hot in what you had on." I take a backwards step toward her desk, my leg running into the back of a chair. "I might need to get a #10 Russell jersey for myself."

I peer over my shoulder and see a trace of a smile flash at the corners of her mouth, her golden-dark eyes sparkling. And then she flicks her gaze away.

"Stop looking at me, creeper," she says, a hint of humor in her voice. "Keep your eyes in the other direction."

"Fine. But it's really hard."

Jade giggles from behind me. "I'm sure it is."

I smile at her wicked retort. While I wait, I hear her rummaging around, hangers clattering together, garments falling to the floor in soft whooshes, and a few small grunts as she changes into something she apparently deems more acceptable. I take the time to look around at the walls of her office and then realize there's a big glass window that's wide open. No blinds or curtains to block the view.

"Jade! The window."

"It's fine. No one can see in."

"Oh," I say lamely, but I peer through the reflective glass to see her leaning over to slip on some heels. Her long, toned legs look fucking spectacular.

When she returns to stand, she grumbles a noise of frustration.

"Dammit."

"What is it?" I ask, automatically swinging my head over my shoulder to find out what the problem is.

My pulse quickens and I can't contain the smile that tips up at the corners of my mouth. Jade is back to her sexy goddess attire, and it sends currents of electricity straight to my balls.

"It's my dress," she laments with a sigh. "The zipper is in the back, and the catch is stuck. I can't reach it."

I spin around and wiggle my fingers in the air. "Lucky for you, I can help with that. Although, normally I'm trying to get a woman naked, not trying to help them dress."

Jade snickers lightly as I take intentional steps toward her. No longer naked from the waist up, she has on a coral-colored sleeveless dress that prominently shows off her defined arms. I remind myself to breathe because she literally takes my breath away.

I gently grasp her shoulders, my fingers fanning a good portion of her arm to hold her in place. I run my fingertips over the cut of her biceps, tracing along the toned triceps. I swallow hard.

"You are so fucking sexy."

She sucks in a deep breath and tilts her head to the side, grabbing a fistful of her thick braided hair to swing it over her shoulder, giving me an unfettered view of the delicate skin of her back. I brush my knuckles down the curve of her spine exposed by the V of the unzipped material, softly caressing the length down her back.

Jade shivers, a tiny gasp escaping her lips.

"Does that feel good?" I ask, bending forward and placing my lips at the base of her neck.

"Yes."

I step in closer pressing against her back, my straining cock nestling into the seam running between the globes of her ass.

"You know what also feels good?"

She hums. "Hmm?"

"What I could do to you with my fingers and my tongue." I drop a hand to the edge of her skirt that flares out mid-thigh, tug it up past her knee, and flick it back and forth with my fingers like a pendulum, grazing over the inside of her bare thigh.

My heart hammers and thuds loudly as I wait for her approval. For her to ask me for more. To grant me permission.

Jade's voice quakes. "What would you do?"

I swallow thickly. "Well, I'd first tease you unmercifully until you could no longer stand it and then I'd fuck you with my fingers. And then once you came, I'd spread you out over your desk and make you come again, only this time against my tongue."

She lets out a deep sigh and presses her ass into my crotch, throwing her hands up behind me to wrap around the nape of my neck.

"That sounds good," Jade whispers, twisting her neck to offer me her mouth. "But what do you get out of it?"

I'd laugh if I wasn't so turned on, my finger inching up toward the heat between her legs. "I get to watch you come apart. And that would be the sexiest thing I'll ever see in my lifetime."

This close to her core I can feel the heat radiating from her pussy and the dampness of her panties. Her breaths have turned rapid and shallow, her breasts rising and falling in quick succession. Her legs tremble under my touch and my cock stirs inside my shorts.

She licks her lips and tugs my head forward, pulling me to her mouth. Her mouth parts on a sigh as my tongue sweeps inside, probing deeply and exploring her heady taste.

I spin her around, crushing my mouth to hers, sucking her plump bottom lip between my teeth to taste her with every swirl of my tongue. My hips thrust and grind as hers arch to meet me.

When we finally come up for air, my chest heaving with exertion, I grin down at this gorgeous goddess, impressed with my good luck. I've never had to work this hard to get a woman before.

I guess it's true what they say. The harder you work, the luckier you get.

And I'm one fucking lucky bastard right now.

I shove my hands up the back of her legs, roaming up under the skirt until I reach the firm globes of her ass. Boosting her up in my arms until she grabs hold of my shoulders, I spin us both around, laying her flat out against the desk, and flick a glance at the window one last time.

"You're positive no one can see us?"

"Hundred percent." She grins, palming my face in her hands. "But it's not sound proof."

I waggle my eyebrows.

"Good to know they'll hear you when you scream out my name and you're begging for my cock."

Jade arches her back, lifting her head to kiss my neck. "I might scream, but I'll never beg for sex."

"Ooh, a challenge. I like that."

Jade laughs before she presses her hands to the sides of

my head and pushes me down between her legs. Then she winks.

My goddess motherfucking winks.

"Speaking of challenges, you have promises to keep." She licks her lips. "Now on your knees and show me what you got."

# 22

J ade

Lordy, this boy wasn't kidding.

After the first orgasm he gave me with his fingers, followed by his oh-so-talented tongue, I find myself on the verge of begging for him to fill me with that massive cock of his.

Somehow, I am able to keep my mouth shut, which was helped by his T-shirt that I balled up and shoved over my lips to muffle my loud and frequent exclamations.

*"That's it, Jaeger. Right there."*

*"Don't stop."*

*"Fuck yes, I'm coming!"*

I am wrung out and limp when he finally stands, wiping a hand over his wet mouth, a sly grin tipping up at the corners of it as his eyebrows lift in that *"I told you so"* kind of way.

I look down at my rumpled state. The pleated skirt of my dress is bunched up at my belly and my legs hang limply over the edge of the desk. I think they call this the afterglow haze.

"You're smiling," he arrogantly crows. "I made you laugh, come, and smile all in one day. That's a triple double in the books."

Pushing to my elbows, I give him a shake of my head and a side smirk.

"I'll admit, you have some talent, Romeo. But my record still stands." I give a toss of my hair and a flirty bat of my eyelashes. "Still no begging from me."

His eyes darken, lids lowering seductively, and I watch with flared eyes as he strokes a hand over the impressive dick print in his track shorts.

"The game's not over yet, Goddess."

If I had any willpower in reserves, I might throw my head back in peals of laughter at his cocky ego.

But it's not funny. I want him more than I have anything or anyone before. My decision was made the minute he stepped in my office and I saw the way his raw unfiltered lust blazed in his eyes. And there was nothing I could do to stop that train except promise myself this would be a one-time thing just so I can get Jaeger out of my head and out of my system.

A one and done we'd move on.

I sit up, wind my legs around the backs of his legs, and dig my heels into the muscular hamstrings. With his shirt off, I get the full view of his tattoos, colorful works of art covering the hard granite of his arms. I trace them with my fingers as I admire his masculinity, exploring over the one word written in script below his heart.

*Trust.*

He asked me to trust him. Maybe for some women that's an easy thing to do. But not for me.

I focus on his body. Lord have mercy, he's a beautiful man with an athlete's physique that includes perfectly sculpted pecs leading to the dips and valleys of an eight-pack that is insanely hard. Like a river flowing over and through mountainous terrain, my finger travels downward, finding the hidden secrets below his waistband. I finally get to reveal what has only been imagined via dick print posts, leaving my imagination to work overtime.

And I've imagined it a lot.

I take pleasure in exploring over this treasure with my fingers, putting both hands to work roaming over the expanse of his torso. He stands with hands casually propped on his hips, studying my movements, allowing me this opportunity to take the lead.

If sex is a game, I'd say we're evenly matched opponents.

When my fingers trail down the soft hairs below his belly, he sucks in a breath as I toy with the edge of his shorts. The shape of his cock jumps underneath the nylon material.

I'm amazed at the control and willpower he exerts. He has a surprisingly deep well of patience for a twenty-four-year-old guy. Most guys I've been with have been Quick Draw McGraws, rushing furiously into sex rather than enjoying the foreplay.

"You gonna show me what you're packing there, Romeo?" I stroke a hand over his erection, boldly squeezing and grazing a thumb over the tip that pokes through at the top of the elastic waistband.

"If that's what you want."

"This is not me begging," I clarify with a raised eyebrow. "But yeah, it's what I want."

He chuckles. I loosen the drawstring and he slips his shorts down his legs, shucking them to the floor.

When he straightens, his straining dick reaches skyward

toward his navel, the tip glistening with moisture. My mouth salivates to taste him.

"Have you been smart about sex, rookie? Do you always wrap it up?"

I clasp my fingers around the hard length and squeeze, then give a long, generous stroke from base to tip, swirling my thumb over the tip. A low and shaky groan expels from his throat.

"Always."

"That's good...then hurry..." I lift my brows expectantly. "I need it."

His eyes pop wide at my admission. I drop my hold on his cock, and Jaeger bends down to rummage through his wallet in his discarded shorts. He returns victoriously with the foil package in his fingers, handing it to me eagerly.

I rip it open, positioning it over his red swollen tip, and roll it down so it snaps snugly over his impressive girth.

The dick print photos didn't lie. Jaeger has a monster-sized cock.

When he positions himself over me, placing his hands on my thighs, he gives me the dirtiest look I've ever seen him wear as he spreads me wide once again.

He drags his thumb through my damp center, circling my clit that should be thoroughly sated but seems to bloom again with teasing, coaxing glides of his fingers. I drop my head between my shoulder blades and moan through gritted teeth and closed eyes.

"Please, Jaeger." My voice is ridiculously husky with need.

I reach a hand around to his ass cheeks, squeezing hard and with a clear demand.

He positions the head of his cock at my entrance but

doesn't push inside yet. Instead, he fumbles with the bodice of my dress, trying to pull it down over my arms.

"I want to see your tits, baby. I need to touch them."

I wiggle the top down, slipping my arms out and sliding the material down just above my belly where it bunches together like an accordion with the lower section of my dress.

"Please don't call me baby."

I'm not sure if Jaeger even hears my request as he stares in rapture at my breasts, covered by a white lacy bra I put on while dressing. His finger traces the generous swells of my breasts as I arch my back off the desk, as I'm reduced to begging silently and with invitation for him to touch more.

And he does. As if a switch is flipped, he goes full throttle, tugging the cups down to expose my breasts, my nipples puckering and tight. He palms them in both hands, plumping and kneading the flesh. I hear a low, husky moan and realize it came from me. He swirls his thumbs over my distended nipples before his lips cover a hard nub, sucking it hard between his teeth before flicking it with a teasing tongue.

I whimper. I mutter curses into his ear. I score my nails down his back as his engorged cock slides through my folds and my wet heat.

Finally, when I just can't take it any longer, I utter these words that I don't even realize I've said.

"Please...Jaeger...*please*..."

The world stops turning on its axis. My breath stalls. My eyes pop open, wide in disbelief the moment the words come out of my mouth, to see the sexy smirk on Jaeger's face.

He pushes himself up with a palm, then reaches for his

cockhead to position it at my entrance before finally breaching inside. All the wind is knocked out of my lungs.

"Did I just hear you beg for it, Jade?"

I have no time to argue because he thrusts inside, taking all my remaining thoughts, and shooting me straight to the moon.

And very soon, I'm seeing the stars.

**23**

———

Jaeger

"What took you guys so long? I thought you left right after us."

Zeke sits next to me on the patio with a beer in hand, his question directed at me but his eyes locked on his son, Gus, who plays hoops in the backyard with his toddler-sized basketball set.

Although I can never imagine having kids of my own, this boy is pretty damn cute. He's got this mop of dark curls that frame his chubby face, and he is the spitting image of Zeke. And every time he waddles up to push the ball into the net, he yells, "swoosh!" Then he runs over to Zeke, then Marek, and finally me for his rounds of fist bumps and high-fives.

The kid's a pretty good diversion from what's going on inside my head. I'm still in too much of a stupor, riding the mellow high of orgasm, to engage in much conversation, so I keep my gaze on Gus while I answer Zeke.

"I had to hitch a ride with Jade since you guys left

without me. And she had to make a stop at her gym to change and do something in her office."

And by do something, what I really mean is, *me*. She did me.

For the past hour, I've done everything in my power to control my unstoppable "I-just-had-the-best-fuck-of-my-life" grin.

And that's saying a goddamn lot. I've been with a fuck ton of women, dating back to my high school days. College girls were everywhere when I played ball in school. And then when I was drafted, it was non-stop hoops honeys any time I turned around.

But none of them can compete with Jade. There are no comparisons to be made. She's beyond beautiful. Competent. Confident. Pushes all my buttons and stirs something inside me that's been begging to climb to the surface all these years. No one else has done it for me.

Unfortunately, there's no more where that came from. She made it very clear that there would be no repeats as we dressed, setting the boundary lines.

Which is normally fine with me. I don't want a girlfriend or even regular hookups with a woman. It makes things messy and complicated, especially when I travel as much as I do.

But now that I've been with Jade, I want to change the rules of the game.

One time won't be enough for me now that I know what it's like with her.

Jade, on the other hand, seems to have forgotten all about me the moment we arrived at Zeke's. She's avoided me, choosing to remain inside the house with Harper and Kendall. The one time she did journey outside was to check on Gus at the request of Kendall, who asked the little guy if he wanted a hot dog or a hamburger for dinner.

I did my best to keep my eyes off her long legs and firm ass when she bent over to pick Gus up in her arms. I worked hard not to salivate when she lifted him in the air, which punctuated the sculpted lines of her defined arms and the mold of her plump breasts against her dress.

Thoughts of fucking Jade turn over in my mind on repeat, like a replay on TV. I envision it as clear as day. I can see her laid out on her desk, her legs spread wide as I lap at her pussy and make her squirm and come against my tongue.

I've completely zoned out of the conversation between Marek and Zeke until Zeke pokes me in the thigh with the bottom of his beer bottle.

"Dude, you're gonna let me get away with that? Did you even hear what I said?"

I turn my head to see both pairs of eyes glued to me with interest. Marek has bent forward in his chair, staring at me expectantly.

"Uh, sorry. No, what'd you say?"

Zeke chuckles, throwing his head back in laughter before clinking his bottle with Marek's, like he'd just won a bet.

"I asked you how it felt to be an MVP who got stomped on by a female basketball player?"

I glare at my teammate over his comment about Jade kicking my ass earlier today.

The truth of it is, I wasn't holding back when I was paired up with her. She gave me a run for the money and didn't make it easy on me. But it's still a sore subject because my ego was bruised a bit.

"Fuck you, Forester. And you, too, Marek. I saw Harper

hand you your ass out there a few times today. *Motherfuckers.*" I scowl, flipping them both off.

And then I remember too late that we're in the company of a small human. My gaze quickly snaps to Gus, who is working on his dribbling skills and then to Zeke. I let out a sigh of relief when it appears Gus isn't paying us any attention, but then he loses control of the ball and immediately repeats it back. Like a broken record.

"*Fuck you, fuck you, fuck you.*"

"Oh shit," I mouth the words to Zeke, offering my apology. "I'm sorry, man. Don't tell Kendall it was me."

Zeke shakes his head, waving a hand. "You think he doesn't hear that from me on occasion? It's fine."

He then stands, heading over to where his son plays with the ball and kneels down at his side, adjusting the little Forester's grip on the ball.

"Hey, buddy, remember we don't say bad words, okay?"

Gus's big hazel eyes lock on mine. "Y'ayer say bad word."

"Well, he's a grown-up. And sometimes grown-ups will say bad things." He turns back to me and shakes his head.

I suck my lower lip between my teeth to hold back my laughter, trying my best to keep my poker face impassive, even though it's the fucking cutest thing I've ever heard.

"Sorry, little dude. I shouldn't have said that. It's a two-point foul."

The kid smiles brightly and throws his hands in the air like he just won the game.

And then all is forgotten when Zeke lifts Gus skyward and they go in for the slam dunk.

～

As DAYLIGHT slowly succumbs to evening and transitions to twilight, the sun begins its journey toward the backside of the Olympic mountains, coloring the sky with orange and pink swaths of color. We finish our dinner of grilled salmon and corn on the cob out on the deck, overlooking the view in the west and the marina below. The conversation hasn't slowed down and the drinks continue to flow as the group begins talking about upcoming wedding plans for Marek and Harper.

Marek looks all too comfortable in the discussion about wedding venues, large or small ceremony, and locations. I swear, nothing fazes this guy. Even when going through the roughest patch of his life, which later we all found out was due to the death of his unborn child, the man never appeared rattled or ruffled. His expression now speaks to his deep love of Harper as his hands intertwine with hers.

Harper peers over at Marek with a girlishly shy grin, rather unlike her usual on-air assertive self, when Kendall asks about their nuptials.

"We don't know yet. Our schedules are always so busy and in flux, and don't line up as well as we'd like them to." She lifts a shoulder. "All we do know is it will be intimate. No three-ring circus. I'll have my two bridesmaids and Marek will have his two groomsmen and it will be outside of the basketball season."

Marek wraps an arm around Harper's shoulder and tugs her in close, placing an adoring kiss on the top of her head.

"Or we could just elope and hold a big reception after we win the next championship."

Harper shoves him in the side as Zeke and I raise a toast. "Cheers to that!"

"I, for one, wouldn't mind avoiding the ugly bridesmaid

dress," pipes in Jade, who sits on the far side of the deck sipping a cocktail.

Jade took one look at the seating arrangement when they came out for dinner and chose the seat farthest from me. It's been harder than I thought it would be to suppress my natural inclination to openly flirt with her tonight, but I've respected her wishes and kept myself from ogling her. Well, not conspicuously, at least. But now that all eyes are on her, I give her my full attention, taking in her gorgeous presence.

An unexpected wave of desire hits me in the chest as she crosses one leg over the other, her dress clinging to her bare thighs, displaying those sexy legs of hers that had been wrapped around my waist as I pounded into her only mere hours ago.

My dick does not agree with this arrangement we made never to fuck again. Not being with Jade again feels like giving up on another chance at a national title.

And that's not something I'm willing to do. When I want something bad enough, I go all in. Balls to the wall. There's no stopping me now.

I've won games on countless occasions where my team was trailing behind and it looked like we would lose. But we didn't. I made sure of it.

So, getting Jade to agree to sleep with me again shouldn't be any more difficult than that.

Right?

**24**

———

J ade

It's going on two days now since I last saw Mary Q and Perkins on their corner on my morning walk to the gym.

That, coupled with the dirty thoughts on repeat of Jaeger and me fucking on my office desk, has me spun up in an anxious ball of energy since Monday morning. I can't concentrate for shit.

*Stop obsessing over the player.*

It's no use, though. There's nothing I can do about what happened with Jaeger, but there has to be something I can do about Mary Q's whereabouts.

During an afternoon lull at the gym, I ask Lars to watch the front and head out to look for my friend. I start down near Alaskan Way where the old viaduct bridge had been located before it was torn down and the road was fitted with an underground freeway tunnel. This area is notoriously overpopulated with several homeless camps and makeshift dwellings.

My goal is to ask around and check in with a few of the

shelters in search of any information on where Mary Q might be. She has a tendency to move around a bit, depending on the time of year, but never has she been gone more than two days.

I strike out at the first and second locations, who said they didn't know who I was talking about. However, I get lucky at the Central Soup Kitchen when I talk to Candice, the receptionist and bed coordinator for the mission.

"Well, hello there, Miss Jade. What brings you by today? I don't have you scheduled until Thursday." Candice gives me a broad welcoming smile from behind the glass partition.

I glance around, hoping by some miracle I'll see Mary Q somewhere in the vicinity, just milling about. Then I turn back to Candice with a cautiously optimistic smile.

"Hi, Candice. I wanted to check on a friend of mine. I'm sure you're familiar with her. Her name is Mary Q and she has a dog named Perkins that's always with her. I haven't seen her around on her usual corner recently, and I thought maybe someone here might have some information."

Candice's expression saddens, her eyes immediately filling with tears as she adjusts the cardigan over her shoulders.

My stomach immediately tightens, clenching at the thought that something is wrong.

"What happened?"

"Oh, honey." She shakes her head, bottom lip quivering. "I haven't laid eyes on her myself, but I overheard a few of our guests talking last night that Mary Q was attacked and beaten up pretty badly. She may have been taken to Harborview, but I can't be sure that's where she is now."

I clutch my shirt, my heart plummeting to my toes in dread.

"Oh shit..." I, thump my forehead against the glass, my braids falling forward with the momentum. "Does anyone know her real name so I can call the hospital and check on her?"

Candice shakes her head. "Not that I'm aware of. The paperwork we have on file is what she filled out the first time she came in. Just listed as Mary Q."

I dig my fingernails into my palms, so angry at the situation I could spit.

Homeless women in general are a vulnerable population, especially the single women, which is why so many of them have dogs to keep them protected and safe.

*Perkins.* Oh no, what happened to him?

I raise my tear-soaked face back to Candice. "What about her dog, Perkins? Is someone taking care of him?"

"I'm sorry, honey. I just don't know any more than that."

Fucking hell. This is exactly why this city needs to do something to establish a shelter dedicated to women, children, and their pets.

*Or I need to.*

The voice inside my head interrupts my regretful lament over Mary Q's circumstances and reminds me that I do have an opportunity at my disposal. A way to advocate for this community.

I have the power to something about it.

But in exchange, I'd have to give up my life's work to fill that gaping hole that this marginalized and vulnerable community needs so desperately.

And partner with the man who can help make it happen.

~

I SLUMP in my office chair, staring down at my desk phone like it's an explosive device ready to detonate. There will be casualties if I use it. And casualties if I don't.

After checking in with Harborview, I was thankfully able to track down Mary Q, aka Jane Doe, who had come in Monday night with lacerations on her face, neck, and arms and broken ribs. She'd apparently been beaten by several drunk men who happened upon her on Bell Street after a night of partying. There were eyewitnesses on the scene and the men were arrested and booked for attempted manslaughter and assault, along with a slew of other things.

Good. Those motherfuckers should rot in hell for how they treated Mary Q.

My luck ran out, though, when I called several animal shelters in Seattle and found none had taken in a mangy gray mutt. But I won't stop looking.

All of it has deepened my resolve to make this deal with Jaeger happen.

Yet I still can't find the motivation to call him. I don't want him to think this is anything more than a business partnership. I'm only doing it for that reason and that reason alone.

It was so much easier when I disliked him. Before I slept with him and now know what a good guy he is.

Now that I've gotten to know him and even worse, learned how good he can make me feel, the lines have blurred, and everything feels messy.

Breathing in a deep inhale, I let it go and pick up the phone, quickly dialing the number Jaeger left me a few weeks ago when he initially tried to make me the offer.

It rings twice and then an out-of-breath Jaeger answers.

"Yo. You got me. Now what do you want with me?"

"Jesus Christ, Jaeger. That is the rudest greeting I've ever heard."

A pause and then a rustling noise, more heavy pants, and loud background noise that is suddenly silenced.

"Jade?"

"Yeah, it's me," I grumble, still pissed at the circumstances surrounding this call. I hate that I'm put into this predicament and need something from him. "What are you doing? You sound out of breath."

A thought crosses my mind. What if he's in the middle of sex? Ugh. I do not need to hear that. My heart has already taken a beating this week with the issues surrounding Mary Q's disappearance. I don't need to imagine Jaeger already in bed with another woman.

He chuckles, low and sexy. "What do you think I'm doing, dirty girl?"

"Dude, grow up and get your mind out of the gutter."

"Mm-hmm...okay." He snickers. "I'll indulge you. I'm in the weight room, lifting with the guys. But I'm alone now if you're calling me for some dirty talk."

I hang up.

Jumping out of my chair, I pace the length of my office, working to breathe in and out to collect myself. Why does he do this to me? The things he says that come out of his mouth make me want to either smack him or fuck him.

The phone rings and I answer without looking at the caller ID.

"Sorry," he says contritely. "I wasn't expecting to hear from you and then you got me all tongue-tied and flustered. I tend to say stupid shit around you."

I snort. "You don't say."

A beat of silence is followed by a long sigh. "I can't control myself around you. You mess with my head."

I chew on my bottom lip, glancing at my desk while memories flood my head and my chest fills with a bubbly effervescent feeling, and my thighs clench together to rid myself of the ache that stirs me inside. Whether he's full of shit or not, the confession is kind of flattering.

"Well, thanks, I think?" I say, twisting a braid around my finger nervously. Shit, this is harder than I expected.

I take a deep breath and let it out. The words seem to get lodged in the back of my throat and I literally have to force them out.

"Listen, Jaeger. I'm calling because...well, because I want to take you up on your offer."

I hear something crash on the other end of the line and a loud curse. I chuckle because I think he may have lost his balance and run into something.

"You want to hook up again?" he asks, incredulously, in a heavy panting voice. "I'd totally be down..."

"What?" I gasp loudly. "Oh my God, no! This isn't about sex. I meant the offer to buy my gym."

"Oh, right. *Riiight*, that offer."

"But there are conditions we have to discuss before I'll sign off."

"Okay. Like what?"

I glance around my office and consider the distraction it's been all week and the memories that surround me every time I step inside for any length of time. Yet, it's the only place we can talk privately about this deal.

"Can you come by my office to talk through it later today?" I hold my breath a beat. "I'll be available after four. Does that work?"

His response is immediate and eager.

"I'll be there whenever you want me to be. Four o'clock it is. See you then."

## 25

———

Jaeger

I left the guys in the weight room without saying goodbye, taking the fastest shower of my life before driving home to grab the drafted contract that's been sitting in a drawer for weeks as I waited, hoping she'd finally want to review it. And honestly, I'm surprised as hell she does.

I'm also more than a little curious to know what changed her mind. As I started the three-block trek walk back to Jade's gym, I consider the next steps and what the future holds if she does agree.

If we end up reaching an agreement today, the gym that will soon be mine.

The possibility suddenly becomes a reality and my stomach pitches with an unexpected nervous rumble.

This whole business arrangement may not have ended the way I'd originally intended, but it still fills me with a sense of accomplishment to check off my first business deal from my list outside of my basketball career.

While I waited on Jade's decision, my brother and I had been discussing other potential endeavors outside of gym ownership. I considered buying a car dealership, a restaurant chain, and even a marijuana growing operation. None of them spoke to me the same way a fitness enterprise does. I shot them all down in favor of proceeding forward with the start of the building renovations.

I'd signed the contract with the construction company I selected and hired, and they began the demolition process a few weeks ago. When I walked by it the other day, I saw they'd already made great progress on the foundation and structure. Based on their project timelines, my hope is to have the walls up by the time my basketball season starts next month.

With work still needing to be done, it's a perfect time for Jade to come on board if that's what she finally agrees to do. It all hinges on the conditions of the deal she mentioned earlier on the phone and the reason I'm on my way to meet her.

My stomach now twists in knots, as I wonder what conditions she has for me.

Truthfully, I may actually be nervous about seeing her again.

Me, nervous to see a woman. Who would have ever thought?

Not only am I nervous but I'm surprised as fuck to hear from her. I thought for sure the offer to buy her gym was dead in the water after everything that's happened between us. She was more than adamant that she would never sell her business to me.

Maybe she had an epiphany sometime over the last two weeks?

Or maybe it was my dick.

I round the corner and laugh to myself. I seriously doubt that, but a man can dream.

And dream I have. Every single night since the day in her office she's appeared in my dreams, usually naked and stretched out across her office desk.

As I open the door to the gym, I hold it open for a woman who is exiting, her hair up in a tight bun, wearing workout clothes, her face shiny and red. She smiles up at me but doesn't show any signs of recognition, just simply nods her thanks and continues on.

"Good afternoon. Welcome to Seattle Circuit."

I step inside and glance up to the receptionist behind the counter as I enter, expecting to see the little fireball I met the last time I was here, but it's not her. This one is tall and whip-thin and maybe a few years older than me.

I smile. "Hi there. I'm here to meet Jade."

"Of course. She mentioned you'd be stopping by, Mr. Matlin, and said you could wait in her office. She has fifteen minutes left in her class."

I check my watch, noticing the time. The class she mentions piques my interest. Obviously, I know Jade is a gym owner, but I guess I hadn't expected to learn she also teaches fitness classes.

"Thanks. I will."

Instead of heading into her office, though, I hang a right toward the gym floor and follow the bank of windows to the far end of the gym where there's a classroom studio.

As I reach the back, I'm stopped short at the sight of Jade in the front of the classroom on a raised platform stage, giving some sort of demonstration with a girl who can't be more than fifteen.

I give a passing glance to the girl but then return them to Jade. She's dressed in a bright coral athletic bra that criss-crosses in the back over her shoulder blades. Covering her thighs and ass is a pair of zebra-striped spandex shorts that cling to her curves so snugly I wonder if she's even wearing panties. Because hot damn, I don't see any panty lines from where I stand.

That thought leads me down a twisted, horny road and has me wondering whether she wears a thong. And if she is wearing one, how much I'd like to skim it down her legs with my teeth before I bury my tongue inside her pussy.

I'm jolted out of my indecent thoughts when a loud chorus of shouts erupts from the room. I peer over the crowd and notice each pair of partners testing out their new moves while Jade, their badass instructor at the helm, observes her students' techniques.

Christ, is there anything hotter than a strong woman in charge?

I never knew I liked that. I see now how it's what makes Jade stand out from all the other women I've been with. She's independent and tough, yet has a tender side with others, and that's sexy as fuck.

The class finishes with a round of cheers and high-fives as the women file out of the room with looks of triumph across their flushed, sweaty faces.

What an incredible sight to witness. Jade gave them all the gift of newfound confidence. She empowered them with something intangible that they may have never known before.

When the last woman exits the room, a short rotund lady who gives me a side-eyed glance, I step inside quietly, crossing over the threshold as I watch Jade begin to clean the equipment used in her session.

"Can I help you with that?"

She startles, her neck twisting to glare at me over her shoulder.

"Jesus, Jaeger. Don't ever sneak up on a woman."

Thoroughly chastised, I move toward the counter where pads and boxing mitts are piled up and stand next to her, but I keep a safe distance between us, covering my nuts with my hand.

Jade returns her attention to the equipment and without looking in my direction, she hands over a well-used sparring mitt and gestures to the disinfectant spray to the right of me.

We clean the equipment in companionable silence side by side until she speaks up.

"How long were you out there creeping on me?"

With a sidelong glance, I see the cheeky grin at the corner of her mouth and bump her playfully in the shoulder with mine. "Long enough to confirm what a badass you are. Remind me to stay on your good side."

She snorts, a smile pulling at the corners of her lips. "You placed yourself firmly on my bad side since the day I met you, Romeo."

"Ahh…" I bark out in laughter, my eyes flickering appreciatively as they scan down her body. "That's not where I was the other day."

She turns quiet and I realize I pushed it too far with the flirting. I return my attention to cleaning a glove and set it aside, picking up another one from the pile to repeat the action.

"How long have you been teaching self-defense?" I ask, looking for a safer, less-intimate topic of discussion.

She keeps her gaze hidden and continues to stare down at the gloves long enough where I think she's evading the question. When she finally answers, her voice holds a small tremor.

"A while now. Maybe three years. I think it's important for young women to know how to defend themselves against…" She pauses thoughtfully. "Men."

I stop what I'm doing, placing the supplies down on the counter, and turn to look at her. With her head bent forward, I can't see her eyes. I lean sideways, ducking my head so I'm in her line of vision and gently pry her chin up with my finger.

"It sucks that women are put in the position to feel like they are always need to be on guard around some men." I run my knuckles along the back of her neck, her skin damp with sweat. She shivers and I drop my hand to my side. "And I think it's great you're teaching them to defend themselves. But not all men are bad guys. Most of us are trustworthy. The bad ones are a small percentage of the whole."

"So you're an expert on the national stats on assaults, abductions, and rape victims?"

"Jesus, no...I don't know anything." Shit, this is what happens when I get nervous around her. I start mansplaining things to her and get tongue-tied, which just gets her defensive. "I only know what I've observed and the men I know in my circle."

She shakes her head with a disgusted huff. "Then you *don't* know. And sadly, neither do most women." She carries an armful of the equipment to the closet, and I follow suit as she continues. "Those men...the bad ones who want to hurt women? They don't wear signs to indicate their evil intent. They usually present as wolves in sheep's clothing. And once a woman finds out, it's too late."

She shoves the remaining equipment in a closet and locks the door behind her. As I follow her out of the studio, I get the sense that there's something deeper that she doesn't want to discuss going on here.

Then a thought occurs to me that makes me want to bust my fist into a concrete wall. Has Jade been hurt before? Abused? Assaulted?

My stomach clenches with a sick roll of nausea at the idea but I brush it away. The Jade I know is too strong and capable. I just can't envision a scenario where she'd ever be put into a situation like that, where she'd be a victim or anyone would do that to her.

No way. If there's anyone out there who can defend herself, it's Jade Russell. My badass goddess.

But still a small niggling feeling breaks free from deep inside my gut and has me wondering if she is hiding something she wants to forget.

**26**

———

J ade

I hate myself for liking Jaeger.

For allowing him the opportunity to get closer, to form this tentative bond we now have together.

I wish I could go back in time when I thought he was just an arrogant rookie man-whore who had an ego the size of Texas who has only one mission: to satisfy his own desires.

But that preconceived notion has been erased now that I know him. Jaeger has shown me through his actions that he's a good guy who cares about more than just himself.

After I showered and changed into clean clothes, we sat down in my office and reviewed the paperwork. We agreed that he would remain the co-owner of the property, since his name was on the deed, and he'd be a board member, along with his brother, Jesse. But outside of that, it was my non-profit organization to run as I saw fit. He would not interfere with any of the day-to-day business.

"You know we'll still need our attorneys to review all

this, right?" I state, glancing up from the document to find Jaeger assessing me with a soft glow in his eyes.

"Of course." He waves a hand at the paperwork. "And while the attorneys do their thing, we can begin discussing the tactical components of your terms for the transfer of the gym, like staffing and classes...your self-defense class, for example."

I point my index finger at him. "That's staying."

"Absolutely. In fact, I was thinking maybe, if you agree, we open the class up as a free class more than just once a month. That's what you're doing now, right?"

I blink, incredulous he'd suggest that. Is he a mind reader? How the hell did he know that was something I wanted to start but haven't gotten around to with everything else on my schedule.

I've been stretching myself too thin for years as it is, running on fumes even on the best days. I'd been meaning to drum up volunteer interest because I can't afford to add another employee to offer more free classes.

Jaeger's brows draw inward with an expectant look. "What? Is that a dumb idea?"

It's the sweet humility in his question that once again has me doing something so incredibly stupid that I know I will regret it tomorrow.

I scoot to the edge of my chair, leaning my elbows on the desk and moving within touching distance of him.

"Come here," I beckon, crooking my finger with a bite of my lower lip. "I need to tell you something."

He quirks his brows but doesn't question, instead shifting the stack of paperwork off his lap and leaning in so his face is inches from mine.

"Jaeger..." I lick my lips. "I fucking love that idea."

Taking advantage of our proximity, I curl my fingers around the nape of his neck and draw his mouth to mine. The kiss is soft and sweet. Gentle and exploratory. A gift of appreciation that quickly morphs into heat and fire, stoking the flames within me.

He wastes little time as his tongue sweeps through the seam of my lips, and my mouth opens for him. The taste of his mint mouthwash infuses with a taste of something all Jaeger. His warmth radiates through this kiss, and I melt into him like butter.

He raises his hands to cup my cheeks, and with my only thought to get closer to him, I rise to my feet and begin to climb over the top of the desk and plaster my body against his.

A phone rings somewhere around us, yanking me from the bubble of warmth his fingers and lips have wrapped me in. I jerk out of his hold as a shiver runs down my spine from the loss of his heat.

Our breaths are rushed and choppy as we stare at each other. I don't know what he sees in my expression, but Jaeger's face registers a flash of disappointment.

"You gonna answer that?" I ask, sitting back in my seat as I open my desk drawer to find my lipstick tube and compact mirror.

With a groan and the drop of his head, he slides a hand in his pocket and extracts his phone, checking the caller ID.

"It's the construction foreman. Can you give me a second?"

With a nod of my head I gesture my go-ahead, then open my mirror and flip open the top of the tube to reapply the color with a sweep over my lips.

"Hey, Jim. What's up?" Jaeger's half-lidded gaze remains

on me, seemingly entranced with my lipstick reapplication. I seductively glide the red color over my lips as he watches. My belly shimmies with lust.

The call takes a few minutes as Jaeger stands and paces the floor, occasionally answering with "*Mm-hmm*" and "*Okay.*"

When I'm satisfied with the reapplication, I smack my lips together, noticing Jaeger has stopped and now stares at me with a hungry look in his eyes. I flirtatiously taunt him with the blot of my lips together followed by a wink and a coy smile. He closes his eyes, throwing his head forward and kneading the back of his neck with a low groan.

A somersaulting sensation in my belly and a tightening of my core results from the delicious sense of satisfaction I receive from this sexy tease.

Flirting with Jaeger is fun. He doesn't make me feel bad about myself for doing it or call me a cock tease or any of those sex-negative terms some men use against women.

All these years I've avoided the flirting game, worried it would backfire on me. Concerned it would be perceived wrong by a guy and he'd have expectations I couldn't meet.

I know I have to learn to forgive myself for the blame I've placed on myself all these years. Blame for what I thought was my part in what happened. The reminder that it wasn't my fault is still a hard pill to swallow even all these years later.

Until I attended the self-defense training certification a few years ago, I had no idea the astronomical statistics around adolescent sexual assault. More than 80% of female sexual assault victims are victimized before the age of 25. And those numbers are only determined by those who reported it. So many victims are like me and never end up going to the police or hospital, which skews the statistics even further.

I've been blaming myself for years, avoiding relationships, pretending to myself that I was fine, lying to my best friend to avoid her suspicions, never coming forward and instead, keeping it bottled up as it continued to hurt me.

For what? Because I was afraid of Ripp?

Or because I felt responsible for what happened to me? I still to this day don't recall what happened that night. It's too fuzzy. Too hazy to remember. I was drunk and passed out. What could I prove? It's the reason I never reported the incident or spoke about it to Harper.

Jaeger's comment to the person on the phone jars me back to the present and out of my head as he finishes up his call.

"Yeah, that would be great, Jim. In fact, I'm just down the street right now and would love to bring along my soon-to-be business partner. Is that okay?"

Jaeger raises his palm as an invitation to me and I nod. I'm done for the day and can manage slipping out early.

"Sounds good. We'll be over in ten minutes."

When he hangs up, he slips the phone back into his pants pocket and grins. If I'm not mistaken, his cheeks flush like I've never seen before. It makes him look boyishly cute.

"Sorry about the interruption. It was my contractor. How would you feel about stopping over to visit the site, then afterwards we could grab some dinner to take back to my place?"

I roll the tip of my tongue over my front teeth and quirk my brows.

"Are you asking me out on a date, Romeo?"

"Damn right I am." He opens the office door to usher me

out. Just as I brush past him, he snags an arm around my waist and tugs me into his side. His teeth latch on my earlobe, and he nibbles at it like I'm a damn snack. "We have lots of unfinished business to take care of tonight."

**27**

———————

J aeger

Jade and I walk down the block side by side, continuing our conversation about our potentially newfound partnership. Everything has changed and there's this new connection we've forged that borders on fun and easy, with a side of sexy. While we're not holding hands and I don't have an arm wrapped around her shoulder, we do have a flirtatious connection as we cross the street toward the construction site.

I was surprised as fuck when Jade pulled me in for that kiss and wouldn't have stopped there had Jim not called me.

Sadly, we'll have to put it on simmer until after we talk to Jim about the permits he's secured and the new architectural plans that came in over the weekend.

Jade seems excited about where things are headed, which has me grinning proudly as we enter the fenced-off perimeter and head over to where Jim stands at the back of his construction truck.

Jade stops walking abruptly, staring at the truck, then swings around to fix me with a look.

"Did you hire Brothers in Arms for this project?"

Caught off guard by the question, I respond, my words more of a question than a statement in return.

"Yeah. Why? Is there a problem with them?" Suddenly I'm worried I fucked up but I was thorough with my research. "They came highly rated with stellar reviews."

A slight smile begins to form on her lips and if I'm not mistaken, it looks like she's about to respond by kissing me again when Jim turns around and sees us standing there.

"Jade Russell? Is that you?"

She spins around and is immediately swept up into the arms of Jim Presly, the man I hired for this project.

"Jim! Oh my God, it's good to see you. It's been a while."

He envelopes her in his burly arms, his construction work hat tipping askew on his head, ready to fall off, until he slaps a hand on top of it. Jade laughs an almost girlish giggle.

A million thoughts run through my head right now, most colored green with envy.

Is Jim a former boyfriend? Or lover? He's much older than her, but I suppose it's possible. The thing is, I can't easily see Jade messing around with an older dude with a receding hairline and a dad bod. Plus, he's sporting a wedding ring.

Something tightens in my stomach, a strange response triggered by witnessing this married man wrap my girl in a very intimate bear hug.

*My girl.*

Fuck, I don't where that came from. Jade would kick my ass in a heartbeat if I ever said that to her. She would hate it if a man felt he could stake his claim and mark his territory with her.

I stand back to give them space, crossing my arms over

my chest, and try to figure out what their connection could be.

When he finally drops her back to her feet, they're both smiling and talking all at once.

"How's the gym?"

"How's Madelyn? Is she in college now?"

"Is my dad here with you?"

I do my best to keep up with their rapid-fire questions but it's the last one that strikes a chord.

*Her dad?*

Finally, as if remembering I'm still in their midst, Jade turns around and gestures between Jim and me.

"Jaeger, this is Jim, an old friend of my dad's and his current business partner. Jim is practically family."

I let this sink in. I don't recall ever seeing the last name Russell on any of the documents I signed for this venture. "Jim, obviously you're familiar with Jaeger Matlin."

I reach out and offer my hand for him to shake. "Good to see you again, Jim."

Jim smiles broadly. "You, too, Jaeger. Glad you could come over on such short notice."

He removes his helmet and cradles it in the crook of his arm, tapping it with his thumb, staring between us.

Then he addresses me directly. "I take it Jade is the business partner you mentioned on the phone?"

Jade and I both glance at each other. "She is. It's complicated, but we're going to hammer out the details this evening."

Along with nailing something else. That may not be an aspect of our contractual agreement but will absolutely be an added benefit.

Jim gives Jade an inquisitive look. "Does Mel know all this? He didn't mention a thing to me."

Jade bows her head, giving it a thoughtful shake. "No. He stopped by a few weeks ago and mentioned that you'd put in a bid for the project, but he never said anything about getting it."

Her eyes flick to mine with a look of guilt and her lips pinch inward. "All he knew at the time was that I wasn't happy with Jaeger's plans to build a gym. Had he been approved, he could've put me out of business."

Remorse stabs me in the heart. Now I feel like a shithead for putting her through all that. Even though it didn't happen in the end, it must've been extremely unnerving for her to go through, knowing her business could have been flattened by another.

"But..." she says with positive emphasis, a smile budding at the corners of her mouth. "Things have a way of working out for the best in the end. Jaeger made me an offer I couldn't refuse."

Jim's eyes shoot daggers at me. "No horses' heads in the sheets, I hope. For your sake, kid."

"Hell no, nothing like that. Scout's honor." I hold up three fingers to indicate my sincerity, promising I wouldn't do something like they did in the famous *Godfather* movie scene. "Hopefully when all is said and done, we'll end up in a business swap. I'll take over her gym and she'll be handed the ownership of this place to run her non-profit organization."

"Jade? Is this true?" His tone is marked with a mix of concern and pride. "You've put everything into building up that gym and have had a great go of it. Your dad said you were even hoping to be nominated for some young entrepreneurial awards this year."

Jade's eyelashes flutter and her hands twist together before she lays one palm on Jim's forearm.

"Thanks for your belief in me, Jim. I've given this a lot of thought though, and what Jaeger has offered is really the best option for my future. Sometimes people come into your life and offer you unexpected gifts"—her eyes flick to mine —"and they challenge you to break your status quo and go a different direction."

Well, shit. That's profound.

As if satisfied by her statement, he nods, giving her one last hug before getting back down to business.

"Okay then. How about we look over these plans and see what you think."

"What a weird coincidence," I acknowledge, wolfing down the Pho we picked up before coming back to my condo. "Your dad and Jim go back to their Army days and formed this company together?"

After our review of the blueprints and build-out plans, Jade and I hoofed up the downtown Seattle hills toward my condo and ordered takeout from the neighborhood Pho restaurant. Now we're both eating in the comfort of my living room, the cartons strewn out across the coffee table, as Jade sits cross-legged opposite me on the couch.

This is the first time I've seen her in such a relaxed state. It looks good on her and makes me smile. It also gives me the opportunity to ask more questions I've wanted answers to since meeting with Jim earlier.

Jade nods, slurping up some noodles between her full lips. I focus down on my own bowl to avoid getting an erection from the thoughts of what those full lips would feel like wrapped around my dick and sucking me off with as much zest.

*Lucky noodles.*

She nods. "Yeah. Technically, my dad's retired, but he invested money into Jim's company and is more of a silent partner. He and my mom now live over on Vashon."

"Is that where you grew up?"

"Nah, I was born in Yakima and we lived there until we moved to JBLM. My dad was there until I left for college, and he retired from the military."

I quirk a brow. "JBLM? What's that?"

"I forget you're not from around here, rookie," she says with a short laugh. "It stands for Joint Base Lewis-McChord. It's a huge base south of Tacoma. My dad got reassigned, received orders to attend the U.S. Army Drill Sergeant Academy school, and we moved out of Eastern Washington when I was a kid when he was transferred and became an Army drill sergeant."

Jade's expression grows dim for a moment as she gathers more veggies from the bottom of her bowl.

"Why'd he do that?"

She uncrosses her legs and leans over to the table, refilling her bowl with more of the Pho broth and holding the container out to me as a questioning gesture of more. I shake my head.

When she sits back, she keeps her feet rooted to the floor, wiggling her toes in an antsy fashion.

"Well, in the military, you do what you do what you're told and my dad was given that opportunity to be promoted. But it also had something to do with my mom and my dad's relationship. My dad met my mom, Annie, when he was first stationed out there. She was working in a bar and, as they tell it, it was love at first sight. They got married within a year, but it wasn't easy. My mom's family basically disowned her."

"Shit, that's harsh. Why?"

Jade's eyes search mine as if looking for understanding of something I don't know a thing about.

"It was because her family are narrow-minded, intolerant people. They didn't want their white daughter marrying a Black man."

My hand stops midway between the bowl and my mouth, understanding now dawning on me. I swallow thickly and drop my chopsticks into the bowl before slowly setting it beside me on the couch. I lean over and place a palm on top of her knee, giving it a supportive squeeze.

"I'm sorry for that loss, Jade. And for the pain your grandparents' prejudicial beliefs and racial intolerance caused your family."

She huffs. "Sadly, we'd probably still be there, and my dad would have been promoted to a higher-ranking position, if that had been the only thing we had to deal with. But it was so prevalent in the community, you know?" She shrugs and sets down her bowl as well, her brow furrowing at the serious nature of the story. "I was just a kid at the time and had a pretty sheltered life since we lived on the base where there were plenty of other Black families and children of multiracial backgrounds. But outside the walls of the base? That was another story altogether."

Taking a chance, I move over next to Jade until our shoulders and thighs touch. I reach for her hand, turning her palm up to lace my fingers through hers. Gently squeezing, I lift our hands and bring her knuckles to my mouth, kissing them softly.

"I can't imagine the heartbreak your parents must have felt. I wish I could have been there to do something to stop those injustices from happening."

Jade twists around toward me and raises a hand to stroke my scruff-lined jawline, her dark eyes searching mine.

"Thank you for saying that, Jaeger. I appreciate it." She stretches up and kisses my jaw. "I didn't mean for our conversation to get so heavy. My plan was just to eat and fuck tonight."

I choke laugh. "Well, we can do whatever…"

She surprises me by sliding off the couch and landing on her knees in front of me. My cock really likes where this conversation is going.

"You know, Romeo. For a playboy, you're very sweet."

I give her my most charming smile as she palms my growing erection. "I do have my moments."

"I think I'm done with dinner," she says, the tip of her tongue sneaking out to lazily glide across her lips. "Why don't you show me what you have for dessert?"

## 28

———

Jade

Tonight's conversation, while it grew deep and a little unsettling for a bit, has proven once again that Jaeger is more than just a hot, young, rich basketball player.

He has heart. A really big one. Which has got me all in the feels—something that's never happened—and which is why I have to find a way out of the deep end.

Sex.

You want to bring a conversation to a screeching halt with a guy?

Show 'em your boobs or go in for the Big D.

Which I have been eager to do, even though I have no logical explanation as to why I'm looking for a second time around with Jaeger. Yes, I realize I'm breaking my own rules.

I thought I'd be satisfied with our one-time hookup. But now I realize that was a ridiculous endeavor on my part. It's like Darth Vader resisting the power of the dark side. Absolutely impossible.

Jaeger's erection is hard and thick under my palm as I stroke the length over the nylon of his track pants.

He drops his head back against the leather couch with a groan, letting his knees fall open to give me access to what's sprung to life between his legs.

I wrestle with the hem of his shirt, tugging it free and pushing it up his abdomen. He takes hold of the material allowing me to admire all the hard muscles in front of me. I trace them with inquisitive fingertips, watching them expand and contract with each touch. Then, unable to help myself, I lift my butt off my heels to lean up and lick the happy trail bisecting his torso.

He sucks in a sharp breath.

"Goddamn, you have fine-ass abs."

I raise my eyelids and see him grinning from above me, his sexy smile sending my pulse racing. "And that's not even my best feature."

"Player, why are you always so damn cocky?" My tone is laced with humor and maybe even a little awe. With a body like this, he can crow a little.

Without warning, he pops up and bends forward, cupping my face in his palms, his lush lips hovering an inch from mine.

"Only to impress you. Is it working?"

He doesn't give me a chance to fully respond before he covers my mouth with his. His kiss is slow and tender, yet it packs enough punch to suck the air from my lungs.

When he pulls back, he leaves behind sensations that spiral through my bloodstream to leave an emptiness in my core that needs to be filled.

"You know what would impress me?" I sit back on my heels and tug down his waistband to free his cock. It twitches as I skim my knuckles over the satiny hard velvet. "You shutting up long enough for me to suck your dick."

Jaeger regards me for a second with a tilt of his head and

then laughs, gesturing with both hands toward his erection pointing to his belly.

"By all means. I'll be a good boy...I promise." He motions with a zipper motion across his tight lips, quirking a brow suggestively. "Unless you want me to be a bad boy."

Then he mutters a muffled curse behind his balled fist as I run the flat of my tongue up the bulging vein of his length.

"Oh fuck. That's so good."

I swirl around the crown, loving the sounds he makes as I tease him while I stroke the tight skin with my fingers and cup his sac with my palm. He eagerly hums through moans and groans, and it gives me all the encouragement I need to continue.

This is as intimate as I've been with a man in years. I don't get on my knees or give a blow job to just any guy. If that doesn't say something about my feelings toward Jaeger, then I don't know what does.

I wrap a tight fist around the base and begin stroking in earnest, simultaneously parting my lips to suck him inside.

I'm immediately consumed by his taste and his scent, a delicious musky-salty combination that sends a rush of pheromone-doused lust through my bloodstream and floods my panties. If my hands weren't already busy, I'd slip one down the front of my pants and get us both off together.

But Jaeger is big, and I work him simultaneously with my mouth and my fingers. My lips stretch wide around his shaft, swallowing hard as I try to relax my jaw and throat to suck him deeper.

I work his cock with everything I have: mouth, tongue, teeth, saliva, fingers, throat.

Finally in need of a breath, I release him from my mouth, but continue to massage his slippery cock in my hand, when he stops me with his own.

"Jade, I'm really close." His eyes plead for something, but I don't know what it is. Thinking he wants me to continue so he can come, I inhale a deep breath and go back in for more, but he reaches under my chin to guide my head back up.

"I want to be inside you when I come. Is that okay?"

My confidence plummets, thinking I'm not good at this anymore. I pop back on my heels, clutching at my shirt. "You don't like this?"

Jaeger scoots forward, the hair on his thick thighs brushing my arms as he encloses me between his legs. He reaches for my hands at my shirt, gently prying them away and placing my palms on top of his thighs. The warmth of his skin penetrates through me and sends shivers up my arms.

"Are you kidding me? Fuck, Jade. I was about to come like a goddamn rookie."

Teasing humor shines in his deep blue eyes and I can't help but smile.

Jaeger cups the back of my neck, guiding me up to my knees so we're at eye level and buries his face in the side of my neck. I tilt to the side to give him access as he kisses and nibbles, moving along my collarbone and then up the column of my throat.

"I loved having your mouth on me...but I want to be buried deep in your pussy when we both come."

I hum my agreement and pull off my shirt, yanking my arms out so I'm down to my bra and shorts. Jaeger gives me that sexy grin of his as he toys with the lace bra straps with his finger.

"You're a goddamn goddess. You know that, right? I'm going to lay you out naked on my bed so I can worship every single inch of your perfect body."

I stand and begin undoing my shorts, and he once again

puts a hand on mine to stop my progress. Then he stands up too, his length bobbing between us, nudging between my legs.

He glides a hand over my shoulder and down my arm, until he encircles my wrist and tugging me behind him.

"Let's take this some place more private. I have no idea when Henri is going to get home tonight." He enters his bedroom and swings around, tugging me into his body before shutting the door. "And I don't want to be interrupted with what I have planned for you."

What a gallant player he is. Gah.

I've totally lost this game.

Or maybe I've won.

**29**

———

J aeger

Just as I imagined, Jade looks like a fucking goddess spread out naked across my sheets, her long arms clutching at the pillows above her head and her legs parted wide, her pussy glistening from the tongue-fucking I just gave her.

And holy hell. The sounds she makes when she comes are like nothing I've ever heard. She's wild and passionate, both eager to please and also be pleasured. It's the sexiest combination ever.

I lick my way up her stomach, paying close attention to her full, round breasts, circling the tip of my tongue over a hardened nipple, then skim the swell of each breast before meeting her lips in a hot kiss.

"Are you ever going to fuck me?" she asks teasingly, her smile wickedly sexy as her fingernails score the length of my back. "Hurry up, Romeo."

When her hands land at my ass, she grabs hold of my cheeks and punches her hips upward, the move grinding her clit against my cock. Her wet center as my cock pulsing with excruciating need to be inside that tight heat. Right. This. Second.

A strangled noise erupts unbidden from inside my throat.

"Yes...fuck...you're so impatient."

I reach over to the bedside table, plucking the condom wrapper sleeve from the drawer, as I feel something sharp dig into my bicep. I glance down to see she bit me in my arm.

"Hey, what was that for?"

She giggles. "I thought you required some prodding."

I shift to my knees between her legs, tearing open the wrapper and sliding the condom over my dick before chucking the wrapper to the floor.

"You keep doing that, woman, and I'm going to flip you over and smack that ass of yours for being so bossy."

An eager hum streaks down my spine when she cocks her eyebrows, pushing herself up on an elbow to trail a hand down my chest and abs. Jade's eyes flicker appreciatively, either at my body or at the promise to spank her. Either way, my cock twitches wildly with excitement.

I grow hungrier and more desperate at the second, my balls tightening with anticipation and ready to nut the minute I'm inside and can feel the clench of her pussy.

"Do it," she urges, dropping her head back to the pillow, heels wrapping around my lower back to the curl into the curve of my ass. Her knees crowd my hips, and her body arches to meet me as I lower my body to hers.

I waste no more time, nudging my covered dickhead into the warm sweet opening of her pussy, sliding in slowly as her inner walls contract around me and stretch as her body accommodates my size to take all of me.

We both let out a collective moan. Why is it like this, so fucking spectacular when I'm inside Jade?

I push the question aside and begin to enter and withdraw in earnest, our bodies syncing with each thrust. Every time I bottom out, a tiny gasp escapes her mouth. I want to bottle that sound up and keep it with me forever.

"You good?" I ask after a few minutes. "Is this okay?"

"More than okay. I want it harder. Give it to me harder."

I hook my arm under the crook of her knee, drawing it up toward her chest. The move opens her further, allowing me more leverage to thrust harder. And harder I go.

"Like this? Is this what you want?"

I don't expect an answer, but she gives one through gritted teeth anyway. "*Yes.* That's perfect. I'm so close."

There is nothing better than to hear a woman say she's close to coming. It gives a man the green light to do everything in their power to make that happen, the incentive to pull out all the stops and help her reach that summit.

Sliding my hand between us, I find her swollen nub and place my thumb over it, gently at first as I feel her quiver at my touch. Jade sucks in a breath as I continue to increase the tempo of my thrusts and begin circling her clit, rousing the brewing desire inside her.

Jade's fingernails scrape across my shoulder blades as she screams out her orgasm. "Oh fuck, yes. So close...*there... there*...yes, right there."

Her entire body trembles from the impact of the climax, tightening and squirming until she reaches that peak and relaxes through the waves of pleasure pummeling through her.

I slow my thrusts, allowing her some time to catch her breath, placing soft kisses along her neck and collarbone and flicking my tongue over each nipple until I decide to see if I can make that happen again. This time for both of us simultaneously.

Sliding an arm beneath her back, I pull out and flip her over so she's on her hands and knees. I wait to see if she voices any objections as I caress her back with my fingers, tracing the length with wet, open-mouth kisses. She simply parts her legs, reaches between them, and guides my dick back into her.

Holy fuck. My pulsing cock is met with wet, tight heat as I slide all the way inside.

"I want your bad boy to come out to play this time," she coaxes, swiveling her head to give me a cheeky grin.

I smack her soundly on her ass and grab hold of her hips, finding purchase so I can begin a pounding pace. The view of Jade's back and ass from this position is so fucking hot, I know it'll take only a few strokes before I'm coming.

I sweep her hair over a shoulder and reach around to plump her breast in my palm. She moans in pleasure when I twist and pinch a nipple.

"Can you come again?"

From her position on her elbows, she raises a hand and slips it between her legs, her fingers brushing over her entrance where we're joined.

My hips punch forward in a furious rhythm as the telltale signs of my orgasm burst free at the base of my spine.

"Oh fuck, baby. I'm so deep. I'm gonna come."

And then I feel Jade still beneath me as I roar out an orgasm that's so hard, I nearly black out from the intensity of it. I drop my forehead to the middle of her back, stars exploding into a million bright lights behind my eyelids.

I take a moment to catch my breath before I grab hold of the condom and pull out.

"I'll be right back," I say, placing a kiss to her hip before scooting to the edge of the bed and walking into my adjoining bathroom.

I take care of business, disposing of the condom before washing my hands and return to my bedroom with a towel for Jade, wearing a gigantic smile plastered across my face. I yawn loudly, the endorphin high waning quickly and morphing into sleep mode. Expecting to see Jade laying happy and content waiting in bed for me, I'm stopped short when she's sitting upright, her arms wrapped around her legs, shaking uncontrollably.

Worry and panic consume me as I reach the bed and sit down next to her.

"Jade, honey? Are you okay? Did I hurt you?"

I try to wrap an arm around her shoulder, but she shoves me off as she scrambles to the edge of the bed and begins searching hastily for her clothing. A wild and almost terrified look flashes in her golden ringed irises, as she stares blankly at the clothes strewn around the floor.

*What the hell is going on?*

I glance around to see if I somehow missed something during my sex-addled haze. Did someone come in and threaten her at gunpoint? Did Henri accidentally walk in and scare her while I was in the bathroom?

I find her bra peeking out from my side of the bed and lay it across the mattress for her to pick up, fearful that if I make any attempts to touch her she'll freak out more.

My voice breaks the silence and tension in the room. "Jade, will you talk to me, please? What did I do? If I hurt you...fuck. I thought...I'm sorry if I was too rough."

Anxiety wrings me out as I consider the possibility that I hurt her. She avoids me and my questions, gathering up her clothes and getting dressed in silence.

I notice there's a slight tremor in her hands. Maybe she's in some kind of shock? I stand up and walk to my closet, pulling out a team zip-up hoodie from a shelf to offer it to her. She accepts it, sliding her arms through the sleeves and zipping it up. The sound of the zipper is almost shocking to my ears.

Without warning, she bolts to the bedroom door as I bend down in search of my briefs. I glance up as I step one foot into the underwear and lose my balance, throwing a hand out to catch myself against the wall. She turns, staring at me with a far-off look in her eyes.

Her voice quivers and is subdued and soft like I've never heard before.

"You didn't hurt me, Jaeger, but you called me a word I asked you never to use."

My mind reels and I look at her in a complete loss. I don't know what I did. What did she tell me never to do? I don't remember through the haze of sex that muddles my head. I run a hand through my hair, scrunching my forehead in question.

Thankfully, she sees that I'm clearly confused and have no memory of what it is she asked me not to do.

Jade turns her head, her hand gripping the door handle, and in a broken whisper, says, "You called me baby."

Baby? When did I do that?

My head spins, the term tumbling around like alphabet soup, as I try to understand. If I use it, I never mean it to be disrespectful or degrading, certainly not in this context. I use it out of devotion and awe. I say it out of adoration.

But before I can ask for further clarification, Jade spins away around the corner, sprint walking down the hallway in a fast clip, as I hear her open the front door and slam it shut.

All while I'm still fumbling with the briefs wrapped around my ankles.

What the hell just happened here?

**30**

———

Jade

I'm still shaking after the Uber drops me off in front of my building and I make it upstairs to my apartment.

The minute I open the door, Tubby is there, his tiny body waggling in delight over my reappearance, whining for me to pick him up.

"Hey, my little man," I coo, scooping him up into my palm and nestling him into the crook of my arm as he cuddles against my chest. I kiss him on the top of his head. "Thank you for always being here for me. You're the only man I can ever count on."

*Lies. Lies. Lies.*

Until I had my little freak-out, Jaeger was doing a damn good job of making me feel more appreciated and valued than any other man besides my dad. Jaeger treated me like a queen.

Carrying Tubby in the kitchen with me, I grab the open bottle of Cab I'd uncorked last night. With one hand, I lift the bottle to my mouth and sink my teeth into the cork and yank it out. Spitting it into the sink, I tip back the bottle and take a long pull of the deliciously fragrant red as the warmth coats my throat and settles the knots in my stomach. My nerves are still shot but the shock has worn off enough now that I can think a bit more clearly.

*What the hell happened to me tonight?*

I open up the kitchen cabinet and extract a wine glass that Harper gave me as a birthday gift a few years back. It says *Queen of Everything.* At the time we joked about it because I was living my best life after my financing for the gym was granted and I started making my dreams a reality.

Funny thing about dreams. Without notice, they can be overshadowed by nightmares.

"Come on, Tubbs, let's go look at the stars."

I unlock and open the slider and we step out onto the balcony. Unfortunately, the cloud cover is thicker than I realized so there are no stars visible tonight.

The phone in my pocket dings with a text notification. Without even looking, I know it's Jaeger.

"Damnit, I shouldn't have given him my number," I grudgingly mutter to myself, knowing realistically there was no way around it. We're technically partners now and he needs my contact information for business purposes.

I didn't think he'd ever use it for personal reasons.

I didn't expect to ever sleep with him again.

Pouring myself another glass, I place the wine bottle down on the small café table, taking a fortifying gulp before reading the text. Or texts. They all come in rapid-fire sequence, preventing me from responding to any of them.

> Romeo: Jade, I'm sorry for calling you that.
> It's all my fault. I forgot. I got carried away.
> Just please tell me you made it home okay.

> Romeo: Are you there? If I don't hear from you, I'm going to come over. I know you probably don't want to see me.

> Romeo: But I will come over if you don't respond. Whatever happened tonight, it seems big. I don't think you should be alone. We need to talk.

> Romeo: But maybe you don't want me there and I get it. I can call Harper and tell her to come over.

> Romeo: Jade, I'm really worried.

> Romeo: That's it. I'm coming over.

"Oh for fuck's sake," I curse aloud, waking Tubby who jerks his head up off my lap, and punch in his number to video-chat him. "Sorry, Tubbs."

Jaeger's worry-stricken face pops up on my screen the next instant and instead of making me squirm with discomfort, it actually makes me feel lighter. A flutter of nerves bounces erratically in my belly.

"Oh my God, Jade. Thank you. I didn't know what to do. You rushed out so fast..."

I shut him up with the universal sign of an index finger over my lips. "I'm fine. Or at least, I am now."

Chewing on my bottom lip, I work to figure out how best to explain to him what happened. Even if I have no clue what it was. But I give him my best guess.

"I think that word—*baby*—triggers something inside me."

This is the first time I've ever said anything about that night or mentioned the aftermath. Even voicing this little detail feels significant in a way I can't even express.

I watch Jaeger's thoughtful expression as he seems to dissect this tidbit of knowledge.

"Um, you mean, like, when the B word is used in a particular setting?"

My lips twitch and I suppress my laugh that threatens to emerge at how delicate he's trying to be. I have somehow misjudged Jaeger all this time, assuming he was just a playboy because that's what the world has said he is.

"You can say it, Jaeger. The word, I mean. As long as it's not directed toward me, you know? Or used during sex."

I reach for my wine and take a sip, pulling my knees up to my chest after Tubby jumps from my lap. I wrap an arm protectively around my shins.

"That's never happened to me before tonight...no one but you has ever said it to me since..."

I stop abruptly, wishing I could redact what I just implied. I do not want to go down this road with Jaeger tonight. I've ruined everything already and there are limits to what I'm willing to share with the guy I just slept with.

"I don't mean to sound ignorant, Jade. But I've heard Harper call you 'babes' before. Is that different than baby?"

Jaeger surprises me with how intuitive and perceptive he can be. I hadn't even thought of the different meanings attached to the variation of the word.

I shrug. "I guess so, yeah. Coming from Harper, because she's my friend, it doesn't hold the same weight or negative connotation. I trust her."

"Ahh, that's it then. When you're with a sexual partner, there isn't that level of trust."

"Yeah," I offer reflectively. "That."

Jesus, Jaeger hit the nail on the head. He is managing to split this onion wide open, peeling back the layers like he's some kind of certified therapist instead of a professional basketball player turned lover.

He runs his fingers through his still tousled hair and hums, like he's putting all the pieces together.

"Listen Jade. I'm not going to ask you what happened, but it's obvious something bad did. Maybe you've repressed it or something. Have you talked to a professional?"

"Aren't you a professional?" I kid, trying to lighten the mood with a laugh. He doesn't take the bait.

Jaeger shakes his head, offering me a tight smile and a patient expression across his face.

"You know what I mean," he admonishes gently. "Have you talked to Harper about it? Or maybe you should give Kendall Rush a call. She can help you."

I let out a grudging sigh. "How did you get to be so wise for a twenty-four-year-old?"

"Age has nothing to do with it. It's only because I care about you, Jade."

This morning, feeling wrung out after all that transpired last night, I sit at my kitchen table and prepare to call Harper.

I need Kendall's number. But I also need to finally come clean with Harper. The timing is for shit though because I hate burdening her with this complicated past, especially with everything she has on her plate with the upcoming wedding.

The other reason for my call to Harper is to share the good news I received that has me bursting with excitement and pride.

As I skimmed through the mail that had piled up on my

entry table the last few days, I noticed one from the Seattle magazine that hosts the Young Entrepreneurs Awards. My pulse raced wildly as I held the envelope in my hands, wondering if it contained the news I'd hoped for or if I'd find a nicely worded letter of rejection.

My hopes were not dashed.

> Dear Miss Russell,
>
> In honor of the work you have done for the community of Seattle and the efforts you've given, you have been nominated as one of our finalists for this year's Young Entrepreneurs Awards. Congratulations!

I sat there with shaking hands for I don't know how long as the feeling of accomplishment filled me with joy. I had realized yet another dream. Tubby probably thought I'd lost my goddamn marbles when I picked him up and danced him around the room, singing my own rendition of Beyonce's *Run the World*.

Although I know other finalists will be announced over the course of the next month, I am filled with hope for the first time in a long time. I've worked for this moment and it's everything I've wanted to achieve, a milestone that feels as big for me as Beyonce's record for being the most-Grammy-award-winning Black female artist in history.

Finally gathering up the courage to call Harper, I take a sip of my now cooled coffee and dial her number.

"Hey, babes. What's up?"

The nickname reminds me of the conversation last night with Jaeger and the weight behind it. I suck in a sharp breath and expel it shakily.

"Hey, girl. Do you have a second?"

"Sure thing. Let me just switch over to my Bluetooth. I just got in the car."

The sound of her car starting, followed by the click of her seat belt and then another ding, provides me the moment I need to calm my nerves. Maybe this isn't the right time to tell her, after all.

"You still there?" she asks.

"Yep, I'm here."

"Okay, shoot. Lay it on me."

So many words and phrases rush to the tip of my tongue, piling up like a traffic jam on I-5. I keep myself from spitting them out one by one in a flurry of news.

*I believe I was sexually assaulted by Matt Rippling in college.*

*I never came forward. I was a coward.*

*And now I'm fucking Jaeger Matlin.*

*He says he cares about me.*

*I think I care about him, too.*

*I don't know how to trust him.*

*I'm scared of being hurt. Again.*

Instead of saying any of that, I go with the basics of what I had rehearsed.

"Well, you know this business arrangement I have with Jaeger Matlin, right?"

"Yeah, of course. I'm surprised, but it's cool what you're going to accomplish by opening the shelter. That's wonderful and you're amazing."

I wish I felt the same.

"Thanks. It's one of the reasons I need Kendall's contact information. I need her help..." I choke on the truth in my statement. I want so badly to get it out. To tell my best friend what happened to me. But now's not the time or the place.

"To refer me to someone who will offer mental health services to our clients."

"Oh my gosh, yes. I'm sure Kendall would love to be involved in the cause. Once I get to the office, I'll text you her contact info."

"Thanks. I appreciate that."

"What are friends for?" she says lightly, but then her tone changes. "And Jade, it might not be a bad thing for you to speak with someone, too."

"What do you mean?"

"Honey, I'm your best friend. You can't fool me." She lets that drop between us as I twirl the ends of my now curly hair that I just spent hours on this morning moisturizing and twisting out. "I've known you for a long time, babes. I've seen you at your best and your worst. I know something traumatic happened to you in college, something you've never shared with me. I see you, Jade."

I swallow back the lump that has suddenly clogged my throat and wipe away the tears that cling to my lashes.

"You're crazy."

She lets out a sad laugh. "No, I love you. I knew it immediately back then, but I didn't know how to help you, so I let it go. That was my bad. But I'm here now."

There's a silent pause that lingers, dropping over the line like a heavy raincloud. I feel the tears prickling at the back of my eyes, ready to spill out in waterfalls of pain.

My lower lip trembles.

"Harp..." I say softly, not sure where to even begin. "I wish..."

That's all I can get out. I don't want to spill it all out over the phone as she drives to work. It would be too heavy and unfair of a burden to release on her right now.

As if she knows how difficult it is, Harper gives me a pass.

"I know, Jade. I wish things were different back then, too. I know it's hard. So promise me you'll talk to Kendall. Deal with whatever happened and learn to love yourself and others again."

I remain silent for a moment, all the emotions springing to the surface like a geyser erupting from the ground. "Yeah, okay."

"You have so much capacity for love, Jade," she says more quietly now. "But if you never open your heart and learn to love, you'll never have room for someone who loves you back."

My mouth drops open and I try to force words out, but they get trapped once again. So instead, I end up spewing the lamest response ever.

"I'm fucking Jaeger Matlin and I was just nominated for the Seattle Digs Biz Mag Young Entrepreneurs Award. Okay, byeeee."

And then I hang up, dazed, confused, and utterly speechless over the strangest conversation I've ever had with my best friend.

**31**

---

Jaeger

Except for the bare minimum in business-related conversations, I haven't spoken much to Jade in a few weeks.

We've been in contact over the non-profit board selections, as well as various decisions related to the build-out, but otherwise, she's been avoiding my attempts at any personal discussions. There've been no secret rendezvous or any new hookups and I haven't pushed.

Not that I don't want to see her again, because hell yes, I do. My previous stance on repeat hookups was tossed out the window the minute I slept with Jade. If I could, and if she'd have me, I'd be in her bed every night.

But after what happened the last time, it's pretty clear even for a dumbass like me that there are some things she has to sort through. My presence would only muddy the waters and I'd just get in her way.

Thankfully, I've been able to keep myself busy coaching the summer Co-Pilots program. It's a two-week-long basketball camp for local youths between the ages of twelve and seventeen who have shown potential in their school programs but aren't given an opportunity to attend the elite-level camps due to the financial limitations of their families.

Glen Roberts in PR roped Henri Pierre, Trenton, and me into volunteering since he knew we were all in town this summer with no family commitments or travel plans. Honestly though, I've been having a great time interacting with these kids. It reminds me of the night I showed up unannounced to volunteer at the soup kitchen when Jade so wisely advised me on the purpose of volunteerism.

She'd said, "It's not what's in it for me, but for them."

I get it now. There's a warmth that burns inside my chest that gets bigger and brighter every day as I help teach these kids about the game of basketball, mentoring them to build their confidence and use new skills both on and off the court. To instill in them the respect for the game and each other.

It's gratifying as fuck. Even though it would be made a hundred times more fun if Jade were part of this.

"What the fuck you smiling about this morning?" Henri asks as he steps out of his bedroom wearing a uniform exactly like mine. He grabs a banana from the counter and peels it back, devouring it in two bites. "You getting some pussy I'm not aware of?"

"No," I grumble because it's a fucking sore spot. "But even if I were, I wouldn't tell your sorry ass about it. I'm just happy, is all."

Henri quirks a brow, ditching the peel into the trash bin.

"I can see that. But why? It's weird, dude."

"It's not weird to be happy, you sourpuss motherfucker," I push back, shaking my head and throwing a fake punch at his arm, which he bobs and weaves away from with a chuckle. "Things are good, bro. I'm having fun this week with the kids. I guess I didn't expect to feel this way."

Henri regards this thoughtfully, his mouth tipped up in a grin. "That's cool, man. I'm glad you're having fun. I, however, grew up with three younger siblings, so I find these pissant brats annoying."

This time I hit the mark and land a flat-handed thump in the middle of his chest. "Maybe *you're* the annoying one."

He snickers. "*Pfft*. Doubtful."

He grabs his keys from the hall table where the stack of mail sits unopened. Turning back toward me, he nods his chin.

"Did you see the mail you got from that Seattle Magazine? Looks important and official."

Grimacing, I pick it up before I close and lock the door behind me. We head down the elevator and jump in Henri's Escalade since it's his turn to drive us to the arena.

I hold the envelope in my hands, curious as to what's inside, then flip it over to slip my finger underneath the flap. They probably just want to schedule an interview or something with me about my plans with the gym. The notification and press release were sent out last week. It seems strange, though, that they sent the request via snail mail instead of contacting my agent.

And if my agent knew, he would have let me know, since we were in contact quite a bit as of late, working on the publicity and press release to notify my contacts in the sports world of the change in ownership of Seattle Circuit. The transfer officially took effect last week. I saw Jade briefly then, when we held a joint meeting with her current staff members to explain that their jobs were safe and that I intended on adding more in the coming months.

Jade said her goodbyes in private and cleaned out her

office while I kept my distance, knowing she needed the space. I'd offered her my help but she declined, as I knew she would.

Unfolding the letter, I scan through it once, getting the gist of what they want from me.

Then I reread it again.

> Dear Mr. Jaeger Matlin,
>
> In honor of the work you have done or are doing for the community of Seattle, you have been nominated as one of our finalists for this year's Young Entrepreneurs Awards. Congratulations!

The letter goes on to extol my virtues and how they are honored I'd use my name and celebrity to start a non-profit agency to help the homeless in the city and that's why I am nominated for the award.

Something niggles inside my stomach. Nowhere in the nomination does it mention Jade or her involvement, and I don't understand why. None of this was my idea in the first place and I don't deserve any of the credit, she does. She was the mastermind behind the non-profit and that was very clear in all the public announcements we've made.

Under normal circumstances when it comes to my skills in basketball, I'm all about the accolades and recognition. I thrive on it.

In this case, the credit feels disingenuous and I'm not the one who should be honored. I'm just the guy literally writing the check.

Henri interrupts my thoughts. "Well, dude? What does it say?"

"Huh?" I ask, my head popping up as I blink the questions away.

"The letter," he says, taking his right hand off the wheel and pointing to the paper in my lap. "What do they want?"

I stuff it back in the envelope, wanting to forget about it and pretend it doesn't exist. It feels completely disingenuous for them to nominate me simply because of my name and claim to fame, not for what we're doing to help others.

The entire thing leaves a bad taste in my mouth and I'm not about to pursue it.

"They just want to sell me a subscription." My lie makes Henri laugh, but it sucks out all the joy I felt earlier and dampens my mood.

I shift in my seat and shove the envelope in the back pocket of my track pants, hoping the out of sight, out of mind move will just make it all go away. I can feel the weight of Henri's gaze boring into my profile, but I don't turn to look. Instead, I stare outside the passenger window and watch the blur of buildings and cars go by.

Before we arrive at the arena, I've come to a decision to ignore the invitation and not respond.

That should put an end to my concern that this unwanted recognition would hurt Jade if she ever found out.

**32**

———

Jade

"What are you doing here?"

I swing the door open to find Harper in my apartment building hallway, dressed in a pair of jeans, a Pilots' T-shirt, and sneakers.

She smiles, holding out a plastic bag from the Pilots' team store. I accept it as I would a basket of slithering, hissing snakes. Cautiously and with fear of its contents.

"I've come bearing gifts that you're going to wear and come with me to watch the Co-Pilots last game tonight."

Harper pushes her way inside, kissing me on the cheek and sidestepping Tubby, who snarls at her but gives her a wide berth, eventually scurrying behind my heels to hide.

"Nice guard dog, you are," I lament, slipping a hand underneath his furry belly and picking him up like a football in the crook of my arm.

I accept the bag by the handle and shut the door with a swing of my hips, scowling with an exasperated sigh.

"I told you on the phone I was busy and couldn't go."

Harper swings her arms wide, gesturing to the empty room around us and then motions down my body.

"Yet here you are, in your sweats and T-shirt, watching"—she glances at the muted TV beside her—"*Love and Basketball* for what, I assume, is the thousandth time." Harper rolls her eyes, then motions toward the bag in my hand with a gloating expression.

"I was right and you're not busy, but you're avoiding, therefore you have no excuse. You're coming with me."

I set the bag down on the floor and cuddle Tubby to my chest.

"Tubby has been depressed and needs me home for some Mama and Me time."

Harper regards me with a lifted brow. "Is that because you've been spending too much time in Jaeger's bed and not in your own?"

"I knew I never should have said anything to you. You're not supposed to use my secrets told in confidence against me. That's a serious offense in the Best Friend's Rule Book."

She *tsks*. "And Rule Number One? Go out with your best friend when she calls."

Harper dusts off one shoulder at a time, a satisfied smile widening across her mouth. I flip her off, which she promptly ignores with a hoot of laughter as she reaches into the bag to extract the T-shirt she brought for me. I'm seriously running out of room in my closet with all the custom team apparel she's brought me over the last year.

She pinches the top of the material and displays it proudly in front of her before flipping it around so I can see the customized back. I squawk in horror.

"Seriously? You're horrible with secrets. You know that, right?"

I testily yank the shirt from her grip and examine it

more closely. It's a blue and gray colored shirt with a deep V-neck. The front has the team's logo and, on the back, in bold type print are the words Jaeger Meister.

"Uh-uh." I shake my head, balling up the shirt and tossing it at her. "No ma'am. You can go fuck yourself because there's no way in hell I'm wearing this shit!"

Harper catches it with her cat-like reflexes and falls on her side across the couch, laughing hysterically.

"Come on, babes...look, we'll be twins." She twists around and shows me the back of her shirt, which reads Talbert's Fiancée.

"Harper," I say, setting Tubby down on the ground before taking a seat next to my soon-to-be-ex best friend. "Nothing is happening between Jaeger and me. It happened once...okay, twice. But it's over and done. We're just business partners now."

Harper pushes herself upright to a sitting position and presses her knees together, placing her elbows on her thighs before reaching out to cover my hands with hers.

"Then tell me what's going on. You haven't said anything since dropping the bomb"—she hooks her fingers in air quotes and choke-laughs—"pun intended, that you slept with Jaeger. Now suddenly, you're holed up here, looking like a girl with a broken heart. Give me all the deets. I want to know what's going on with you so I can help."

I sigh, my eyes misting up unbidden. "It happened because I was weak and gave in to his charms. I don't even think I like him very much."

As if seeing right through my lie, she shakes her head and purses her lips.

"Bullshit...what don't you like about him?"

Pulling my hands from hers, I tick off the reasons with my fingers.

"One, he's young and immature."

"He's only five years younger than you. That's nothing." She waves her hand dismissively.

Ignoring this, I continue. "Two, he's annoying and uses his celebrity status to get what he wants."

Harper tilts her head. "But he's given a lot in return."

I can't argue this one, but it does drive me nuts that everyone sees him or his name and goes bonkers for him. And he turns on the charm to seal the deal every single time. Even Mother Martha went gaga over him like a screaming teenage girl.

I hold up the third finger. "And three, he's..."

"A good lover? An excellent kisser? Knows how to use the D?"

*Yes. Yes. And goddamn fucking yes.*

Now I'm distracted with the memories of Jaeger's kisses. The way he used his mouth to bring me to my knees. And his dick?

The best I've ever had.

But I will not admit any of this because it does me no good. I need to move forward and forget it ever happened.

"He knows how to use the D because he's a player and a certified man-whore. You know my rule about dating ball players."

Harper picks up the discarded shirt and holds it back out to me. I accept it, albeit unwillingly, still not thrilled to wear it. She knows I will, though, and will go with her to the game, too. She's my ride or die and I won't turn her down.

"That rule of yours seems like it's long overdue for an overhaul. We're ten years out of college, babes. Jaeger isn't a college dirtbag. I think you should give him a chance."

"He's also my business partner. That could just create a ridiculous amount of drama. I'm not a drama llama."

She stands up and points to the bedroom. "Seems to me that you've already brought the drama by fucking him twice, girl. Now go change." Harper flicks her hand and shoos me down the hall.

I get on my feet reluctantly and throw the shirt over my shoulder as I head back to my bedroom, grumbling the entire time how she's the worst friend ever. I don't bother closing the door because Harper and I had been roommates for years. Changing in front of her is no big deal.

"I bought you the size smaller, so it'll show off your boobs and guns," Harper hollers from the other room. "And wear a sexy bra, too."

"Isn't this a kids' charity game?" I counter, opening my lingerie drawer to select a racerback sports bra. Once changed, I examine myself in the mirror, smashing my boobs together. She's right. My arms and girls look amazing.

When I step back out into the living room, Harper whistles and waggles her eyebrows.

"That's exactly what I'm talking about. You look so hot, I'd even fuck you." She bats her eyelashes and blows a kiss in the air.

"Good because I'm done with men."

Famous last words.

THE ARENA WASN'T full to capacity like it normally is for season games, but the crowd still brought the excitement with their wild yelling and chanting, calling out the names of the players and raising the roof with their enthusiastic roars of appreciation.

The game wasn't your typical four-quarter basketball game, either. The first two quarters were played solely with the kids who participated in the camp. Then at halftime, the players, coaches, and various other volunteer personnel did a rehearsed dance to a popular Lizzo song, and the crowd erupted into cheers and laughter.

Admittedly, it was pretty funny watching all those guys make fools of themselves. But who am I kidding? My attention was centered directly on Jaeger, who wore a pink and yellow tutu and a unicorn headband, strutting around the center court like someone who gets off on public attention.

During the final two quarters the real Pilots players joined in on the game, equally dividing their talents amongst the two teams. Jaeger's team lost by three points but to watch Jaeger encourage and root those kids on, you'd think they'd won the national championship.

My heart squeezed and spasmed inside my chest as I watched him interact with the kids. A deep swelling of pride had me smiling, honored to be wearing Jaeger's name on the back of my shirt.

"For someone who came against their own free will, you look like you're having fun," Harper comments as we leave our seats to head down the bleachers toward the court where Marek stands waiting for us.

I give her a look of acquiescence. "Fine, maybe it was a little fun."

"See? When I'm right, I'm right."

I give her a gentle slug against her bicep, and she laughs before jumping down the last step to throw herself into Marek's waiting arms.

"Hey, gorgeous," he greets, kissing her solidly on her mouth. When they break apart, he grins at me, his arms still full of his fiancée. "Good to see you, Jade. I wasn't convinced Harper would be able to get you to join us tonight."

I roll my eyes. "I didn't have a choice but I'm glad I came. This was pretty fun."

Harper jumps from his hold and wraps her arms around me.

"And she has no choice but to join us for drinks at the bar, either."

I'm about to decline because I've done my bestie duty tonight when the crowd parts and there in front of me stands Jaeger. His handsomely square face, accentuated by his dark blue eyes, is only second to the way his towering body glistens and glows all glorious with sweat and tatted muscles.

When he notices me, he winks and gives me that thigh-clenching smile.

My brain says hell no, but my body reacts with a resounding yes.

## 33

---

J aeger

"How about we get out of here?" I ask, whispering in a low, tight voice into Jade's ear.

My body has been vibrating and ready to snap after nearly two hours of sitting next to her in a small six-person booth.

If it's not my imagination, her body has been buzzing as loudly as mine, the heat sizzling between us igniting and scorching every place where our touch meets and mingles. Arms. Thighs. Legs. Even fingertips, which toyed and teased hers under the table, out of sight from everyone else's unsuspecting eyes.

In response—and retaliation—her fingers spread out over my thigh, which twitched under her touch. My cock strains against my waistband, the heady desire of our hidden secret ratcheting up my libido to a thunderous level. If I don't get inside her again in the very near future, I might go crazy. I inhale a deep breath when her fingernails score into my flesh, which I hope is a good sign.

"I think I'm ready to take off," Jade says to the group in

our booth, staring straight ahead at Harper, faking a yawn. "I need to go. Time for bed."

To me, her message is clear. She wants to go to bed with me.

I shift in my seat and slide my hand to cup her knee in my palm, gliding my fingers up to the juncture of her legs.

Harper looks shrewdly at Jade before her eyes dart to me, then back once again to Jade's. She's obviously aware that something is going on, but others seem oblivious to all the foreplay happening under the table. I continue to run my finger back and forth on the inside of Jade's thigh.

"I should go, too." I add.

Henri raises the full beer that was just delivered to his lips.

"Let me finish this beer and we can head out."

"It's good, man. If Jade doesn't mind, I can catch a ride with her." I peer into Jade's warm honey-brown eyes, hoping she'll not refuse my request.

She lifts a shoulder nonchalantly like she could take it or leave it. God, I love that about her.

"Yeah sure. But I didn't drive. I suppose we can share an Uber."

I can feel her hand slipping in mine, her fingers interlacing tightly and squeezing.

It's weird to hide this from my friends. They all know we work and spend time together, and I'm sure it's obvious by the way we've joked and laughed all night that we have a strong connection. But can they see how enamored I am with Jade?

I feel that's written all over my goddamn face.

Have I ever felt this way about a woman before?

I've never spent enough time with anyone to find out who they are and what makes them tick.

It's not just the sex with Jade. I enjoy being with her when we're not in bed together. She has a biting sense of humor and doesn't take shit from anyone. Watching her and Marek argue and disagree incessantly over just about everything is like some kind of comedy routine with Harper in the middle. Harper acts like a ref on the court trying to squash their supposed beefs.

Henri seems to have picked up the chemistry between me and Jade as he sat throughout the meal quietly observing us from across the table. At one point, when I looked up, he wore a smirk that told me he knew exactly what was going on.

Now, as we get up to leave, Henri cocks his head to the side, gesturing for me to lean down so he can tell me something.

"Text me if you need me to stay out for a while," he murmurs, his lips twisted in a knowing grin. "I'm sure I can find something to do if you need the space."

I peer over my shoulder at Jade, who is saying her goodbyes to Harper and Marek. Patting him on his back, I laugh.

"It's all good, man. But thanks."

He shrugs and turns back to the table to finish his half-empty beer.

Jade waves and then blows a kiss to Harper. "Later, babes. Catch up this weekend? You guys should come check out where we're at in the building progress. It looks really good, doesn't it, Romeo?"

The entire table stops talking all at once and stares at Jade with curious looks at the nickname for me that she uses with such familiarity. I step behind Jade, her body blocking everyone's view as I give her ass a squeeze. "It definitely looks good."

Jade elbows me in the ribs and I bite my lip to fend off the laugh that wants to burst free from my lips.

"That sounds great. Text me when you get home, so I know your *Romeo* here hasn't taken advantage of you." Harper pins me with a hard stare. I raise my hands to feign innocence.

"What? I'm a good boy."

Everyone at the table laughs.

"Laters," I say, wheeling around on my heel to head off toward the front entrance, glancing back once to find Jade catching up to me.

When we're out of earshot and view, I stop to face Jade, spinning her around and shoving her flat against the hallway wall. Then I cup her face in my hands and kiss her hard and impatiently.

"That was the longest two hours of my goddamn life," I mutter hastily before releasing her from my grasp. "And I'm gonna lose it if I don't get inside you in the next ten minutes."

I encircle her wrist in my palm and tug her to follow me out the main door and down the street toward the waiting Uber car I'd ordered.

Opening the door, Jade ducks inside, and as I scoot in the back seat alongside her, I lean over and make my intentions known.

"You know you won't be sleeping alone tonight, right?"

Jade licks her lips. "Who plans on sleeping?"

"OH FUCK, woman. I'm addicted to this pussy."

With my face between her legs, I cup her thighs in my hands, my tongue sweeping up her wet seam, flicking over her sensitive clit in hopes of drawing out another one of Jade's impressive orgasms.

Her fingernails clutch the short strands of my hair, tightening each time I circle her nub with the tip of my tongue and then dip down inside her entrance where two of my fingers eagerly thrust in deep.

"I think it's kind of addicted to your dick too." She tugs my head up and stares down at me, her eyes dark with desire and need. "I'm addicted to you, too."

I remain still for a moment, feeling the beat of my pulse in my neck, stunned by her frank admission. It's not something I'd expect to hear from Jade. She's not a woman I've found who often shows vulnerability or weakness. Except for that one night, I've only known her to be strong, stubborn, and always in control.

"Jade..." I begin to say but she shakes her head.

"Shhh," she requests softly. "I'm close. Then I want you inside me."

I give her a smoldering smile. "What the lady wants, the lady gets."

I settle myself back at her warm and wet center, her heels locking around his back, as my lips suction over her clit until her legs begin to shake under my ministrations and her breath quickens before she screams out an orgasm into her pillow.

From just behind her bedroom door, I hear the disgruntled whine from her dog, Tubby, as his tiny nails scratch at the woodwork.

"Holy hell, Jaeger. That was so good."

I swipe the back of my hand over my mouth, and then kiss my way up her belly, licking around each distended nipple until my cock is nestled at the heat between her legs. She lifts her hips, positioning my straining dick right where she wants me. I groan from the sensation.

"You know what else is good?" I lean down and bite her earlobe, sliding my length up and down her seam.

"*Mmm*...what's that?"

"My cock."

She moans. "I agree...let me have it."

I lean over toward the night stand and realize we're not at my place, so I have to scrounge around the floor in search of my discarded pants for my wallet. Without bothering to look, I feel around and snatch it from the pocket, handing the condom to Jade for the assist.

She unwraps the protection and slips it over the head and down the shaft, teasing my balls with a flutter of her fingers when done.

I position the tip at her entrance, bracing myself up on my palms as I stare down at her beautiful face.

"Are you still okay with this?" I ask, voicing my concern, not wanting to trigger any further emotional responses like what happened the last time we fucked.

Now that I know she doesn't like being called baby during intimate moments, I've kept myself in check and have avoided all terms of endearment outside of her name. Baby is completely off-limits and I respect that.

I also want to respect her boundaries. On the way over, she mentioned she'd been seeing a therapist about her PTSD, but I'm not dumb enough to think she's completely cured of those past issues. It could take years for that shit to finally be dealt with and left behind.

With that in mind, I've been extra-careful and gentler with her this time. I let her call the shots and give me the okay on what she wants and doesn't want me to do.

Jade grabs my ass cheeks in her hands and pulls me

inside, her legs falling open as I thrust into her entrance with a groan.

"Give it to me, Jaeger. I want you to give me the full Romeo experience."

And I do.

But what she doesn't realize is that she's the only recipient of that experience these days. And I have no plans on changing that.

**34**

———

J ade

Sore. Wrung out. Sated and completely satisfied.

That describes me to a T after last night's non-stop sex fest with Jaeger, interrupted only by a few trips to the bathroom, a short nap, some snacks, and a quick potty break for Tubby.

There is something to be said about Jaeger's stamina. That boy used everything at his disposal to wring five orgasms out of me. His tongue. His mouth. His fingers. His cock. And then after a short break, he confidently came strutting out of my bathroom holding my vibrator in his hand like it was a magician's wand, and there was no stopping his desire to bring me to climax again using that, too.

I now finally understand what all the hubbub is about. The way a good night of fucking can change your entire mood and change your viewpoint on love and all that domesticated shit. The idea that you can trust a man with your body and mind and enjoy sex that is good for you both *together*.

Now I realize why Harper fell so hard for Marek.

While she doesn't share every single detail about their sex life with me, I know enough to know that it's a big part of their intimacy, love, and devotion that make their relationship so solid. It also boils down to communication and trust.

I'm getting there with Jaeger. Maybe not love quite just yet, but it's a close relative to that particular emotion. And he's proven that I can trust him, too. He's been gentle and patient with me and never once pushed his own agenda in the bedroom last night.

He wants only to make me happy.

The only problem is things will soon change because next week he'll start Pilots training camp and then a new season of play and travel will begin. It has my chest tightening in a foreign feeling of loss, like my empty heart was just filled with a bottomless peace and satisfaction and soon will deflate with his absence.

Oh Lordy, I've turned into a fucking romantic sap.

"I can hear your wheels turning," Jaeger says quietly, his body spooning mine from behind, one arm tucked around my middle, as we watch the early light of morning stream through the blinds. He taps my forehead with his finger. "What are you thinking about?"

I exhale a long sigh of contentment. "Honestly? That you're the first man I've ever woken up with in my bed."

"What?" He shifts, pulling me over onto my other side, his arm secured behind me. I burrow into his chest, breathing in his warm, masculine scent. "How is that even possible?"

I choke out a laugh. "Easy. I've never let a guy sleep over. You're the first one."

Jaeger twists sideways, propping up his head with his palm. His other hand glides over the curve of my hip, gently up and down, tickling me in the sensitive spots that send shivers down my spine.

"So you're saying I'm special?" he winks, the corner of his sensual mouth tipping up into a smile.

Instead of sarcasm, I go with sincerity. "Yeah. That does make you special. Don't let it go to your fucking head, Romeo."

Jaeger toys with the ends of my dark twisted curls. "You're pretty fucking special to me, too, Jade. In fact, it's something I've never felt before."

He reaches for my hand that lays at his chest and drags it up to cover his heart.

"What's that?" I ask, spreading my fingers over his pec, feeling the rise and fall of his chest and the *thump thump thump* of his heart.

Jaeger's voice is husky but his gaze steady. "I think it's called love."

I stiffen for only a moment, my eyebrows rising in surprise.

But when he covers my mouth with his, sinking his tongue inside, I relax into his kiss. He rolls me on top, my legs straddling his lap as he cups my ass. Our lips remain locked together, tongues dueling, as my hips instinctively move with urgency. His cock lengthens between us, and I reach between us to bring it to my entrance.

I have an overwhelming need to be closer to him. To feel him stretch me wide and pulse inside me. The same thing that he's done to my heart. He's found a way to pry open my closed off heart and fill it with joy.

He stares down at where his cock disappears between my legs. Then his eyes travel up my body until they reach mine gazing longingly at him.

"You sure? I should get a condom."

"I'm on birth control. I'm okay with this if you are. I know you were just tested and I'm good."

Jaeger closes his eyes and inhales, as if fighting something internally. When he opens them again, the dark blue of his irises burn hot with sensual need.

"Fuck yes. I'm okay. I'm all yours, Jade. All fucking yours."

With one swift move, he's buried deep inside me, nothing between us but our desire for one another. A bond that can't be broken. An intimacy neither of us have ever shared with another before.

And I fall...

So far...

So fast...it's almost frightening.

But I can't stop it and I don't want to, either.

JAEGER LEFT SOMETIME after that heart-obliterating lovemaking that knocked me into a sound sleep.

He said he thinks he loves me.

Holy shit. I think I'm in love, too.

When I woke earlier, I found Jaeger had snuck out while I was sleeping but left me a note on my kitchen table saying he'd call me later after practice. Since getting out of bed, I've literally been walking around in a weightless, dreamy state of euphoria, going from room to room and remembering every single moment from last night.

When I catch sight of myself in the bathroom mirror, I'm shocked at what I see. I'm actually smiling like a girl in love. I haven't even had my first cup of coffee yet.

"Listen here, girl." I point at my reflection which wears the perpetual smile of a well-fucked woman. "Don't go getting any crazy ideas about love and marriage. He's still a player."

I take a long hot shower, lathering my body with my favorite tropical-scented wash, and enjoy the delicious ache in my muscles and the body parts that were thoroughly taken care of last night by Jaeger.

That boy does indeed have a super dick.

I grab my towel and step out of the tub, drying off before I go through my extensive routine of lotions and oils to keep my skin soft and smooth. Then I grab a pair of panties from my bureau and slip them on, pulling them up before I toss on a clean T-shirt. I glance around the floor and notice all the clothes scattered around from where they landed last night in our haste to get naked in bed.

I'm just about to pick them up when my phone dings with a text message. It produces another dopey grin as I think it might be Jaeger checking in after practice because he already misses me.

My smile diminishes only slightly when I see it's from Harper.

> Bestie: Well? Don't lie to me, girl. I know you hooked up with you-know-who last night.
> How was it?

I consider ignoring her just to make her wait it out, but now I'm too worked up and over-sexed not to dish to my best friend.

> Me: Holy shit. I get it now. I understand why you're such a heartsick girl over Marek's dick.

> Bestie: REALLY??? (Eggplant emoji) It was that good, huh?

Me: Eggplant emoji times fifteen. It was incredible.

Bestie: Call me when you can. I want to hear the whole scoop.

I call her immediately and she answers on the first ring.

"Hey, lover girl," she sing-songs, doing her best to imitate Taylor Swift. "I'm on my way to the airport so you have thirty minutes to fill me in. Tell me everything."

It honestly feels like I'm reliving my teenage years, dishing on the boy I like with my best girlfriend.

"Harps, I think I might be in love."

"What?" she squeals into her speaker, a sound I imagine every car in a 10-block vicinity just heard. "You? And Jaeger? The guy you despised? The ball player? That Jaeger?"

I let out a deep sigh. "Yeah, I know. It's fucking crazy. But he does it for me, ya know? I don't know how it happened, Harp, but he wormed his way in. That man has it."

Harper shrieks in delight. "Oh my God, girl. I can't believe this. It was fate. All because of your gym." She pauses for a second. "As a matter of fact, I think your gym is like some kind of love factory. First me and Marek, and now you and Jaeger. You should convince Jaeger to rebrand and market it as a love-match gym."

We laugh in unison at her antics. "I'll keep my nose out of that one. It's his gym to do with what he wants now."

"You know what we'll have to do?" she asks animatedly. "We have to plan a double date. Or, maybe even a triple date if we can get Zeke and Kendall to come out, too."

"Slow your roll there, girl. I don't want to jump into the deep end on the whole dating thing with Jaeger. We haven't even discussed where this is going or if we are even officially dating. It's too soon."

"But you just said you think you love him. And you trust him. That says a lot. Plus, you two have been working together all summer long, which means you know what he's like. Why wouldn't you go public now?"

I sit down on the edge of my bed and set the phone to speaker, considering her question as I bend over to pick up the Pilots T-shirt off the floor. The one I wore last night that was tossed to the ground in a rush to get naked.

My belly flips at the memory.

As I pinch the fabric between my fingers, tugging it out from underneath the bed, I notice a piece of paper visible from the end of the bed. I don't recall bringing any mail or letters into my bedroom, so I pluck it with my fingers as Harper jabbers on about when you know, you know. *Blah, blah blah*.

When it comes into view, I realize it's an envelope. It's like the one I received a few weeks ago from the Seattle Digs Biz magazine. But this one isn't mine.

It's addressed to Jaeger.

My curiosity piqued, I slide down on my ass with my back pressed against the side of the bed, holding the letter in my hand, contemplating what to do.

Harper telling me she needs to go seals my decision.

"I'm in the parking garage. Gotta run. I'll see you in a few days. Love you, babes."

"Mm-hmm, love you too," I add distractedly, reaching over my head to the phone and pressing end before returning my attention back to the envelope.

It's already open and unsealed.

It was found in my room, and therefore, I'm not doing anything illegal by reading it. Possession is nine-tenths of the law, as they say.

If I just peek at it, no one will be the wiser.

I pinch the edge of the letter and extract the contents, dropping the empty envelope on my lap. Then I carefully begin to unfold it one flap at a time, until it lays flat across my thighs.

All those butterfly feelings that had been flitting around in my belly earlier now sink like lead and I almost feel sick to my stomach as I read.

> Dear Mr. Jaeger Matlin,
>
> In honor of the work you have done or are doing for the community of Seattle, you have been nominated as one of our finalists for this year's Young Entrepreneurs Awards. Congratulations!

What the ever-loving fuck is this?

Jaeger is up for the same award I am?

How long has he known about this?

And why hasn't he told me?

The letter weighs heavy in my hand as I reread it a few more times, all the joy I felt from earlier plummeting to the ground,

He knows how much this award means to me and how badly I've wanted to be nominated. He knows how long I worked my ass off to prove myself, to finally be acknowledged as a successful business owner in my own city.

And then he just arrives on the scene, strutting in with a wink and a smile and a big fat bank account, and snatches a nomination of his own.

Fucking hell.

Fuck Jaeger Matlin for never having to work a day in his life and fuck his goddamn privilege.

And fuck this stupid committee for nominating men whose only contribution is through their fucking wallets.

I'm done.

I've had it with Jaeger Matlin. He doesn't deserve my trust when he didn't even have the decency to tell me about this to my face. Instead, he just fucked me good and then fucked me over.

If he wants to be my competition, then so be it. I'll go back to being his motherfucking rival.

## 35

Jaeger

Our first day of training camp kicked my ass and my teammates enjoyed the extra torture and smack talk they've dished out to me.

Especially our veteran co-captain, Carch, who has been busting my ass all day.

"Where's all that cocky MVP energy, Jaeger Bomb? Is the Meister a one-hit wonder?"

I glare at Carch, who holds the ball in the crook of his arm in front of me in a taunting gesture and snickers at my inability to catch my breath.

To be fair, I've already done about a hundred sprints, stair climbs, push-ups, and burpees this afternoon. It wouldn't normally affect me like this, but I didn't pace myself after the lack of sleep from last night.

Am I exhausted today? *Hell yes.*

Do I regret it? *Hell no.*

The only thing I regret is having to leave Jade this morning while she slept naked in her bed, curled up on her side with her hands in a prayer position at her cheek. She looked like a gorgeous sleeping princess, all her dark beauty on display against the white of her sheets.

It took every ounce of my willpower not to climb back into bed with her and hold her until she woke again so I could fuck her while she was warm and pliant.

But duty called and I had to head home first to shower and grab my workout clothes before I drove to the arena.

Coach Green blows the whistle and calls us into a huddle in the center of the court. We're a sweaty, smelly bunch of overworked basketball players, but the excitement to begin the new season is palpable among us.

"I won't say it was the best first practice I've ever seen before but it wasn't the worst, so congratulations, men. Now before we finish the day, I have a few announcements and an introduction to make."

My gaze flies to the three people walking out from the bench to make their way to center court where we all stand. Coach turns to the side, allowing for the full view of the owner of our team, Marvin Spurlock, heading our way along with Marek. Walking between them is a tall, slender young woman in a gray pantsuit, her blonde hair pulled back into a severe bun. From her appearance, she could be anywhere between early twenties and maybe thirty, hard to guess. But she is beautiful and someone in the back blows out a low whistle, clearly meant for her.

Coach clears his throat. "Team, many of you already know Marv, our owner. And of course, no introductions needed for Marek. The announcement, however, is to introduce you to Miss Karis Spurlock, Marv's niece, who, it will be announced later today, is taking over the reins of the Pilots organization. Karis, welcome to the Pilots."

Coach tucks his clipboard under his armpit and claps, signaling that we should all do the same.

I swing my head over to Henri, lifting my eyebrows in a "who knew" question. He shrugs back.

"Thank you, Coach Green. Hello, players and welcome back to our championship-winning team," she acknowledges with a wave of a delicate hand, and a chorus of whoops and hollers fly through the arena from all my teammates. "And welcome to our newest rookies. We are excited to include you in our new season's roster and look forward to another winning season ahead of us."

Cheers and loud applause erupt among us as the team celebrates and encourages one another, getting each other pumped up for our new season.

"I want to thank both Marv and Marek for working with me over the past year as I've learned the ropes and ins and outs of the organization from behind the scenes. I'm impressed with Marek's and Coach's intuition and abilities to continue to dominate in the league. I won't be in the fore-front of the team much this year as you're already in capable hands. But if there's anything you need or want to address, my door is always open."

After a brief pause, Karis continues, "Anyway, I just wanted to say hello and welcome you all back from your summer vacations to wish you all a great start of the season." She glances down at the phone in her hand and then says something completely unexpected.

When she raises her head, she scans the crowd and locks her gaze straight into mine.

"I also just heard this morning from Glen in PR that our MVP from last year, Jaeger Matlin, has received a very important nomination for the charity work he's done over the summer. Let's hear it for Jaeger."

This of course brings a bunch of sarcastic *oohs* and *ahhs*, bumps in the shoulder, pats on the back, and teasing jeers from my teammates. *Fuckers.*

I throw my hand in the air and wave it off, hoping to downplay the importance. "Thanks, Ms. Spurlock, but it's nothing. Really."

Her red lips tip up into a charming smile. "No need to be so humble now, Jaeger. I've seen your post-championship TV interviews. We all know you like the spotlight."

This brings the crowd to uproarious laughter at the jab toward my cocky behavior. I laugh it off, too, but my heart pinches at the remark, especially coming from a woman who doesn't know anything about me personally.

I suppose if that's all she knows of me, it would seem that I'm still that cocky and arrogant kid from last year.

But I feel I've done a lot of growing up this summer, especially working with Jade, who has taught me a lot about showing care and having compassion for others.

Her assessment of me may have been true once, but it's not anymore. I used to strut around like a peacock, enjoying the accolades. But not anymore.

I clear my throat a little nervously. "Actually, that nomination wasn't meant for me. All the credit goes to my business partner, Jade Russell. She's the one who earned it."

Karis tips her head and narrows her brows before she nods with a practiced smile. "Sounds like you have a great partner by your side. Kudos to her."

That I do.

As long as Jade's on my side, I feel I can accomplish anything.

"Hey, Matlin. There's a visitor outside wanting to see you," calls out Ansel Warner from the other side of the locker room.

With the exception of my damp hair, I'm dressed and ready to go, still waiting to hear back from Jade, who I texted over an hour ago after practice ended.

I'm not expecting any visitors today. My dad is on the East Coast, my brother at school, and I don't think my agent would just show up unannounced.

"Who is it?"

Ansel's voice is now muted as he walks into the bank of showers. "Don't know, bro. Some pissed-off chick. Probably someone you never called back after you slept with her."

Worry worms and twists inside my stomach. I haven't slept with anyone this summer except Jade. There'd be no reason I can think of for any of my previous hookups to find their way into our practice session today to call me out on something.

I close the door to my locker and grab my gym bag, throwing it over my shoulder and nodding to the guys still dressing.

"See you guys tomorrow."

They all say goodbye in their own fashion and continue their conversations.

"Catch you at home, bro," I say as I pass Henri, giving him a fist bump on my way out the door.

"I won't wait up." He chuckles and slaps at his knee.

The thing I like about Henri Pierre is that he's not only a great player and teammate but also a thoughtful roommate and friend who knows when to get personal and when to butt out. He's basically there when I need him and not up in my business otherwise.

I run my fingers through my damp hair one more time,

shoving the wet strands out of my face as I open the door to the hallway.

At first, I don't see anyone until I look down the hall and see Jade, standing with her back against the wall, staring down at something in her hands.

"Hey, ba..."

Two things happen at once.

First, I catch myself before I greet her using the term baby, even though it comes so naturally to me, because I know she doesn't like it. And the second thing is the expression on her face when she raises her head, and her eyes meet mine.

I'm expecting a very different look with her greeting. Something that says she's happy to see me, as happy as I am to see her. But instead, her gaze reflects a thunder cloud, anguish and disappointment all swirling in the depths of her golden-brown eyes.

The smile falls from my face, and I immediately close my mouth to keep from saying anything further. I'm not sure what happened from the time I left her apartment this morning to now, but it was big, whatever it was.

"Why, Jaeger?" she asks, voice quaking with pent-up emotion. "What did you have to prove with this? Was it just your way to show me up? Is that it? To take me down a notch?" Jade stops in front of me and slaps an envelope into my chest. I reach for it as she lets go to prevent it from falling to the floor.

Her voice quavers now with confusion and dubiousness. "I trusted you, Jaeger. I thought I..." Her words fall off to a broken whisper. "Loved you."

I stare at her with pleading eyes before dropping my gaze to what's in my hand. It's the letter I shoved in my back pocket on the way to the Co-Pilots game yesterday.

What the hell is she doing with it?

I thought I threw it away. Didn't I?

I thought I'd discarded it, along with any intention of ever accepting the nomination. I don't want to be part of it, knowing as I do that Jade is the one deserving of the recognition. Not me.

When I lift my gaze back to Jade's, tears stream down her face. Fuck me. How do I get out of this mess and make her understand I only want her?

I take a tentative step forward and she immediately steps away. Raising my hands in the air in a defensive move.

"Jade, it's not what you think." I shake my head, imploring her to hear me out when I tell her the truth. "The committee..."

She scoffs. "Oh please. Save it for someone who doesn't understand how these things work. I know exactly what the committee did. The question is, what did you give in return?"

"What? Nothing...not a thing. I didn't even ask to be nominated."

"It figures." She gives her head a frustrated shake, chewing on her bottom lip as if deciding on her next move. To bail or to pounce.

Jade crosses her arms over her chest and pointedly looks away, down the length of the hallway, when the locker room door opens. A few of the team come sauntering out, glance our way, notice the tension, and turn in the other direction. Smart guys.

"Whatever, Jaeger. You can keep that fucking joke of a nomination for all I care. It's obvious anyone can buy their way in without exerting any real effort, so what's the point?"

She spins around on her sneakers about to leave when I stop her with one last attempt.

"Jade, please...wait. We can resolve this. Please, let's just talk this through. Don't let it ruin the meaning behind this award for you or allow it to break us apart."

She stands at the doorway with her back toward me, staring down at her feet.

And then the bottom drops out on me when she skewers me in half with her response.

"There's nothing to break apart, Romeo. Get over yourself. There was never going to be an us."

**36**

———

Jade

"What's going on with my baby girl? It looks like you're carrying the weight of the world on your shoulders."

My mom comes in from the kitchen carrying a glass of wine and the bottle, setting it down on the coffee table in front of the sofa, where I'm curled up on the couch binge-watching several seasons of *Love & Hip Hop Atlanta*. I started watching it in college when I needed a break from reality and haven't been able to keep up the past few years. But I need all their train wrecks and booty-call business to keep my mind off my own messy life.

I've avoided everyone's calls over the last week by shutting down and holing up at my parents' house on Vashon.

Sometimes the only thing that will help is eating my weight in my mom's homemade gingersnaps and my dad's BBQ ribs, which I've been filling up on like I'm vying for a spot in some world record book.

I've tried to avoid speaking about it with my parents, but they know me too well. They read it on my face. I'm gutted. I literally had everything in my grasp and now I have nothing. At least, nothing that's truly mine. My gym is gone and my brainchild non-profit doesn't even have my name on it. And then there's Jaeger...having infiltrated every part of my life, had me falling for him and breaking my rules on dating an athlete, and is now the reason I'm a flipping mess.

Even the shape and weight of my heart has been forever altered by the sudden loss of my trust in Jaeger.

What'd I expect? I got played by the player.

My mother, Annie, is a petite white woman, whose heart is a size extra-large. To this day, when we're together in public, no one believes I'm her daughter. The only striking similarity we share is the color of our golden hazel-eyes. Otherwise, I have my dad's tall build and a similar skin tone.

But regardless of the differences, my mother has always protected me fiercely through thick and thin. She's defended me when I couldn't do it myself and left the only home she ever knew when she realized I wouldn't be given a fair chance as a biracial child. I was too young to know it then but I understand now that the small-town ignorance and passive-aggressive racism was alive and well.

She sits down next to me, throwing an arm around my shoulders, and gently encourages me to lay my head down on her lap. Her sweet touch and tender strokes of my hair have my eyes welling up with tears.

"I trusted a guy and he screwed me over. And I'm to blame because I promised myself I'd never do that again."

My mom is silent for a bit, simply brushing through my hair in rhythmic patterns.

"Did you love him?" she asks intuitively.

One lone tear slips under my lashes and falls down my cheek. I swipe it away and sniffle.

"I was falling in love with him."

She hums. "Hmm...and was that feeling mutual?"

I lift a shoulder. "I guess. He said it was. But it was a lie, otherwise he wouldn't have done what he did to me. He broke my trust and hurt me."

"I can see that, honey," she coos softly, empathy lacing her words. "Trust and love go hand in hand. You can't have one without the other. But you also need to include a good portion of forgiveness in the mix, too. Because we're all only human, Jade. We make mistakes and sometimes those mistakes hurt those we love."

I push myself up to sit, shifting so I can look into my mom's eyes. Her blonde hair hangs loosely at her shoulders, a touch of white framing her temples. She's beautiful and graceful like an old-time movie star.

A thought occurs to me. "Did Dad ever make a mistake and hurt you?"

She gives me a small smile and chuckles. "Of course, he has. You can't have a thirty-year marriage and not make some mistakes along the way. Both he and I have. But we've learned to communicate, apologize, and forgive each other, then we do our best not to repeat it."

I contemplate her words, chewing on the corner of my lip. She raises a dainty hand and caresses my cheek.

"Giving someone your trust isn't easy. It requires vulnerability on your part and accountability on theirs for their actions and their role in the relationship."

"You sound like my therapist," I joke, and then realize what I've let slip out, slapping a hand over my mouth. My eyes snap to hers and she cocks a questioning brow, encouraging me to continue. "Yeah...I've been talking to a therapist for about a month now. Someone who is helping me deal with a past trauma."

My mom's eyes well up with tears, her lips pinching in

sadness as she takes my hand and places it in her lap, covering my knuckles with her palm.

"Oh Jade, honey. You don't know how happy I am to hear that. You've carried that pain for far too long."

I jerk in surprise. "What? How do you know?"

"Honey, a mother knows these things." She offers me a wan smile and pats my hand with a sad laugh. "I knew something was wrong the summer you came home after college graduation but I didn't know what. You came home so sullen and that light inside of you had dimmed. I was worried about you and tried to get you to talk, but you're so stubbornly independent. I knew you'd sort it out in your own time. You're resilient that way."

I dip my head to her shoulder. "I'm sorry I didn't tell you. I just couldn't. Honestly, even to this day, I only know bits and pieces. But according to my therapist, I've carried around the guilt and shame of the experience, as well as a lot of self-hatred for allowing it to happen. It's prevented me from forging any fulfilling adult relationships."

She leans over and embraces me in a motherly hug.

"I'm so sorry you went through all this alone. I wish you would have told me sooner."

"It's not your fault, Mom. And it wasn't mine, either. My therapist, Patty, has given me a lot of healing advice, and I was starting to see improvement until everything blew up with Jaeger."

"Sometimes it takes a step back to move forward again," she says sagely. "Until you learn to love and forgive yourself first, no one else will have a chance, either."

I chuckle softly because that's in essence exactly what Harper said to me recently.

"Yeah, so I've been told. But look where it's gotten me? I tried and now everything's ruined between Jaeger and me."

She shakes her head, shifting back and cupping my cheeks in her palms.

"Stop that right now, Jade. It is never too late. Whatever mistake Jaeger made, if he's willing to apologize, then you should be willing to hear him out and forgive him." She tilts her head. "If you still love him, that is, and you think he's deserving of your forgiveness."

Images of Jaeger replay like a film reel in my head. His cocky smile and swagger. His charm and sweet nature. His sexy hot bod. His big heart and generosity. His willingness to listen to me, respect what I have to say, heed my advice, and treat me like a valued business partner.

And then I see his face the day I gave him the letter. The sincerity in his voice and the devastation written in his expression.

Admittedly, in my anger and haste at that moment, maybe I was too overwhelmed to listen to him. I was so caught up in finding out he lied and didn't tell me about the nomination that I shut down. I wouldn't hear him out.

Now that I've had some time to calm down, maybe there was truth in his response. Even if he didn't seek out the recognition on his own, regardless, it still hurts that he received it.

But I'll never truly know what was going through his mind unless I give him the chance to explain.

Tubby's head pops up as I jump to my feet, a shot of adrenaline spiking through my veins as I consider my next steps.

"Mom, I think you're right. I need to give him an opportunity to explain himself. Because in the end, we are still business partners, and he did me a solid by gifting me his property for the shelter."

"That's my girl. Go with your gut. And then, if your

instinct feels that it's the right thing to do, allow Jaeger to begin repairing your connection and earning back your trust." Her lips tip up into a smile. "And maybe your heart."

We hug each other tightly before I begin the frantic packing of my things in hopes of catching the nine o'clock ferry back to Seattle tonight. But first, I need to respond to Harper, whose texts and calls while I was here and she was in San Francisco covering a baseball game have gone unanswered.

God, I'm such a shitty friend.

The last she knew before she left on her trip was that I'd fallen into bed and head over heels for Jaeger, my business rival turned partner turned lover.

What she doesn't know is how he fouled out of the game big time and fucked with the one thing he shouldn't have: my heart.

But I'm feeling generous and have decided to heed my mom's advice by giving him a second chance to earn back my trust.

And maybe become my MVP again.

**37**

———

Jaeger

Between training camp, practice, flying to LA to film a new endorsement commercial, dealing with the gym, and acting as board president for the shelter, I've had no time yet to resolve the unfinished business between Jade and me.

And it's driving me crazy that we've left things like this.

I know I need to make amends and hopefully find my way back into her good graces, but our schedules just haven't connected.

When she finally returned my texts earlier this week, stating she wanted to meet up, I tried everything I could to make it happen. Unfortunately, we couldn't find the time.

The only chance for me to see her is today at the official ribbon-cutting ceremony for the shelter.

Which gave me an idea earlier this week that I ran past Glen Roberts, the VP of public relations for the Pilots. When I asked him, he initially rolled his eyes like I was some kind of lovesick puppy, but he agreed to help me carry out my plan.

Jade will probably hate it and hate me for doing it, but I need to prove to her that without her, none of this is possible. Honestly, without her, this nonprofit shelter never would have been on my radar or been an option as a way to help the disenfranchised women in this city.

That's where she's right about me. I do live a privileged life and see the world only through my lens. I've been given advantages in my life that most haven't. But she helped me to see the importance of giving back and making a difference in the lives of others.

With the help of my contacts and the list of resources Glen provided me, and Harper and Marek's assistance, I was able to get everything ready for today's event.

When I arrive at the site, I notice I'm one of the first to arrive, along with two of the members from the board, Shante and David, who still seem a bit enamored with my celebrity. They both fawn over me in a way that used to make me feel like a king but now gets under my skin with how annoying it is.

Did I once actually like this attention?

Jade never behaved like this around me. Like a giggly teenage girl, flirting and vying to win my approval. She's just straight-up cool.

"Jaeger, we're so excited to watch you play this season," chirps Shante, a woman in her late forties who is the head trauma nurse at one of the big hospitals downtown. "My nephew nearly passed out when I said I know you. He'd love to get an autograph at some point if you can."

I give her a nod, moving some chairs that were delivered into formation in front of the podium for the presentation today. David follows behind me as I set up chairs, adding a pamphlet we had designed that lists all the donors and contribution credits for the event. One of them, of course, is the Pilots organization.

"Yeah, sure. Not a problem. But probably not today."

Shante titters nervously. "Oh, of course not. This is your big day. I'm just happy to be included in your event. It's been such a treat working alongside you. You've honestly changed my mind about professional athletes."

I stop abruptly and turn around to face her. Her head snaps up at me, a smile still on her face. "Thanks, but don't forget about Jade. It's more her event than mine. She's the brains, heart, and business director behind it and deserves all the credit."

It pisses me off that I need to say this. Especially to one of our very own board members.

Shante's mouth dips into a frown. "Well, sure, that goes without saying. Jade has been doing a fantastic job."

I turn away and grumble under my breath about favoritism, now finally seeing with my own two eyes what Jade has been trying to tell me all this time. I finish with the chairs before checking my phone to see if Jade expects to arrive soon.

She had texted earlier that she and Harper would be picking up the catering for the event—sandwiches and some snack items—while I worked to get things set up.

I look around, satisfied with the arrangement of chairs, and wipe my hands together. Then I remember the banner I'd stashed neatly in the box up near the podium.

"Hey, Shante? David?" I ask both members, opening the top and carefully removing the six-foot banner and rope. "Could one or both of you help me hang the banner?"

They practically trip over themselves to get to me. It's almost comical.

"You bet." "Absolutely," they say at the same time.

We make quick work securing the banner across the length of the building wall, stretching out wide so all the lettering is visible.

*Jade Russell's Living Room*

I smile thinking of the night we spent putting our heads together to come up with a name for the shelter. We wanted something inviting and warm. The feeling you'd get when you walked into a friend's house.

Jade had argued at the time that it should be my name on the building to bring more notoriety to the place. I wholeheartedly rejected the idea. My name was already in use down the street at Jaeger's Gym, the name I changed it to after buying the place from her.

It only took a few glasses of wine and my mouth between her legs to get her to warm up to the idea.

"That looks good from down here," calls out a familiar voice from below. I snap my gaze to the ground from the third rung of the ladder and smile at the goddess standing below me.

I give her a wink, uncertain of where things stand, but wanting my feelings to be known. "The view is pretty spectacular from up here, too."

The only acknowledgment that she heard this is the roll of her eyes before she turns and walks off to drop off the food. I fold the ladder back up, toting it over to my truck and sliding it in the bed of the truck. Then I peer into the window to make sure the gift I brought is still there.

Satisfied everything is in its place and set to go, I head back out front and notice our crowd has grown in size. Harper waves at me and I wave back with a smile. I do a quick scan of the crowd but don't see Marek or Glen yet, or any of my teammates. But they all promised to be here.

And Henri texted me twenty minutes ago to let me know

he'd picked up my dad and Jesse at the airport and they all were on their way here.

Everything is on track for the ceremony. I work to tamp down the nerves that flutter and spin in my stomach as I get ready for my grand gesture of appreciation that Jade doesn't know is coming.

~

JADE HAS JUST FINISHED with the introductions of the board members that are here and given a speech about a woman named Mary Q and her dog, Perkins, who were what inspired her dream to make this shelter a reality.

And then she pauses momentarily, collecting her thoughts and clearing her throat, before she turns to the side of the platform, her gaze landing on me.

"I may have had the dream of someday opening a shelter for women and their pets, but in all honesty, it would've taken me years had it not been for the generosity and monetary gifts from my *rival*, Jaeger Matlin." She raises an eyebrow as the crowd chuckles. "Without him, none of us would be here to celebrate this win today. Truth be told, when I first met Jaeger, I thought he was...well, it wasn't flattering."

My leg begins to bounce nervously because I have no idea where her speech is going or what she's about to say. But it doesn't sound great. I can feel my face heating in shame.

I know she doesn't trust me after finding that nomination letter, but will she call me out on it here? At this public forum?

"Ladies and gentlemen, Members of the Seattle City Council, fellow Board Members, and members of the Pilots' organization. I need to make one thing very clear. My first impression of Jaeger Matlin was wrong. I misjudged him and drew conclusions about who he was based on social media accounts that sensationalized his behaviors off the court for their own monetary benefit.

"But let me tell you...he's the real deal. He's kind, respectful, intelligent, and a very special person in my life. So thank you, Jaeger. Thanks for proving me wrong."

Jade steps off the platform to a round of applause and walks toward me. I get to my feet, buttoning up my sport coat before embracing her in my arms. We don't hug for long, but long enough for me to whisper in her ear.

"Don't go far. I have something else planned."

She eyes me with suspicion, and I proceed to the microphone.

I give a brief statement, then look to Marek and Glen in the front row.

"And now I'd like to invite one of our major sponsors to the podium for a special recognition. Please welcome, from the Seattle Pilots basketball team, GM and President, Marek Talbert, and VP of Public Relations, Glen Roberts."

I watch them walk up single file, with Marek holding in his hands the box he snagged from my car at my request.

And then I take my seat next to Jade, who leans in to whisper in a disgruntled tone, "This wasn't on the agenda, Jaeger. What did you do?"

I lift my shoulders in an innocent shrug and give her a smug grin.

"It's not about what I did, but what you did."

## 38

J ade

I've always been proud of my accomplishments. It's part of my makeup and my drive to succeed to see how far I can push myself. And if accolades come along with it, then I'll happily accept them with a smile. I flourish under the recognition.

But right now, I'm not smiling. It's like watching a scary movie when you know some creepy dude is about to pop out from around the corner, but you don't know when it will happen.

While I am in my chair, nervously toying with my dress, Jaeger sits with an all-too-eager smile slashed across his face, his knee bouncing a mile a minute, his foot bumping mine on purpose.

"As a new basketball franchise in the City of Seattle, the Pilots organization is continuously on the lookout for good causes, charities, and ways to invest back into the community. And when we found out that our very own team member, Jaeger Matlin, had such a cause, we jumped in to help out. In doing so, it seemed like a logical platform to acknowledge and recognize future leaders in the community who demonstrate the values that we hold dear."

I scan the crowd surreptitiously, locating my parents in the front row sitting next to Harper. They all wear bright, proud smiles. Other friends are peppered throughout the crowd, including Jim Presly, a few of the gym staff, and two women from my Black Women in Business group, La'nissa and Daniele. And then I notice two men, one older and the other in his very early twenties, that must be related to Jaeger. The similarities are striking.

My belly flips with nerves to think I might have to meet them after the ribbon-cutting ceremony, and I wonder how Jaeger will introduce me.

What am I now to him? Business partner? Girlfriend? Friend with benefits?

Jaeger and I haven't had a chance to have a conversation about what happened last week. I'm on pins and needles wanting to resolve this and work through it with him. To maybe start again from here and see where a relationship leads.

Returning my attention back to Marek, I stare curiously at the very large award plaque Glen removes from a plush velvet blue box, proudly displaying it in the air.

"With that in mind," Marek continues, gesturing to the plaque, "we've created the first annual Co-Pilot the Cause Award, based on an idea brought to us from Jaeger. And the recipient of this year's award, along with a ten-thousand-dollar donation to her nonprofit organization, is none other than Jade Russell."

The crowd erupts in applause, cheers, and whistles, with Jaeger jumping to his feet and extending his hands for me to grab and stand up. My feet don't seem to want to work, so Jaeger places a palm at my elbow and guides me up to the podium again, where I nervously shake hands with Marek and Glen and then accept the plaque.

Jaeger spins around to return to his seat, but I grab onto the top of his shoulder to hold him back.

"Uh-huh. You're staying right here with me, *Mr. Meister*."

The audience chuckles at the request, with Jaeger happily obliging with that trademark sexy grin of his stretched across his mouth and playful shrug. I make him hold the award while I try to come up with something profound to say in appreciation.

"I don't know what to say. Today was only supposed to be a ribbon cutting," I tease, pinning both Marek and Jaeger with a look that says, "*I'll talk to you both later*." I inhale deeply and return my attention to the crowd. "First off, thank you to the Pilots' organization for this truly unnecessary and unexpected gift of recognition. I am incredibly honored and humbled by the support of this new charity. It means the world to me and those women who deserve a chance for a safe environment. As I mentioned before, none of this would have been possible without Jaeger Matlin's investment."

I take a quick breath, and locate my family in the front row, their watery smiles an indication of how proud they are of me. It fills my heart with overwhelming gratitude for the love they've always given me.

And then I turn to face Jaeger, whose eyes shine with the same admiration and respect. But in his gaze, I see so much more. A different kind of love.

I lean back into the microphone and decide it's about time I overcome this fear of commitment. To learn to trust that my instincts about Jaeger are right. That his heart is true and he is the kind of man I want to be with.

"Jaeger, thank you for everything. For seeing what truly

matters. For meeting me halfway. For proving to me that even cocky ball players have big hearts and the capacity to love." I clear my throat, twisting to look up at him, and slip my hand through his. "I love you."

His eyes grow wide from the unexpected public admission. But his shock is soon squelched when I wrap my arms around his back and press my mouth to his.

The audience goes wild with cheers and wolf whistles, but I don't give a damn.

I'm announcing to the world that Jaeger Matlin is my man. He's mine.

And my heart belongs to him.

"It's a pleasure to meet you, Jade. I'm very happy that my son has found such a truly remarkable business partner," Jensen says, letting the last word linger between us. "A woman who is as intelligent as she is kind and will keep him on his toes and his head in the right direction."

"Dad, please. I'm not an idiot." Jaeger rolls his eyes with a disgruntled huff.

Jensen Matlin pokes his son in the ribs. "Well, duh. You somehow managed to get Jade to fall for you, so you must have been smart enough for that."

I giggle at the way his dad teases Jaeger. The older Matlin obviously loves to poke fun at his son in a trash-talking manner, but it doesn't come off as derisive or demeaning, just good-natured jabs.

Jaeger, however, seems to have had enough of the incessant jokes and stories at his expense. He pinches the bridge of his nose and inhales a deep sigh.

"Remind me again why I invited you here?"

His brother, Jesse, pipes in. "Because you're a glutton for punishment and you missed us."

Jaeger snorts and he swings an arm around Jesse's neck as they pretend to wrestle each other.

Boys. They never truly grow up.

"Where will you two be staying while in town?" I ask Jensen, who is laughing at his sons' antics.

He grins and gestures with his hand. "Jaeger for some reason didn't want us to stay at his place so he booked us a suite at the Four Seasons." He raises his eyebrows. "Just as well. Who knows the last time Jaeger washed his sheets."

Jesse and Jaeger finally pull apart and Jaeger swings an arm around my back, pulling me in close and placing a sweet kiss on my forehead.

"They've been washed for obvious reasons."

I let out a squeak of mortification. "Oh my God, Jaeger! Shut up."

The guys all laugh, and I hide my eyes from their scrutiny.

"Speaking of which, Jade and I need some alone time tonight. So you two shitasses are on your own for dinner."

"Don't be rude," I counter, sneering at him. "They came all this way to be here for you."

Jaeger gives his father and brother passing glances and returns his gaze to me.

"They'll be fine. Henri will probably take them to the clubs. But you and I have some unfinished business to take care of."

I suppose he's right. We do have to talk about my freak-out over the letter and I need to hear him out. It's the only way we can move past this if we want to make this thing between us work.

Although, it's clearly obvious that I've already forgiven him considering I expressed my love publicly.

Forgiveness is a remarkable concept and has so much power over our emotional well-being. I seriously feel lighter and happier than I ever have in my life.

I hadn't realized how my heart had been held captive in a constant state of turmoil and pain all these years. It's finally been freed through forgiveness. Of myself. Of Jaeger.

And maybe someday, I'll be able to forgive Matt Rippling. But that will take some time.

For now, we make our rounds, giving hugs of thanks and goodbye to Jensen and Jesse, my parents, and Marek and Harper. It's been a good day.

I smile as Jaeger escorts me back to my car, parked behind the building next to his truck.

"Your place?" he asks, opening the door for me.

"Yeah. But do me one thing first before we go."

He bends his head to look directly into my eyes. "I'd do anything for you."

I reach up and place a kiss on his nose. "Call me baby."

Jaeger cocks his head to the side, eyebrows pinching together.

"You want me to call you baby?"

Nodding, I cup his face in my hands, staring into his loving eyes, seeing a future I never knew could exist with him.

"Yes. Say it. Please."

"Well, if you're gonna beg for it..." He snickers when I punch him lightly against his pec. "Let me take you home, baby, and give you something you'll really want to beg for."

I close my eyes and smile. "You know I only beg when I need it really, *really* bad."

He crushes my mouth in a searing kiss that leaves me both breathless and amped with anticipation.

"Baby, you know damn well you're always gonna need this from me."

"Always."

# EPILOGUE

Jade - December

"Thank you for not making me wear a hideous bridesmaid dress. I'm not sure I would've agreed to come if you did."

"Well, that's the true spirit of friendship right there," she says wryly.

Smiling at my best friend, I give her a gentle hug before pulling away to examine her one last time in private before the ceremony begins.

We're in a Vegas hotel suite getting ready to head down to a private chapel where approximately twelve people are gathered, waiting for us to arrive. Marek is presumably already down in front, with Ballas, his best man, at his side and Zeke Forester next to him.

A knock on the door is followed by the sweet giggles of little girls and the sound of the heels of their black shoes charging down the hallway.

"We're in here, girls!" I shout from the large bedroom suite, adding a few of the baby's breath flowers to the crown of Harper's head.

Her nieces round the corner and both run at full speed directly into their auntie's legs, their arms wrapping around her body.

"Auntie Harper, you look like a princess!" the youngest, Holly, coos in awe of her beautiful aunt.

"So do you. Give us a twirl." Harper spins her pointed finger around and both Holly and Hazel comply, their skirt bottoms fanning out wide as they dance.

We smile and laugh, watching the girls have fun, when Jaeger's voice is heard from the main suite.

"Everyone decent in here? Your escort is here."

Harper gives me a look. "Depends on what your definition of decent is, but yes, *I* am."

I stick my tongue out at her and both girls giggle at my childish behavior.

When I look back into the doorway, my heart flutters like a flock of birds at the sight of my handsome boyfriend as he steps in wearing a dark navy suit, crisp white dress shirt, and a royal blue tie that matches the color of his striking blue eyes. His dark blond hair is slicked back to one side and all I want to do is rush into his arms just like the girls did to Harper and never let him go.

Hannah nearly runs into Jaeger's back when he stops abruptly and stares between me and Harper. It's his sexy leer that scans me from head to toe that has me melting from the heat in his gaze.

"Holy shit, you two are hot as fuck."

All three adult women in the room scold him. "Jaeger. Watch the language, bro."

He slaps a hand over his mouth, an apologetic look across his face. "Oops. Sorry."

He moves toward me, and wraps me in a hug, whispering in my ear.

"Baby, you look so fucking beautiful in this dress. But fuck if you think I'm going to make it all night with all the dirty thoughts I have of getting you out of it." He skims his lips over my neck. "How about we run back to the room after the ceremony for a bit? For our own celebration."

I cluck my tongue, wagging a finger at him. "Sorry, Romeo. You'll have to wait until later because this dress was hard as hell to get into. I'm not doing it twice."

He glides his palms down my back and over the curves of my hips and ass and tucks me into his body, where I feel the ramrod strain of his cock.

"Don't give me ideas, woman."

"Hey, you two. We do not need to see that. Get a room or something."

"That's exactly what I was trying to convince her to do," he responds to Harper, who slips her feet into the shoes that her sister holds from her crouched position in front of her. "But apparently there's something important going on right now."

The girls jump up and down clapping. "Yay! Auntie Harper's getting married!"

She swings her head over to me and gives me a nod. "Okay...I think I'm ready to go. Let's get this show on the road."

Jaeger slaps my ass for good measure and then strides over to Harper, hooking her arm under his as he escorts her out the door and down to the ceremony, where I'll witness the nuptials of my best friend to the man of her dreams.

And I'll be right alongside my own dream man.

"THE ZIPPER'S STUCK. FUCK," Jaeger howls, his oversized fingers trying to pry the zipper of my dress down far enough so I can wiggle out of it. "If I don't get inside you in the next ten seconds, I'm gonna die."

"You're such a drama queen when you're horny."

He snorts before he begins to devour me with his mouth. His lips skim the column of my neck, skating over that sensitive flesh and sending shivers down my spine. The moment we got inside our hotel room, he disposed of his clothing and stood naked before me while I was still trying to extricate myself from my red dress. From my vantage point, I admire his golden tan chest that is now adorned with a new tattoo.

*Baby.*

In fact, it's identical to the one mirrored under my left breast.

We got them together the day we arrived in Vegas two days ago. It may just be a term of endearment for most, but the connotation is so much bigger for us. For me. For him.

He's mine and I'm his.

Baby now defines what it means to love and be loved. To be devoted to someone else. It means conquering our fears of commitment and finally opening our hearts to trust another.

Still fighting with my dress that is so tight-fitting there's no way I'll be able to pull it down my torso without a working zipper. However, if I remain standing, I may be able to wiggle the bottom up over my hips to free the rest of my body up for his taking.

"Here, try this." I work at the hem, working the fabric up inch by inch so my legs are free. "If you're in such a hurry, Romeo, pick me up and fuck me against the wall."

Jaeger smiles devilishly and does as I suggest, boosting

me up with his palms underneath my ass so I can wind my long legs around his back.

He glides his hand up and down the back of my hamstring, circling around to the front, then dips his finger underneath my panties to find me wet and ready.

"Oh fuck, baby. You're so goddamn wet. Have you been like this all night?" He slips a finger inside my tight heat and thrusts in and out, drawing out a gasp from my mouth. I drop my head forward and bite the warm skin of his neck.

"All fucking night."

He adds a second finger and my back bows as I rock my hips against his palm, seeking more friction.

My body welcomes the intrusion as his fingers slam in and then ease out, turning me into a needy, moaning mess with every curl of his finger.

A low fireball of sensation begins to build and cascade through my limbs, an urgent need to come climbing up my spine.

"I'm close, baby," I moan, my fingernails digging into the bunched muscles of his shoulders.

"Don't you dare come yet, woman...wait for me."

Jaeger removes his fingers from my hot center and my inner walls cry and clench at the empty feeling.

"Hurry. Give me your dick. *Please*, Jaeger."

He drags his mouth over mine as he rubs the crown of his cock around my wet entrance before he slams inside, thrusting his hips forward, filling me once again. I cry out in sweet relief.

We kiss and suck with mouths and teeth, pull and tug with greedy fingers and hands, and I rock my hips to rid myself of the throbbing ache that's built to intolerable levels between my legs.

One more stroke of his cock and an explosion erupts

inside me. I don't know which end is up as white-hot sparks surge through my body. I grip his hair as I ride out the wave after wave of delicious release. And then with a hoarse roar that rumbles from his throat, Jaeger's own body stiffens, and I feel the heat of his climax pulse inside me.

A slow, languid smile spreads across his kiss swollen lips. I smooth a hand over his unruly, sex-ruffled hair, massaging his scalp, my own satisfied smile meeting his. He leans in and nuzzles his nose into my neck.

"Did I just hear you beg for it, baby?" he muses against my ear, his breath labored and fanning over my skin in puffs of air.

"We've been over this before, Romeo. I only beg when I really, really need it."

"Mm-hmm...yeah, that's right. Seems to me you always need it."

I roll my hands down the back of his head and undulate my hips in a lazy pattern. Then I clutch the hair at the nape of his neck and tug his head back, pinning him with a serious look.

"Jaeger Matlin, I will always need you. Don't you know that by now?"

"Does that mean if I proposed this weekend, you'd say yes?"

I quirk an eyebrow. "If you can find a way to get me out of this dress and fuck me again in the shower in the next two minutes, I might consider it."

In the time I've known Jaeger, I've learned the trick to getting him to do the things I want him to do.

I simply give him a challenge that he thinks he can win.

Jaeger is a true competitor and never backs down from a friendly competition. Especially when sex is involved.

It takes him exactly one minute and forty-five seconds to get me naked.

*Game over.*

We both end up as winners.

## The End

# WANT MORE PILOTS ROMANCE?

If you enjoyed this story, please be sure to leave a review. It means the world to small independent authors such as myself.

And be sure to check out the entire Puget Sound Pilots series now available on all retailer platforms.

You can also get a FREE bonus book, *Above the Rim*, and read about Pilots rookie, Tra'Von Matthews prior to him being drafted by the team.

Download **Above the Rim** HERE

# ACKNOWLEDGMENTS

Many thanks to my sensitivity editor, Renita with A Book a Day Author Services. Without her help, Jade would not have had the depth of character she did, nor would I have been given the honest feedback I required to do her backstory justice.

I knew Jade's past would be tough, as would her current situation in dealing with the tricky balance of her professional and personal life. Renita helped me at every turn and I am grateful beyond words for her assistance.

To Autumn and Roxie at Wordsmith Publicity. Thanks for all you do and helping me along in the journey of this story.

Thanks to my editor, Sandy Bennett, for your polish and expertise in making the words on the pages so much better than they were before. I humbly thank you.

Amy Q from Q Designs: you always rock the covers. Thank you for making Jaeger's cover so yummy.

To my author friends who listened to me panic and fret along the way. This book took me six months to finish. from beginning to. end because I wanted to get it right. My friends kept me from veering off the path and throwing in the towel along the way.

Every day during the writing of this story, I had to ask myself: WWJD. (What Would Jade Do?) She'd never give in or give up. #belikeJade

# ABOUT THE AUTHOR

Sierra Hill is a *2020 RONE Award-Winning* author of *Game Changer*, as well as over 30 novels, including the award-winning college sports series, *Courting Love*, and the twice award-finalist erotic ménage serial, *Reckless – The Smoky Mountain Trio*.

Subscribe to her email list and download a FREE book here: http://www.subscribepage.com/sierrahillreaders
And don't forget to look for me on one of these socials:

# ALSO BY SIERRA HILL

**The Puget Sound Pilots (Sports Romance)**

The Girlfriend Game (Book #1)

The Wife Win (Book #2)

The Rival Romeo (Book #3)

**Change of Hearts (A College Campus Series)**

Game Changer (Book #1)

Change in Strategy (Book #2)

Change of Course (Book #3)

**Courting Love (College Sports)**

Full Court Press

The Rebound

Pivot

Fast Break

Jump Shot

Playmaker (A World of True North Moo U novel)

The Boy Next Door (All American Boy Series)

Stuck-Up Big Shot (A Cocky Hero Club Novel)

**Find ALL Sierra's books and series's on her website here:** https://www.sierrahillbooks.com/books

www.ingramcontent.com/pod-product-compliance
Lightning Source LLC
Chambersburg PA
CBHW072210150726
48002CB00005B/1744